SIX
MONTHS
LATER

NATALIE D. RICHARDS

sourcebooks
fire

Published by Sourcebooks Fire, an imprint of Sourcebooks, Inc.
P.O. Box 4410, Naperville, Illinois 60567-4410
(630) 961-3900
Fax: (630) 961-2168
teenfire.sourcebooks.com

Library of Congress Cataloging-in-Publication data is on file with the publisher.

Printed and bound in the United States of America.
VP 10 9 8 7 6

For my Dad and David.
Thank you for believing.

CHAPTER ONE

· ·

I'm sitting next to the fire alarm, and my best friend is going down in flames. Irony or divine intervention? I can practically feel the metal handle under my fingers. It might as well be whispering my name.

Tempting. One strategic arm stretch and I could send this whole school into an evacuation frenzy.

I could end Maggie's nightmare *right* now.

At the front of the classroom, she swallows hard. She is as pale and shaky as the paper in her hands.

"The social p-pressures and isolation encountered b-by male n-n—"

I can't let her suffer like this.

Maggie shakes her head and tries to shrug it off with a sheepish grin. "S-sorry."

"It's all right," Mrs. Corwin says, playing with the cat pendant around her neck. "There's no reason to be scared."

She thinks stuttering is a fear problem? Aren't teachers supposed to know about speech issues and all that crap? Then again, what can I expect from a woman who has professionally framed pictures of her beloved Siamese, Mr. Whiskers, on her desk?

Maggie takes a breath. "The p-pressures and isolation

encountered by male n-nurses in a predominantly f-female occupation is a compelling argument f-f-f—" She trails off, going crimson.

Someone snickers from the front.

"Go on, Maggie," Mrs. Corwin says. Again.

I'm going to do it.

Beside me, Blake Tanner shifts in his chair. I know this partly because I have good peripheral vision, but mostly because I have freakishly sensitive Blake radar. I hesitate, breathing in the clean hint of his cologne, watching him softly drum a thumb on his desktop.

My face goes hot. I can't do this with him sitting here. I'm completely invisible to this guy. And now I'm finally going to get his attention by, what? By pulling a fire alarm? Yes, I'm sure that will send a great message. To the guy who's been on the student council since the eighth grade.

Maggie tosses her hair back, forging on. "It's a compelling argument f-for s-s-sexism against men. In most modern contexts, concerns about s-s-s-s—"

Maggie goes pink and then red. Tyler and Shannon laugh in the back, and my eyes start to well up. Screw it. I can't sit here for one more second of one more minute.

I sink down as far as I can in my chair and start sliding my arm back along the wall. I reach up, but I'm grasping blind. It kind of hurts. I touch something cool and metal. Bingo. Two seconds and this misery is over.

Blake clears his throat and I bite my lip. Is he watching me?

What's wrong with me? Of course he's not watching me. I'm invisible.

I turn my head because I'm sure I feel someone's eyes on me. I do.

Adam Reed. He's slouched low in his seat, his dark hair in desperate need of the business end of a pair of scissors.

Adam arches one of his brows at me. The half smile on his lips asks me what I'm waiting for. I don't really have an answer, so I curl my fingers over the alarm handle and pull hard. And then I kiss my detention-free junior year good-bye.

• • •

Maggie is waiting outside the principal's office. She's got a couple of notebooks clutched in her arms and a pencil securing her strawberry blond waves into a bun.

The office door is barely closed when she starts in on me. "What were you thinking? You c-could have been expelled."

I sling my backpack over my shoulder and offer our school secretary, Mrs. Love, a wave. Maggie takes the cue and follows me briskly back into the hallway. Students are slamming locker doors and texting madly in the few minutes between periods.

Someone whistles, and across the hall, Connor holds two thumbs up. "Let's hear it for fire safety!"

The hallway bursts into a smattering of applause and wolf calls. I blush but give a little bow with a flourish of my hand.

We make our way to the stairs, climbing them two at a time.

"So what happened, Chloe? How b-bad is it?"

"I got a week of detention and a lecture about applying my interest in psychology to evaluating my episodes of acting out."

Maggie looks away, and I can tell she's biting her tongue.

I know that look. It means she's working hard to say something in a way that won't offend the hell out of me.

"Spit it out. You're obviously dying to insert commentary."

She sighs. "Look, I know you w-wanted to help me, but you've got to start thinking about yourself, Chloe. Sometimes it's like you're running away from everything you want."

I try not to look as hurt as I feel. "It's not like I'm afraid of being good, Mags."

She just laughs and takes my arm. "You jumped off the Third Street Bridge on a *dare*, which proves you're not afraid of anything. It also proves you're insane."

"Watch it."

I take a breath as we pass the drinking fountains, heading close to the last stretch of lockers in the hall. An otherwise unremarkable place in this building except for the fact that it's the Blake Zone.

As if on cue, he closes his locker door and appears, the tall, popular king of this lonely hallway. He laughs at a joke I don't hear. It's a perfect laugh that matches his perfect teeth and his perfect everything else.

I sigh. "Did Blake seem…disappointed?"

She blows out an impatient breath and rolls her eyes at me. "I didn't really think to dissect Blake's expression in the chaos and p-panic of the fire evacuation."

Blake laughs again, and I turn away, my cheeks burning. "Right. Sorry."

She gives me a sly grin. "Want me to go ask him?"

I slump back against the wall with a sigh. "How is it that I'm not the one who talks to boys? I'm the bridge jumper, the alarm puller—"

"The streaker," Maggie adds.

"That was one time! And technically, I was in my undies, but yes. How is it that you, High Queen of the Honor Roll, are better at this than me?"

"The stutter makes me a wild card," she says, winking. "No one ever sees me coming. And you talk t-to plenty of guys."

My gaze lingers on the stretch of Blake's polo across his shoulders, the ends of his hair curling over his collar. "Yeah, well. Not that one."

"I've got to g-get to class," Maggie says. "Speaking of which, did you remember to pick up your GPA at the office this morning?"

I feign a big, carefree smile. "Gosh, I must have completely forgotten. But I totally signed up for the SAT study group you told me about."

"And somehow forgot t-to ask for your GPA?" she asks, clearly unconvinced.

"Oh, who cares about a GPA anyway?"

She blinks at me, arms crossed. "Uh, every college you'll be applying to."

"Right. Well, finals aren't until next week. I can fix it."

Her eyes go dark. "Fix it? How bad is it?"

"Um, I—" The warning bell rings, saving me from another lie. "Gotta dash. Study hall and all. Yep, that's me. Study, study, study."

I slip inside the door and hear her calling after me. "You're running out of time, Chloe!"

She's got a point. I have exactly six days left of my junior year to turn my GPA into something that won't doom me to serving bad eggs at Trixie's Diner for the rest of my life. The urgency should inspire me to use every minute of my study hall period. It *really* should.

I pick up my biology notes, but it's all *cellular* this and *genetic* that, and my eyelids feel heavy after two lines. Why can't I get my act together?

Everyone around me is in full-force cram mode. Of course they are. Even Alexis, who spent the whole year reading *Vogue* behind her textbooks, is flipping through a stack of note cards. I'm officially the last slacker standing.

Maybe I could make a waitressing gig awesome. Except I don't want a waitressing gig. I only want one gig, and it doesn't involve rushing baskets of fries to hungry truckers.

It involves a doctorate degree in psychology.

How am I going to get through twelve years of college if I can't even stay awake in study hall?

Too bad I can't make a career out of sleeping in class undetected. I could tutor people in *that*. It's all about the posture. Chin in palm says bored. Chin on knuckles says deeply in thought.

And that sunbeam drifting through the window next to my desk? It says, *Go to sleep, Chloe.*

I tilt my head, watching the late May sunshine stroke my arms with soft, golden fingers. I do have all weekend to study. And I've got that stupid study group tonight, so I'm taking steps in the right direction. How much harm could one *teeny* little catnap do?

I give into the warmth and let my eyes slip closed. I'll worry about my lack of self-discipline after the bell rings.

But the bell doesn't ring.

There's no sound at all to wake me, just a cold sinking feeling in my middle. The hair on the back of my neck prickles, and my heart changes rhythm. Skips one beat. Then another.

And I know something is horribly wrong.

CHAPTER TWO

. . . .

'm afraid to open my eyes, but I do.

Darkness closes around me like a fist. Even still half-asleep, I know this isn't right. I blink blearily, but everything feels off. The room, the air…me.

Dreaming. I must still be dreaming.

Outside the window, everything is dark. Wait, that can't be right. It can't be that late.

Can it?

A slate-gray sky stretches beyond the glass. I see bits of white trailing through it, drifting down like glitter against velvet.

What is that? Flowers? Dust? No, it's just snow.

Snow?

I bolt out of my seat, the scrape of my chair legs shattering the silence. I'm alone. Goose bumps rise on my arms as I stare at the emptiness.

The clock above the whiteboards reads 9:34 p.m. Mr. Brindell, who I've never seen anywhere but behind his desk, is gone. I look around, realizing that it's not just the teacher. *Everyone* is gone. Every*thing* too. Books, papers, backpacks dangling from the corners of chairs. I'm in the belly of a skeleton, the remains of a class long over.

Panic shoots through me like a shock from a bad plug, white hot and jangling every nerve.

No.

No, this can't be happening. It's a scary dream. A mistake.

I lean closer to the window, but the snow refuses to be anything other than what it is. It falls thickly on the brown grass, clinging to the spindly branches of barren trees.

Where are the leaves? For that matter, where is the freaking sun?

Please let me wake up. I *need* to wake up.

But I won't. I feel it in my bones. My heart screams, *Nightmare!* but my mind says otherwise. This is happening.

I press my hand to the glass then snatch it back in shock. My nails—they're filthy. I examine the black half-moons of dirt wedged under each nail, black streaks caked into the creases of my fingers.

Okay, this is too creepy. Like horror-movie creepy and I need to get out of here. Right now.

I reach for my backpack, but it's not there. Gone too is the strappy sundress I zipped myself into today. I'm wearing a black sweater and jeans now. The feel of the soft knit beneath my fingers makes my stomach roll. This isn't right. Nothing is right.

I find the comforting bulge of my car keys in one pocket and my cell phone in the other. Thank God. I pull it out with shaking fingers and turn it on.

Light blooms on the screen, and I deflate in relief. Outside the world is still screaming all its wrongness at me, but this little glowing rectangle is my anchor. I hold it tight.

I inch farther away from the dark window with its impossible snow, my fingers hovering over the keypad on my phone.

Now what? My parents flash through my mind, but they still think I'm crazy after last fall. I might as well just call the psychiatric ward at Mercy Hospital and save the extra step. No, I can't call my parents.

Maggie.

My speed dial for her doesn't work. Too impatient to figure out why, I scan through my recent calls. But she's not on here.

Impossible. I haven't gone ten minutes without calling or texting Maggie since we both got phones in the ninth grade. I texted her on my way to the principal's office like two *hours* ago.

One glance at the window reminds me that wasn't two hours ago.

I keep paging, stopping only to make sure this isn't someone else's phone. Because the list of names in my recent calls cannot belong to me. Finally, on the sixth or seventh page, I find my mom's cell phone and a couple of calls to my house, but no Maggie.

I pull up the detail on one of my calls, and fear slithers through me like a living thing. 11/10—6:32 p.m.

As in *November* 10? No. I read it once and then again. A bunch of other calls are all from November too. I glance up, panicked, finding a calendar on the wall and a flyer for a winter dance that should still be eight months away.

The evidence hits me like icy darts, needling me toward the impossible truth. I've been asleep for six months. A coma or something. Somehow, I've missed *six months* of my life.

But that can't be right either. They wouldn't leave me uncon-scious in a classroom. I'd be in a hospital, hooked up to machines and watched by nurses. But if I wasn't asleep…

Amnesia?

Maybe I've also got a terrible case of consumption too. Or malaria. I need to get serious here—no one gets amnesia! But what else could this be? The longest lasting roofie of all time? Alien abduction?

A sinister possibility whispers to me. One word, two syllables, and an endless river of humiliation.

Crazy. I could be going crazy.

I heard it enough last year, whispered behind my back. I saw it on their faces too, expressions that ranged from pity to contempt as they looked at the "troubled girl." But troubled is way better than insane, and *what else could this be?*

Sane people forget what they ate for breakfast. Or maybe the names of their new neighbors. They don't wake up in a dark class-room without a damned clue where they've been or what they've done for six months.

Adrenaline flares through my middle, making my joints tickle and my stomach cramp. I feel my body poising for flight, my lips going numb, my heart pumping faster with each beat.

It won't stop there. Not with me. Familiar bands squeeze around my chest in warning, and I clench my fists. I have to calm down before this turns into a full-blown panic attack.

I close my eyes and do all the things my therapist told me to do. I remind myself that I am okay. That I am not sick or dying.

My body is giving me extra energy to figure this out, and it's good energy. It's okay. I don't need to be afraid.

"Chloe?"

My head snaps up at the sound of my name and at the person standing in the open doorway of the classroom. Adam Reed. Six feet and a couple of inches of something that scares me half to death.

I feel the blood drain from my face as he makes his way into the room. The light from the windows seems all too happy to highlight his model-worthy cheekbones and broad shoulders. Adam's so pretty he looks like he could sprout wings and a halo. But angels don't usually come with criminal records.

Is he here because of the fire alarm? He's looking at me like that again, with a little bit of a smile on his face. And Adam never smiles, so what gives?

"What do you want?" I ask, my voice small and frightened.

He chuckles. "You called me, remember?"

The idea of me calling him is so ridiculous I can't even respond. We don't even nod at each other in the halls. Why would I call him?

Despite my little fire alarm adventure, it's not like we run in the same circles. I get along with almost everyone. Adam can't seem to move through the hallways without starting a fight. I sometimes walk dogs at the animal shelter. He sometimes gets pulled out of class by the *police*. We aren't just in different social groups; we're in different solar systems.

He tilts his head, and I take a breath, feeling my shoulders relax. Which is maybe crazier than anything else happening right now. I shouldn't feel safer with him here. I should feel completely freaked out.

So why don't I?

"What are you doing here?" he asks, and though everything about his heavy black boots and ratty cargo jacket screams don't-give-a-crap, he *sounds* interested. Maybe even concerned.

"I'm…" I search for something that sounds better than *I'm losing my mind* or *I'm stuck in some* Twilight Zone *time warp*, but nothing comes. And I don't need to explain myself to him. I don't even know him.

"Why are *you* here?" I ask instead.

"Because you called me," he says, laughing again. Then he nods down at my hands, smirking. "Have you been making mud pies while you waited for me to get here?"

I flush and hide my hands, but I still take an instinctive step toward him. And then I remember that he is a juvenile delinquent and, for all I know, a psychopath. I should be running *away* from him. He doesn't look like a psychopath though. He just looks like Adam.

He crosses his arms and smirks at me. "You *do* remember calling me, right?"

Fear snakes its way up my spine, making my tongue thick and my throat dry.

No. I don't. I've never had a conversation with him, or hell, even stood this close to him until tonight.

Maybe he's wasted. He's got to be, right? But he looks absolutely sober. No red eyes or twitchy fingers. Kind of odd, now that I think of it, because I would have figured him for the type.

He smirks at me then, his blue eyes glittering. "I'm impressed you jimmied the cafeteria door without my help. I was beginning to think you'd never figure that out."

What? I did what to the what?

This is nuts. Completely nuts. I've never *jimmied* anything in my life. And if I did, it wouldn't be the door to my high school cafeteria.

He braces his hands on the back of a chair and tilts his head. A rush of déjà vu washes over me. I take a breath and hold it in, watching him drag his thumb along the back of the chair. I've *seen* this. I've seen him here, looking at me like this. I'm sure of it.

I stare at his hand, feeling my cheeks go white and cold. Apparently he senses the change because his smile disappears, his eyes narrowing.

"You all right, Chlo?"

My nickname sounds right on his lips. Natural. He shouldn't even know I have a nickname, let alone feel right using it. But he obviously does.

"You look scared to death," he adds, frowning down at me.

I'm not sure *scared* is the right word. I'm not sure there *is* a right word for all the things I'm feeling.

"I'm fine. Just tired," I lie.

He walks right up to me, and I swear to God, I can't remember how to breathe. My heart is pounding and my fingers are shaking, but somehow the world feels steady anyway. I'm not afraid. I should be, but I'm just not.

"Do you need to talk? Is that why you called?" he asks. "You know you can talk to me."

"I know that," I say automatically, the words coming from a place I can't find, a great empty space in me where I'm sure a memory should be.

I feel inexplicably sad at this yawning hole, this absence.

What's happening to me? What happened to make me forget?

I bite my lip and feel my eyes burn with the threat of tears. Adam's expression softens, twisting into something pained. Not once have I dreamed him possible of this kind of look. Hell, of anything in the same zip code as this look.

He opens his mouth to say something, and my whole body goes tense, my belly a knot of fluttering things. What is going on with me?

He reaches across the desk between us, almost but not quite touching my fingers. Every centimeter between our hands feels charged. Electric.

"We can't keep doing this, Chloe," he says softly.

The words sting and I don't know why. I don't even know what he means, but I desperately want to argue with him. I want to shake my head and grab his hands and—this is crazy.

Way beyond crazy.

My whole world is sliding into a flat spin. I can't have this guy, this total freaking *stranger*, at the center of it.

If I don't get away from him, I'm going to do something stupid. Something I won't be able to come back from.

"I have to go," I say, retracting my hands into fists and starting toward the door.

"Chloe," he says, touching my bare wrist as I pass.

Something warm rushes through me, making my ears buzz and my face heat up. I hear Adam laughing in the back of my mind, like the sound track to a movie I can't see. I whirl to face him, ready to snap his head off for making fun.

But he's not laughing. Not now. The memory of his laughter fades away even as Adam's hand drops from my shoulder, a hurt look crossing his face.

He lets me pass without another word. My footsteps are even and steady as they carry me into the hall. I wish my heart would follow the example.

CHAPTER THREE

. . . .

My car isn't in its normal spot. Then again, I've misplaced a couple of seasons, so why should this surprise me? I finally find the aging Toyota in the south lot, resting under a thin blanket of snow. So I haven't been here long.

Only six months or so.

Panic rushes again, squeezing hot fingers around my throat. I force myself to count to ten. And then twenty. Finally, I give up on trying to harness my inner calm and I pry open my frozen car door.

I start my engine and find my scraper in the backseat and set to work shaving the ice from my windshield. I'm shaking so hard that my teeth are rattling.

I stop once to call Maggie, getting her voice mail twice in a row. The fact that she doesn't answer is as stupefying as everything else. She doesn't take a shower without propping her phone on the sink. Now, three calls and nothing?

I hear the roar of an engine and look up like a trapped deer as a pair of headlights turn into the parking lot. My heart flies into my throat. It stays there, pumping hard, while the red Mustang cuts a slow arc toward me.

Blake?

Oh God, please not now. Not when I'm completely frozen and totally unstable thanks to an acute case of freaking amnesia.

For some reason I can't even fathom, the Mustang is pulling straight toward me. How would he even see me from the main road? It's like he knew I was here.

The car rolls to a stop and the door opens. Maybe it's his sister or his mom or, God, maybe someone stole his car and is now about to kill me. Every one of those options would be preferable to this.

But it's not someone else. It's him. The blond-haired, dimpled lacrosse player and not-so-secret crush of at least half of the girls in this high school.

"God, Chloe, I was worried sick," he says, slamming his door shut and striding toward me.

Before I can speak or blink, he hauls me into a tight hug. He smells just like he did this morning, like real cologne, the kind most of the guys around here can't even afford to look at. And yes, before this moment, I would have given everything I own for even a sideways arm-around-the-shoulder hug from him, but right now, it's just too much. His cologne, his supersoft down coat. I feel suffocated.

I lift my hands to push away, but he pulls back first, his face a weird mix of worry and irritation. I take a step back, my ice scraper still dangling from my left hand.

He reaches out, tucking some of my dark hair behind my ear. The strands drag along my neck, leaving goose bumps in their wake. They shouldn't reach my neck. I hacked my hair into a chin-length bob last week, but it isn't short anymore.

Blake smiles, and I try desperately to force one in response, but I can't.

Behind me, I hear heavy footsteps approaching from the direction of the school. Blake's hand falls off my shoulder. I don't need to look to know who it is, but I can't seem to resist.

I wish I had. The expression Adam's wearing turns my stomach to stone. I know this feeling creeping through my middle, but it can't belong to me. What would I have to feel guilty about?

Adam flips his dark hair out of his eyes and offers us a half-hearted salute. He slings his backpack over one shoulder and turns to lope through the school yard in his half-laced boots.

He'll freeze in this snow. Where's his car?

And why do I care? He's a stranger, and I don't care where his car is. Except that he's not a stranger. And I obviously care a lot.

A touch to my arm brings my attention back to Blake. He's also mostly a stranger, but not the kind I need to be afraid of. He's the poster boy of nice. Good citizen. Class president. He probably does commercials for the Boy Scouts when he's not helping little old ladies cross the street.

He's the one I should feel safe with.

"Chloe, are you okay?" he asks me, his hand resting just above my elbow.

"No. Not really," I admit.

"Is your head all right? Why are you muddy?"

As soon as he says it, I reach for a spot just above the nape of my neck. My fingers graze a swollen lump, and I wince in pain. What the hell? When did that happen?

"Easy," Blake says, and I step back from him, wary. He ignores me, reaching forward to take my hand. "You bumped it pretty hard. I can't believe you didn't go straight home. Maybe I should get you to the hospital."

"I didn't bump my head," I say, even though it's clear I did.

And it's equally clear he saw me do it.

He looks really concerned now. Like daytime TV worried, his brow all puckered and eyes sad. He doesn't know me well enough to worry about me like that. Or to hug me.

The world starts a precarious tilt, so I rest my palm on the roof of my car and try not to pass out.

"Chloe, I think I should take you to the hospital," Blake says slowly. "Do you even know why you're here? And why are you so filthy?"

I prod the tender bump, hoping that the pain will jar my memory.

"I don't know. I remember..." I trail off because what am I going to say? I remember falling asleep in study hall. On the last Tuesday in May.

"Do you remember the walk we took at my house tonight?" he asks.

A walk with Blake Tanner? Not possible. If Blake passed me a napkin in the cafeteria line, I'd dissect it with Maggie for three days. I wouldn't forget a walk.

"Do you?" he repeats softly, and I feel his fingers lacing through mine.

His hand is warm and large and everything that a boy's hand is supposed to be.

"Do you remember slipping on the porch? That's when you hit your head. I don't know how you got so dirty though."

I touch my head again, this time conscious of the cold, black stains on the knees of my jeans. Is that what this is? A stupid head injury or whatever?

I want it to be true. I need it to be true.

"I…I slipped. By the sidewalk," I say, the lie spilling out of me automatically as I brush at my filthy jeans. "I'm really tired. My brain is just fuzzy."

"Let me take you home," he says. "At least there your mom could take a look."

I glance back at my half-scraped car and then over to his snow-less, clearly garage-stored Mustang. The dark interior is probably toasty. Maybe if I just sit for a moment, I'll figure this out.

"Okay," I agree. "If you're sure it's not too much trouble."

He laughs at that, like it's ridiculous for me to even think it. "No, Chloe. It's not too much trouble to take my girlfriend home."

Girl-what?

Girlfriend. He said *girlfriend.*

It's a joke. This whole stupid thing is an enormous prank but why? Because I have a crush on him? Who doesn't?

No, that can't be it. Blake isn't into that kind of juvenile crap. He's on the Bully Patrol, for God's sake.

But it can't be anything else.

Blake doesn't seem to notice me standing there gaping like a goldfish. He takes the scraper from my hand and turns off my car, locking the doors when he's done. And since he doesn't fumble with the locks or my ignition, which tends to stick, I'm guessing he's done this before. He hands me my purse with a frown.

"This was on the floor."

"Thanks."

He smiles and guides me over to the Mustang. I fidget and watch him open the passenger door, and then he helps me into the seat like this is all routine. Like I wouldn't normally be stumbling over myself in rapture at the chance of setting foot in his vehicle.

When I sink into the leather seat, I don't feel rapture. If anything, I feel a little uneasy. Maybe even nauseous. I shift my feet, painfully aware of the mud on my boots and his pristine carpets.

It's deliciously warm though, like sitting by a fire. I smell new car and Blake, and I don't know why, but I don't like the mix. Blake slides behind the wheel, and we both fasten our seat belts in silence. Then he tugs something out of the backseat.

"You left your coat when you ran out tonight," he says, and then he hands it to me. "You must have been freezing."

I run my hands down the rough red wool. It's my coat, all right. I spent a small fortune on it at the beginning of my sophomore year, so it's not something I leave lying around.

"Oh, thanks. I really must have hit my head harder than I thought," I say, baring my teeth in something that I hope passes for a smile.

Blake turns up the heater and rolls out of the parking lot without another word. He turns right on Main before I can direct him and makes the immediate left onto Birchwood, proving that he knows where he's going.

When he slides his hand to my knee, my whole body goes cold and tense. I watch him out of the corner of my eye, but he doesn't look like someone playing a prank. His body language is relaxed. Touching me is comfortable for him.

For some insane reason, I'm pretty sure Blake believes this. He thinks I'm his girlfriend.

I ignore my swimming head and Blake's squeezing hand, and stare out the windshield. Out of the corner of my eye, I can see him watching me.

"What a crazy night," I say, figuring I can't just sit here in silence forever.

He doesn't react at first, but I see a muscle in his jaw jump when I turn to him.

"Yeah," he finally says. "What all do you remember?"

It's a weird question. And a short list. Darkness. Snow. Terror. Adam.

I linger on that last one longer than I should, my mind forming a picture of him. "It's kind of a blur."

He sighs in a way that borders on theatrical. "I just wish you'd tell me why you're so tense. Is it still about your SAT scores?"

"My SAT scores?"

He turns to me, half rolling his eyes. "Mine aren't that much better, you know."

"I haven't taken—"

I cut myself off, realizing that I probably did take the test. Like everything else, I might just not remember it.

"I'm just stressed," I say weakly, half expecting that awful itchy anxiety to return. Instead, I feel numb. Heavy and slow, like I'm half-asleep.

Huh. I must be going into shock. Fine by me. It's infinitely preferable to the flailing and panicking.

Blake pulls to a stop in front of my house. I look up at the dormer windows and black shutters. Mom's Thanksgiving wreath hangs on the door, and the windows give off a warm, yellow glow. In my whole life, home has never looked so sweet.

"Want me to walk you in?"

"It's all right," I say. "I'm really tired."

He nods and then tilts his head. "Hey, stop worrying about your scores. You're in the top three percent, Chloe. You're one of the elite."

I open my mouth because I have no idea what he's talking about, but before I can say anything, he's kissing me good-bye. And I can't remember what I wanted to ask him about now because this is Blake. Blake Tanner. Kissing me.

I've imagined him doing this for as long as I can remember. I never dreamed it would feel so horribly wrong.

CHAPTER FOUR

nsistent electric beeping wakes me. It can't be seven o'clock yet. I'm too tired. Too snug and content here in the cocoon of my blankets.

The clock blares on, unmoved by my silent protest. I roll over and mash the snooze button and then burrow back into the blissful warmth of my quilt. Two more minutes and I'll get up. I mentally catalog my sandal options. Is my blue tank top clean? Maybe. Or I could—

My thoughts cut off as I remember. The snow. The darkness. Blake. *Adam.*

I sit up, scanning my room as I kick the covers off my legs. It's cold and dark. *Too* cold and dark for seven o'clock in May. I shiver as I rise from my bed, padding across my wood floor. My curtains are tightly shut, not a sliver of daylight showing around the edges.

I pull the drapes open quickly, like I'm ripping off a bandage. Outside, it's still winter. Inside, I die a little.

I press my palm to the cold windowpane with a sigh. The street looks magical, every house and mailbox dipped in a snow so white it looks like sugar. It's like a Christmas card.

But I'm not ready for Christmas. I'm ready for jean shorts and sweet tea and long, sticky nights with cicadas singing in the grass.

I return to my bed, curling into a ball. It wasn't a nightmare. I'd known that, of course, but nothing else seemed possible when I'd stumbled in here last night.

Now, the newness of the day hits me like teeth, gnawing at the unwelcome truth. I'm missing time. A lot of it.

"Chloe?"

My mom's voice drifts up the stairs, familiar and just a little scratchy so she probably hasn't had much coffee.

"You want breakfast, honey?"

No, I really don't. I want my six months back.

I try dialing Mags again before giving up and heading downstairs. Mom is peering into the fridge, her hair in a towel and her shirt buttoned wrong. Nothing newsworthy there. Until she turns at me and breaks into a grin.

"Morning, Superstar. Need some oatmeal to keep that brain churning?"

Uh, what? I blink several times, and she just laughs, pulling out a carton of blueberries and a couple tubs of yogurt. Which is… weird. We don't do breakfast. Not together, anyway.

"Too early, I guess." She nods at a cup and saucer on the counter. "Your tea's ready."

Tea? We have tea in this house?

I don't know what she's talking about, and I'm too tired to care. The coffeepot is sputtering, so I head over to get myself a cup. One whiff and a wave of queasiness rolls through me. I push the pot back onto the burner.

"What's wrong with the coffee?" I ask.

My mom sighs and takes another sip while my stomach cramps in protest. "Don't start again, Chloe."

My hands are shaking now. I can't handle this. It's just too scary.

"Mom, I need to talk to you."

"Is it about Vassar? Honey, I know it sounds hoity-toity, but with these scores, you've got to consider—"

"It's not about Vassar, Mom. It's about me. I'm having some trouble."

She looks up, her gray eyes clouding with worry. "What kind of trouble? School trouble? The kids in the SAT group?"

I can't blame her for asking. If I go down in the yearbooks for anything it'll be Most Likely to Not Live Up to My Potential. "No. I'm just…I'm forgetting some things."

Her relief is palpable, bringing pink back to her cheeks. "Of course you're forgetting things. You're exhausted, honey. You've been studying day and night, putting in extra credit."

"I think it's more than that," I say, though the idea of me investing in extra credit is just insane. I'm a Play Now, Work Later girl, and she knows it better than anyone.

She takes a breath, hands moving absently to her throat. "You don't think it's those *panic attacks* again, do you?"

She says it like a dirty secret, almost whispering it. I feel like she's poised on the edge of a knife. One wrong word from me now and she will return to the mother I remember. Quiet. Distant. Disappointed.

"Maybe I just need some sleep," I say with a sigh.

Mom nods so quickly it's like she spoon-fed me the answer. She clears the table, though I've barely touched my yogurt. Typical. I get a smile and a pat that's supposed to be reassuring. And then she's up the stairs and I'm left on my own.

Across from me, the fridge whirs to life and I glance at the clutter strewn across the doors. I watched a *Dateline* episode once about how criminals could learn everything about you from digging through your trash. They'd have better luck looking at our fridge.

Bills, birthday pictures, concert tickets, notes we leave each other, it's all stuck up there, layered so thickly most days, it's hard to find the handle to get the darned thing open. And today there are some new things to the mix, one in particular that I can't stop staring at.

It's a printout from a website placed front and center on the left door. I remember the logo in the corner from the information they passed out in homeroom. It's the SAT website.

Blake's words from last night play through my mind. *You're in the top three percent, Chloe.*

My scores. My SAT scores are on my fridge.

My heart starts pounding harder and faster. Even from here I can see my name at the top and a series of numbers circled in red in the middle. There are comments from both of my parents, stars and exclamation points all over the place.

I stand up and head over, frowning at the four digits that spell out the impossible.

Two thousand one hundred and fifty-five.

My mouth drops open. No, it can't be right. I'd hoped I'd

manage maybe 1650. Anything over 1700 and I would have lost my mind, but this?

I check again. My name, the scores, the dates. It's all there.

It has to be a mistake. What else could it be? This is the kind of score genius kids get. Future rocket scientists and surgeons and…psychologists.

I press my thumb over the four numbers and think of the row of psychology books lined up above my computer desk. I think of that first panic attack when I sat there panting and shivering in the girls' locker room, sure I was dying and desperate to understand how something like this could happen to someone like me.

When I pull my thumb away, the numbers remain.

2155.

Maybe I don't remember that test, but I took it.

This score? It changes *everything*.

● ● ●

My shower is beyond brief. I spend a minute checking myself over in the mirror. My hair is at my shoulders now, but it's still dark and curly enough to be a hassle. The rest of me seems unchanged. Green eyes, narrow nose, and dimples I've hated since I first noticed them in the second grade.

My phone rings when I'm finishing my hair, buzzing on the sink.

"Mags," I breathe, scrambling as it skates across the vanity. I catch it and search for her name, but it's not Maggie. It's the number I saw over and over in my phone last night. The one I obviously call all the time these days.

I answer it, hoping that Maggie's number has changed—that she'll be yelling at me for not calling and asking me what we're doing for lunch.

"Morning." It's Blake. My shoulders sag, and he goes on, not waiting for me to respond. "How are you feeling?"

My eyes search for the mirror. I look tired and pale. Maybe even a little scared.

"I'm okay."

"You sure? Did you have your mom look at your head?"

I test it with my fingers, but it's barely sore now. Not likely a brain injury.

"She did. It's fine," I say, because lying is easier than explaining I totally forgot about my head after his good-bye kiss completely squicked me out.

"Good," he says. "So you want me to come in? I've got your breakfast."

My spine goes stiff. "Come in? Are you here?"

He chuckles at that. "Your car's at school, babe. Did you think I'd make you walk?"

Babe. Girlfriend. All kinds of impossible words that feel too ridiculous to be believed. They also feel sort of…nauseating.

"No," I say, forcing the word out through a tight throat.

Blake makes a noise on the other end of the phone, something between a snort and a sigh. "Are you sure you're all right? I hate to say it, but you're acting like a total head case."

The word pinches the last nerve I've got, but I'm sure he can't mean anything by it. And he's got a point. If he really thinks I'm his girlfriend, then I am being a head case.

I force a stiff chuckle. "Sorry, I didn't get enough sleep. I appreciate you stopping by. Can you give me two minutes?"

"I'll be here."

I don't need two minutes, but I take them to get my nerves settled. I slide in a pair of silver hoops, noticing new pictures tucked into the frame of my dresser mirror. The three new group shots turn my skin cold at one glance.

I don't belong in these pictures. These aren't pictures of my people. I'm not a social leper, but I'm not the girl that belongs in these pictures. They're filled edge to edge with the rich, the beautiful, the brilliant…and *me*.

Blake stands next to me in every last one, his arm around my shoulder and my head tipped toward him. It's the kind of pose that leaves no question to our status. We're together.

Un-freaking-believable.

My memory decides to have some sort of massive file corruption and *these* are the months I missed? What about my years in braces? Or the summer my dog and grandmother died a month apart? No, I get to miss the six months that turned my life from train wreck into perfection. Lovely.

I glance out my window where Blake's Mustang is idling at my curb. Things definitely could be worse.

I make my way outside to his car. He opens the door for me, a doughnut in his mouth and a paper bag held out for me to take.

31

"Good morning," I say, forcing myself to kiss him when he leans in. It's still stiff and awkward, but it will get better. It has to. He's Blake Tanner, for God's sake.

I bury my nose in the bag and inhale. "Smells awesome. Thank you."

"Hop in. We're going to be late."

I've never been so grateful for a blueberry scone. I savor every bite, chewing slowly so that I don't have to say anything. I need to fill in a few more blanks before I talk myself into a corner. It works like a dream, and before I know it, we're in the parking lot.

Blake drops me near the doors, and I automatically take his trash with mine. I feel like we've done this dance a thousand times. My body knows the steps, even if I can't hear the music.

Salt crunches beneath my feet as I climb the stairs two at a time out of habit. I doubt it matters if I'm late now. With the scores I've got tacked to my fridge, I could probably schlep off a month of school and still pick almost any college I'd like.

And apparently those pictures on my dresser weren't a joke. I'm *popular*. Not just, *Oh, hey, there's Chloe*, but, like, squealing and waving and air kisses from girls who barely nodded at me before. Even Alexis gives me a shoulder squeeze and a "Hey, girl!" as I pass her.

By the time I get to my locker, I feel dizzy with all the greetings that have been aimed my way. I'm getting so much in-crowd attention, I feel like I should have pom-poms and a pleated skirt.

I approach the locker that's been mine since freshmen year and grin when the combination hasn't changed. Okay, I can do this. I can figure this out.

And then, when I didn't think things could get any better, I see Maggie across the hall. Her strawberry blond hair is six inches shorter, curling just above her shoulders. But I'd never mistake the set of her shoulders or the half smile that always seems present on her lips.

"Maggie!" I shout.

She looks up at me, and for one second, the world is right. Maggie will drag me to the bathroom and borrow my lip gloss or ask me if she should go a shade darker with her hair. Then I will tell her about my stupid amnesia, and she will help me diagram every major event I've missed. My secret will be safe. Everything will be perfect.

I think all of those things in the nanosecond before our gazes lock. And then Maggie's eyes go cold and flat. Her mouth purses into a frown I've rarely seen, and she looks away.

• • •

I'm standing in the hallway, staring at the empty space where Maggie once stood, when the bell rings. Lockers slam, classroom doors close, and then I hear the soft drone of more than one teacher addressing their students.

My feet feel glued to the ground. I could force them to move, but where would I go? I don't know which class I belong to. I don't know what to do, and I can't ask for help, not without giving myself away.

Stupid! What was I thinking coming here? Thinking I could get away with this?

Tears are stinging the backs of my eyes, choking my throat. I need to get out of here. I need to get help because I am *not* okay.

A classroom door opens in front of me. A hall check. And here I am, in the hall when I should be at a desk in one of these rooms. I can see it all—the principal's office, the questions. The end of this perfect life before I have one second to enjoy it.

I hear someone rushing up behind me and then a strong hand sliding between my arm and waist, poking at the books I have clamped to my side. I fumble, watching everything fall to the floor. Mr. Fibbs pokes his balding head out of his classroom, a look of wariness in his eyes.

"Hallway collision," someone says behind me. "My fault. We're just getting her books."

Adam. Relief rushes over me at the sound of his voice. Wait, not relief. It has to be something else. It kind of feels like relief though.

His arm brushes my calf as he crouches down, carefully collecting the notebooks and folders he just forced me to drop. I stare, mute and dazed as he gathers my things into a neat pile.

"Move fast," Mr. Fibbs says, and this time he leaves his door cracked as he returns to class.

I hear nothing but my own breath and the soft hiss of paper against paper, his long fingers pulling them together.

I've never been this close to Adam. He's kind of famous around here, our resident criminal and all. I've never thought much about it, or him for that matter. But when he tilts his head and looks up at me, I wonder how in the world I *haven't* thought about him.

Because I can barely imagine going an hour without thinking about him now.

He smirks then. "You're never going to convert him."

"What do you mean?" I ask, staring a little too directly into his unbelievably blue eyes.

Adam stands up, and I have to tilt back my head to hold his gaze.

He hands my books back. "Mr. Fibbs. He still doesn't buy the new, *improved* you."

He says the last bit with a wink, almost as if it's a little joke between us. Of course we don't have jokes, and even if we do, I don't remember the punch lines. I don't laugh. But when he starts down the hallway, I automatically start walking too.

He stops at a corner, arm brushing my shoulder before he turns to face me. "So when are you going to tell me why you called me last night?"

"Last night," I echo, feeling confused.

"Did something happen at Blake's place?"

"At Blake's place?"

Oh my God, I'm like a freaking parrot. *Words, Chloe. Find some and spit them the hell out!*

Adam's face goes hard. "Look, you called me. If you changed your mind, just say so."

"That's not it," I say, because I hate his expression. But what am I going to say? I don't know why I called. Heck, I'm still having a hard time figuring out how I ended up with Adam Reed's phone number in the first place.

"It's not a big deal. Blake's fine," I say, hoping maybe that's the missing connection. Maybe he's friends with my boyfriend. Maybe he's upset about Blake?

But no, he wasn't upset. I know that because *now* he's upset. His eyes narrow to dangerous slits. When he steps closer, I feel the distinct need to hold on to something. Since he's the only thing within reach, I refrain. Instead, I squeeze my books so hard that the sharp edges press into my arms.

"Blake's fine? You're going to go with that, Chloe?" he asks, voice too soft for the hardness in his eyes. "You're going to stand here and pretend like nothing's happening?"

It's like all the air is sucked out of the room. I want to explain, and he's obviously waiting for me to respond. But even if I can manage to make my mouth work again, what am I going to say? I don't remember whatever *happening* he's talking about. And I wish to God I did because whatever's happening right now is making it hard for me to breathe.

"Just talk to me," he says, and he reaches out like he's going to touch me. I want him to. So much that my skin aches for it. When he pulls away, it's all I can do not to grab his arm to yank him back.

"Am I interrupting something?"

Blake's voice startles me. He's suddenly right behind me, his hand pressing into my lower back possessively. It feels as hot and unwelcome as a branding iron. It takes every ounce of strength I've got not to lurch away from him and closer to Adam.

"Am I interrupting, Reed?" Blake asks again, a cold edge to his voice.

"No," Adam says, but his eyes are on me. "Apparently not."

His long stride takes him down the hall. I watch the distance stretch between us and feel like I should call after him. Or run to him. It makes absolutely no sense.

"We're late for English," Blake says, pointing me toward a door at the end of the hallway.

So now I know where to go. I guess that's one mystery solved. Only eight billion or so to go.

CHAPTER FIVE

. . . .

There are serious advantages to being popular. Having people magically appear after every bell, happy to chitchat all the way to my next class, is really handy when you have no clue where to go.

The downside? Maggie wasn't one of those people. Not even once.

I dig through my purse for my car keys and thank whatever forces might be listening that Blake has some sort of sports practice after school. Because I'm not ready for another dose of *him*.

Just as I start the engine, someone taps on my window. I glance up, forcing a smile to my face.

Abigail Binns. Star of *42nd Street* last year and high-flying, handspringing cheerleader since junior high. I like Abbey. We're not friends exactly, but she's been on my bus route through three schools now. It's hard not to like someone who volunteers at the children's hospital and bakes cookies for her neighbors at Christmas.

I roll down the window. "Hi."

"Hi, Chloe. I'm so sorry to bother you. My brother was supposed to pick me up, but he got stuck at work. Is there any way you could drop me by my place on the way home?"

"Sure," I say.

Abbey flashes a million-dollar smile and hops in the passenger side of my Camry. My dad bought the car when I was born, and I think he's determined to make it last until I die.

"Thank you so much," she says, pulling on her seat belt as I start backing out.

Someone strolls right behind my car, and I slam on the brakes, coming way too close to hitting him. All I see is a charcoal gray hoodie pulled all the way up. It's more than enough to send my pulse into a sprint. Adam drops the hood back and flashes me a look I can't read. It doesn't settle my heart down at all.

Abbey shakes her head. "Not an ounce of common sense in that guy."

"Tell me about it," I say, but I crane my neck to watch him walk away all the same.

"I still can't believe he's in so many AP classes," Abbey says.

I tear my eyes away from the rearview mirror to look at her. "He is?"

"Well, yeah. His GPA this quarter is a 3.98." Abbey covers her mouth the moment she finishes her sentence, looking shamed. "I shouldn't have said that. I overheard it in the office. Honest, I wasn't trying to be a snoop."

I smile my first genuine smile since this whole thing started. And why shouldn't I? The walking Gossip Girl of Ridgeview, Ohio, just landed in my car.

"That's okay," I tell her. "It wasn't like you divulged some dirty secret."

She giggles. "He probably thinks his grades *are* a dirty secret. I'll just never understand. So did you hear about James and Kelsey?"

I drive as slowly as possible while Abbey fills me in on all the latest social happenings of our school. She's got juicy stuff on absolutely everyone, which would be sort of fun if she wasn't so determined to put a positive spin on every last bit of that dirt. Also, she might look seventeen, but after listening to her talk, I'm pretty sure she is an eighty-five-year-old widow who attends church three times a week.

"Bless her heart, we all make mistakes. It's really a shame those two can't work it out," she says as I turn onto Belmont Street.

Cookie-cutter two-story and Cape Cod houses like mine give way to sprawling historic giants. Mom calls them the Belmont Beauties. She's not wrong.

This is where Abbey lives. Where all the Ridgeview lifers live. These homes have been in their families for generations. I gaze out the window, passing wide, wraparound porches, most festooned with Prowler Pride flags and "Keep Ridgeview Clean" signs.

And then of course, there is the queen of them all. The white, columned mansion flanked by lilac bushes in the spring and crowned in glittering lights at Christmas. The Miller house. Iona, Quentin, and their daughter, Julien. Julien holds more academic and athletic titles than my entire homeroom class. It's not surprising. Her parents were legends too.

What is surprising is the lack of pumpkins and cornucopias on the lawn. Mrs. Miller lives to keep her house appropriately festive for every conceivable holiday and—wait a minute. Where are her curtains?

Something small and white near the mailbox catches my eyes.

I slam on the brakes, gaping at the wooden realtor sign with its bright red FOR SALE message printed at the top.

"Omigosh, Chloe, what is it? Is it a dog?" Abbey asks, hand to her chest and eyes searching the road. "Did it get away?"

"Where are the Millers?" I ask, waving wildly at the house.

Abbey's too busy worrying about the nonexistent dog to even look at me. "What are you talking about?"

"What am I talking about? I'm talking about the *Millers*, the family that's lived here for, like, twelve billion years!"

Abbey turns, looking at me like she's seen a ghost. Her dark eyes go very round.

"You're joking right? They left in *August*, Chloe."

"Left?" I say, because I can't even process that word. The Millers do not *leave*. They organize every charity event and holiday parade in this little nowhere town. If they left, the whole damn city would slide into Lake Erie.

"California," Abbey says slowly, looking a little pale. "Remember their big move to California?"

I blink but say nothing. Because I'd believe in Bigfoot before I'd believe this. The Millers wouldn't move *two blocks* away from their ancestral abode, let alone two thousand miles.

"Chloe, you came to the going away party. You and Blake." She looks genuinely frightened now. "Are you kidding around or something?"

She wants me to be kidding. Heck, *I* want me to be kidding. So I sigh and give an awkward laugh. "Uh, of course. It's just... weird seeing their house empty like that."

Abbey deflates like a balloon, shaking her head so that her blond hair swishes. "You're terrible, Chloe. Frightened me half to death."

I force a smile, but it feels too tight on my lips. My palms go slick on the steering wheel. Between that and my shaking knees, I don't know how I drive the next half block to Abbey's place.

She stops after she's out, holding the door open with a manicured hand. The air is icy, and my head is throbbing now. I just want her to go.

"You know, I thought the move was weird too. Julien seemed so off that whole month, like she could barely remember her own name. You can't imagine the kind of stuff she couldn't remember. It was…uncanny."

I can actually feel the ice forming in my veins. I force myself to respond. "Yeah, well, I'd be off too if I was moving thousands of miles away."

"Yes, but…" She trails off, waving a hand dismissively. "Oh, never mind."

"No, tell me," I say, though I have a bad feeling I don't really want to know.

Abbey tips her head. "Well, do you remember that psychology course we took last year?"

I nod impatiently because of course I remember it. It was the first time in my life I've ever leafed through a textbook ahead of time. Just for fun.

"Remember the day we discussed phobias and fears, and Julien said her mom had a terrible case of that, um, sizme..." She pauses, searching for the word.

"Seismophobia," I say automatically. "Fear of earthquakes."

Abbey nods. "Don't you think it's weird that someone with a fear like that would move out to California? I mean, isn't that where all the earthquakes happen?"

It is.

I look at Abbey and think of the empty house, something cold and prickly creeping up my spine. I feel like it's somehow reaching at me, begging me to tell the rest of the story. But I don't know the rest of the story.

Or at least, I don't *remember* it.

Abbey shifts her books and laughs. "Probably just silly of me to think it. I'm sure they have their reasons. I guess you never really know what happened if you weren't there."

"No, I guess you don't." Especially not if you're me.

When she closes the door, I pull my phone out of my purse and dial Maggie's number. It rings straight to voice mail, her soft voice lilting out of the tinny speaker. I wish I'd thought about this longer because I don't know how to say this. I only know that I have to.

"It's me. I know something's going on with us, and I'm pretty sure you don't want to talk to me, but I had to call." I take a shuddery breath. "I'm scared, Mags. I think something happened to me, and I think whatever it is, I think it might have happened to Julien Miller too."

• • •

Dad and Mom are home early when I get the house, which I expected. It's Taco Tuesday. We started this when Dad worked horrible hours and Mom was still going for her master's degree, one meal a week when we'd all be together.

At first we'd trot out the good dishes and make a chips and salsa bar and a buffet of taco toppings. Most of it fell by the wayside after a couple of months. But I guess old habits die hard, because we still get Mexican takeout every Tuesday night, and we usually end up on the couch together watching something on TV.

They look up at me with matching smiles as I head in, hanging up my purse and my coat. I smell salsa and can see a spread of chalupas and chips spread out on the coffee table. It's a happy, easy scene. I'm about to fling a flaming wrench into the middle of it.

I don't want to do this. What I want to do is be this new version of me, the one they've probably been hoping for all along. They probably think I've finally got it all figured out. Except that I can't even figure out where I sit in my fourth-period trig class.

"I think something's wrong with me," I say, because there's not much sense in beating around it.

Mom turns first, a crease forming between her brows. Dad follows, his smile quickly fading when he sees I'm not joking.

They watch me with a look of growing fear that probably matches my own expression. Ever since I saw the Millers' empty mansion, I've been scared to death. And I know I look it.

• • •

Four hours later I'm strapped down in a hospital testing room that smells like disinfectant. The gown scratches at my skin even though I'm trying to hold still like they asked.

"You're doing great, Chloe," a tinny voice assures me over the speaker. "Still okay?"

"I'm okay."

Total lie. This is not *okay*. Anytime you spend four hours getting poked and prodded while wearing a gown that leaves your butt flapping in the breeze, things are *not* okay.

At least in this dark machine no one will come in to shine a light in my eyes. Or ask me the same five questions the last ten doctors and nurses have asked.

I thought about writing a list to save myself the trouble. No, my vision is fine. No, I am not sleepy. No, I've had no nausea. No, there isn't any pain. Yes, I'm having some trouble with my memory. Dad and I started making up a song about it after the fourth person, but Mom shot us a look that could wither an evergreen, so we stopped.

The scanner grinds and buzzes around me. I try not to think about it. Instead, I wonder if I should have told them the whole truth. I mean, I said I had *some* missing time, but I was pretty vague about it.

"You're all done," the speaker voice says, and then the little tray I'm on whirs me out of the machine.

From there, they cart me to another room where I wait alone for at least a year. Maybe two.

"How are you holding up?" Mom asks when she arrives. "I

45

knew we shouldn't have gone to the cafeteria." She looks like she cried the entire time I've been in the CT scanner.

"I'm fine," I say. "I'm not dying, you know."

"Of course not. I know that," she says.

Behind her, my dad rolls his eyes, making boo-hooing gestures that make it crystal clear how *fine* she is.

"Contraband," he says, tossing me a Mr. Goodbar.

"You're my hero," I say, shredding the wrapper and scarfing down half of the candy bar in one bite. "I'm starved."

"George, she's not supposed to eat," Mom says.

"I know," I say around a mouthful of chocolate. "I'm such a rebel. First, Mr. Goodbar."

"Next she'll be robbing banks," Dad says, finishing my sentence.

Mom sniffs, crossing her arms over her chest. "It's not funny."

But it is. Pretty soon we're all laughing. I think they're buying it. I think they totally believe that I'm not scared anymore.

The neurologist who ordered my CT scan walks in holding my folder. He's got the longest, thinnest fingers I've ever seen and a mustache that looks penciled on. I can't help thinking he'd be a perfect Disney villain.

"The good news is, I don't see a concussion," he announces. "Your scan looks perfectly normal, Chloe."

Apparently the stress that's been holding me upright evaporates, because the minute I hear *perfectly normal,* I drop back to the pillow like my bones have melted.

My relief doesn't last. I prop myself back up on my elbows, frowning at him. "Wait. Then what's wrong with me?"

The doctor tips his head back and forth, like he's weighing something in his mind. My parents squirm in their chairs. Oh no. I know that look. I also know my parents probably filled out a lot of helpful information regarding my mental health history.

The doctor clears his throat and glances at my file. "Your parents tell me that you had some trouble with panic attacks. A little over a year ago?"

"Yeah, I had panic attacks. I didn't start *losing time*."

Nobody speaks. They all just look at me in that careful, guarded way. The way kids at school looked at me after the ambulance took me after that first attack.

I shake my head, frustrated. "I'm not crazy."

"No one's saying that," Dad says.

Mom says nothing.

The doctor dons an expression of neutral compassion that they probably bottle and sell in pill form at medical school. "Doctors don't like to use words like *crazy*."

Yeah, not with people they think *are* crazy.

He tucks my file under his chin and looks thoughtful. "Chloe, stress can manifest itself in hundreds of ways, and the effects are very real. As a high school senior, you're at a critical turning point in your life and that creates pressure. I think you need to find ways to cope with these issues."

Unbelievable. I'm missing time, and this doctor, this highly trained medical *professional*, wants to pat my hand and tell me I'm stressed? He's still talking, but I'm done listening. All I can think about is my medical chart, of the section on panic attacks that's going to stay with me for the rest of my life.

I take a breath, and I can almost smell the chlorine from the pool that first day it happened. Everything should have been fine. I mean, yeah, I had stuff going on. My homecoming date backed out, I failed my first two history quizzes, but it was just stuff. It wasn't tragic.

Every girl in my class swam their timed lap and got out, except me. Halfway down my return lap, I felt my whole body curl in around a crushing pain in my chest. I was tumbling in agony, sputtering wildly for the surface. Our gym teacher, Mrs. Schumacher, had to drag me out of the pool, and I screamed like a banshee; it hurt that bad.

They stretched me out on that rough cement beside the diving board, and I stared up at the dripping swimsuits, sure I'd die.

I didn't. I did, however, end up with several months of behavior therapy and a brief starring role in the gossip highlights of Ridgeview High.

"Chloe, do you understand what the doctor said?" Mom asks, interrupting my trip down memory lane. Her voice is pinched and tight, just like her smile.

I manage a nod, and everyone nods with me, looking oddly relieved. Did they expect me to say no? Maybe to run around screaming or something?

They hand my mother discharge papers and shuffle me to the door. My dad reaches forward to shake hands with the doctor.

"Dr. Kirkpatrick says she could squeeze her in this afternoon," the doctor says softly.

"We'll take her right over," Dad promises.

CHAPTER SIX

. . . .

've read that in a therapy session, *everything* is analyzed, from the chair you choose to how long you wait to answer a question. So now, instead of actually focusing on real issues, I'm wondering if I'm sitting in a way that says relaxed and healthy or disturbed and potentially sociopathic.

I glance at the clock and realize I've already looked at it three times. A possible indicator of obsessive-compulsive disorder. What else could I have? Paranoia? Generalized anxiety disorder? God, I wish she'd just say something so I can stop the diagnosis roulette.

Dr. Kirkpatrick sits back in her chair. She's got some issues too, I'd bet. I've seen her a total of thirteen times, including this session, and in that time, she's had three drastically different hairstyles. Talk about identity issues.

The last time, she had an auburn pixie cut. Now her hair is jet-black and angled harshly around her chin. She looked friendlier before, like a fairy just a few years past her prime. I can't help feeling like this version of Dr. Kirkpatrick should slap on some red lipstick and pull a gun on me or something.

"It's been a while since we've talked," she says. "Would you like to catch me up?"

I glance at the clock again. It's four minutes after. Just long enough for me to stop looking around the office, but not so long that I've had time to get nervous or rehearse answers.

"Um, sure. School is going good."

Dr. Kirkpatrick nods and watches me. Which means it's still my turn, I guess.

"My grades are great. My classes are fine. I'm applying at a lot of colleges, I guess."

"Your grade point average is substantially improved from last year. The study group did good things for you," she says. Bizarre. Do they keep that in my file? Apparently they do because she glances down at it pointedly. "How do you feel about that change?"

Here we go. How do I feel about my grades? My teachers? The paint in this room? This could go on for days. I'm convinced she could find meaning in the way I feel about a carton of french fries.

I've read more than anyone I know about anxiety, and I have a pretty hard time believing that a therapist is going to tie gaping holes in my memory to last year's anxiety attacks. I tried to explain this to my parents in the car on the way over from the hospital, but my mom only sniffled harder into her tissue.

So here I am.

"Chloe?" she asks.

Crap. That'll be noted for sure. Excessive pause before answering her question.

"Well, it's not like I have anything to complain about. I'm going to be able to get into pretty much any college out east. Plus, I'm dating Blake, who's great."

"Oh, really?" She doesn't look surprised. She looks like she's feigning surprise and it's…weird. All of this is just weird. "Have you and Blake been together long?"

"Oh, I don't know…" Which is the God's honest truth.

"Would you like to tell me about him?"

Yeah, I'd love to. Except I can't because I don't know a darned thing that I didn't read in my yearbook or the school paper.

I don't want to say that though. There is something in the set of Dr. Kirkpatrick's jaw that's different from last time. And I'll bet it's got everything to do with the new report in my chart, the one that was probably faxed over from the neurologist. Somehow I'm betting giant memory lapses rank a wee bit higher than anxiety episodes on the how-screwed-up-is-your-patient scale.

Before, I was a typical angsty teenager. Now I'm a *real* case.

"Actually, I was hoping I could talk about losing my memories."

She smiles a little. Just a little. I can tell she's pleased though. Point for me. "Sure. Why don't you start by telling me a little more about it."

I bite my lip and do my best to look thoughtful. Truthfully, I don't need to think about this. I thought about it all the way here. If I tell her too much, it will destroy everything. They'll start talking in-patient therapy and medication, and I can kiss my senior year good-bye.

I don't know how I became the girl with the killer SAT scores, but I'm not stupid. This is my ticket to my own perch in a chair like Dr. Kirkpatrick's. I'm not about to throw it away.

I take a breath and tilt my head, schooling my expression to sincerity. "I feel busy. So busy sometimes that I'm starting to lose track of things. Sometimes I forget so many things it's scary."

"Things at school?"

"Conversations, mostly," I say, forcing a mild look onto my face. "Social stuff."

"Do you still have time for your friends?" she asks, searching for something on my chart. She must find it because her eyes pop up to meet mine again. "Do you still see Maggie?"

Maggie.

"No," I say, swallowing hard. "No, Maggie and I don't talk much anymore. Too busy."

She sits back at this, watching me while a minute or two ticks by. "It sounds like you aren't happy with how busy things are, Chloe."

I nod, my mouth still thick and dry at the thought of my best friend. My ex-best friend, I guess.

"What do you think you can do to change things?"

"I don't know. But I want to do something about it. About the forgetting thing mostly. I was hoping there'd be an exercise that might help."

"That's a great idea," she says, as I knew she would. She *loves* exercises. "If you're open to the idea, we can try one now. Just sit back and close your eyes for me."

It's a comfortable chair. Probably purchased with this exact kind of exercise in mind. I close my eyes and follow her instructions to let my mind drift a little. To let go of my classes one by one. Then the hospital and the tests.

It sounds like nonsense, but sometimes it works. I saw it in my elective psychology class last year. And now, I'm feeling it myself, loose and warm around the edges, kind of lost in a soft limbo.

"Now, I'm going to say a few words. I want you to pretend you're one of those old slide projectors or those viewfinder toys where you flip through picture discs."

"I had one of those," I say. Mom bought them for long car rides to the beach.

"Good. I want you to pretend you're looking into one of those right now. When I say a word, think of an image. Just one. You don't have to tell me what it is. Just see it in your mind."

"Okay." I try to stay relaxed. It's hard because I'm excited. This could help. I mean, it's not a guarantee, but it could happen.

"Home," she says.

Click. I have a picture of our backyard, the picnic table with peeling paint, and a plastic pitcher of sun tea sitting in the middle.

"Fun."

I see Maggie and I posing with our tongues out on prom night.

"School."

A row of lockers, posters of varsity teams stretching above them.

"Love."

A boy looking up from a book. Dark hair and a killer smile. Adam.

I jerk my head up, eyes flying open. Dr. Kirkpatrick is writing in her book. Her face is serene. "Are you all right, Chloe?"

"I have no idea."

• • •

Maggie's house is probably not the best idea. But where else can I go? My parents are busy grieving the mental decline of their briefly perfect daughter. I could call my boyfriend, except that I barely know him. And since I'm associating the word *love* with an entirely *different* guy, I'm pretty sure I'm not as close to my boyfriend as I should be.

I ring the doorbell and plunge my hands back into the pockets of my coat. Footsteps echo in the entry inside just before Mrs. Campbell's face shows in the sidelight window. She looks surprised and delighted in equal parts.

"Chloe," she says as she swings the door wide. She squeezes me in a hug that smells like the bakery she owns. "It's been so long. Come on in, honey."

I swallow hard. "That's okay. I know it's kind of late. Is Maggie home?"

"Of course, sweetie. Come in out of the cold." I step inside and stand on the rug while she heads for the stairs. She seems to think better of it, stalling halfway to the steps and tilting her head at me. "Why don't you just go on up?"

"I'm not sure—"

Mrs. Campbell ghosts a hand over her reddish hair and smiles at me. "You know, whatever this is, it's long past time for you two to work it out. Go on, Chloe."

I nod and take the stairs slowly while Maggie's mom disappears into the kitchen. Even with her words bolstering me, I feel like I'm climbing my own gallows.

I should have waited another day. Maybe then I wouldn't be

so wound up by my memory of Adam. But why? Why would I picture *him* with love? I mean, just how messed up am I?

I turn left at the top of the stairs and see the collection of bumper stickers on Maggie's door. Too late for second-guessing now.

She tells me to come in before I even knock. There's a squeaky board right outside her door so she always knows when someone's close. We used to call it the parental alert system.

I open the door and stand there, looking over Maggie's pillow-strewn bed and the posters of obscure punk bands hung above it. Her enormous white dresser looks as buried as it always does, lost under a sea of silk scarves and discarded earrings. She's flopped sideways across the bed with her laptop open in front of her.

She looks up, and the shock of me being the visitor registers quickly in her face. "Why are *you* h-here?"

I shrug. "You didn't return my call."

"That usually means someone d-doesn't want to t-t-talk to you."

I frown and look at my feet. She's stuttering. She doesn't stutter this much. Not with me. I bite my lip, feeling bruised all over.

Maggie shifts on the bed, sitting up. "I think you s-said plenty the last t-time we talked."

I take a breath, trying to keep my voice steady. "I don't know what came over me then," I say, which is totally true. "But I want to talk to you, Mags. I miss you."

"No, you d-don't," she says. "What do you really want, Chloe, b-because I'm not going to be your p-pet project?"

I can't believe this. I can't process that this cold, mean girl is Maggie. "I don't…I don't know what you mean."

55

She laughs then. It's usually one of the friendliest sounds on earth. Today it burns like acid.

"Maybe I'm not smart enough t-to explain it," she says. "Why don't you go ask one of your study b-buddies, like Julien…Oh, wait, you c-can't ask Julien anything anymore, can you?"

Her words punch at my gut like a cold fist. My mouth goes dry with fear. "I think something happened to Julien, Maggie. That's what I was trying to tell you in my voice mail."

She crosses her arms, obviously not affected. "Yeah, Chloe, I g-got your voice mail. About three months t-too late."

"Why are you acting like this? What if she's in trouble, Maggie?"

"Why are you acting like you c-care? I told you all of this, Chloe. I t-told you *months* ago."

"I was confused," I hesitate, desperate to know what she knows before I say too much. "Confused and distracted, okay? But I'm trying to be better, and I want to talk about it."

She folds her arms over her chest and glares up at me, her face closed off like a wall. "Well, tough shit. I d-don't."

Eight years. That's how long I've known Maggie. We fight like sisters, but she has never shut me out like this. Not ever.

"You should go," she says.

I open my mouth, ready to plead my case, but then she leans forward. "I *want* you t-t-to go."

Tears blur my vision, but I shake my head, feeling my chin tremble. "Maggie—"

"Just go, Chloe!"

And I do.

I fly down the stairs and right past her mom. I'm desperate to be out of this warm, familiar house and all of its memories. Away from Maggie's hard words and hate-filled eyes. Mrs. Campbell calls after me, but I ignore her. I fling the door wide, rushing into the cold darkness beyond it.

I thunder down their porch steps, wiping tears as I run for the sidewalk. Sobbing and half-blind, I run until I slam blindly into someone's back. Whoever he is, he's tall and broad and he barely shifts at the impact.

"What the hell?" he says, and I leap back because I know that voice.

Adam turns around, shaking his hair out of his eyes and rubbing the back of his arm where I plowed into him. I stumble back in fear, and he catches me, fingers curling around my arms.

"God, Chlo, what is going on with you?"

I jerk myself free, feeling my eyes go wide. "How did you know I was here? Why are you following me?"

"Following you? I live here," Adam says, narrowing his eyes.

I shake my head, panting hard and feeling like a trapped animal. "No, you don't. I'd know if you lived here."

"You do know," he says, frowning. "I live in the apartments on the other side of the middle school."

He looks like this is all very obvious. But it's not. Nothing's obvious except that I'm crazy. I'm totally crazy and I'm not getting better.

I'm supposed to be better. I did everything they told me to do a year ago. I went to therapy, and I wrote insanely long journal entries.

God, I even did yoga! And it had worked. Dr. Kirkpatrick had said my results were so good that I didn't have to come anymore.

And now this. How in the hell am I going to fix this? When will she ever say I don't have to come again?

Pain rises up my chest, right into a little ball in my throat. Adam is just standing there, watching me closely while I choke all over my own breath.

I shake my head. "Stop looking at me like that!"

"Like what?"

"Like I'm supposed to know things I couldn't possibly know. Or like you know me, which you don't, okay? You don't know anything about me."

"Hey, hey," he says, dropping his backpack and rubbing his hands briskly up and down my arms. "Calm down. Just breathe."

I glance at Adam's hands on my arms. I don't have that feeling of someone invading my personal space. Adam's touch feels good. No, it's better than good. His touch feels like home.

He steps in even closer and slides his hands down to the cuffs of my coat. He tells me again to breathe.

This time I listen. I inhale, long and deep. And something smells…familiar.

"I smell something," I say. Something sweet and spicy that prickles at the back of my mind. I can almost remember it.

Adam laughs. "All right."

Just like that, I get it. This clean mix of soap and leather and cinnamon—it's him. This is *Adam's* smell. And it's curling in my mind like a memory.

"Just wait," I say, and for some crazy reason, I take his hand.

His skin is warm and rough, though it can't be thirty degrees out here. But he's not cold. His strong fingers wrap around mine without a bit of hesitation. This time, I don't think about how insane it is to touch him. All I can think about is that image I saw today. The one that sent me running to Maggie's house in the first place.

I close my eyes and grip Adam's hand tighter, trying to focus.

The picture forms in my mind again, and I exhale slowly, willing it to move.

Nothing.

"Chloe—"

"Please," I whisper. "Just give me a second."

He doesn't owe me a second, or anything else, and I feel my cheeks going hot. I know I'm being weird, but he sighs and stays still. His fingers go soft, sliding until they interlace with mine. Our palms close together, and I shiver though I don't feel cold at all.

And then I remember.

A classroom. Study hall from last year, but it's nighttime. And the posters are different, so it's not last year. It's this year.

Adam's bent over a book. I can hear myself talking about something. Science, maybe. But Adam's ignoring me, his eyes scanning the pages.

"Ugh, I can't focus," I hear myself say. "I feel all jittery and distracted."

Adam doesn't look up when he speaks. "Why's that?"

"Do you really have to ask?"

59

He looks up like he doesn't trust me. Like maybe he's heard me wrong. But then he lets himself smile, just a little. I feel warm and bright to the point of bursting, like the sun is rising somewhere deep inside my chest.

"One of these days we're going to have to do something about that," *he says.*

I'm sure he's right.

It's over as soon as it starts. Back in the present, I'm cold and panting, standing on the sidewalk. Every part of me is shaking. I blink up at Adam, our hands still locked.

"I remember something," I say. "Something about you."

Adam's expression is so intense, I swear it could power small cities. I feel his gaze crackle through every cell in my body. I don't know if he's mad or happy, or maybe both of those things mixed up, but when he steps closer, I forget where I am. Hell, even *who* I am.

"I can't figure you out, Chloe," he says softly, shaking his head. He reaches up, fingering the tips of my hair. "I can't figure you out at all."

I feel the delicious weight of his hand on my face for one soul-blistering second. He lets me go and turns toward the sidewalk, shoving his hands into the pockets of his jacket. I expect him to leave, but he doesn't.

"You coming?" he asks.

"What?"

"C'mon," he says, sounding half-distracted. As if he didn't just have his hand on my face and the promise of more in his eyes. "I'll walk you home."

CHAPTER SEVEN

. . . .

My parents look up from the news when I come in. Mom's been crying. Again. It's getting seriously melodramatic in this house. I'm half expecting a mournful instrumental score to play every time I leave a room.

Mom pushes on a bright smile, but this isn't my first rodeo. She cried every night for a week after I was diagnosed with panic attacks and anxiety. Now they don't even have a *name* for what I've got. Come to think of it, it's probably a miracle she's not in a padded cell rocking back and forth.

"Hey, you," she says, trying for brightness. She's a terrible actress. "Was Maggie ready to talk?"

"We talked for a minute."

"Well, baby steps are best," she says. "So how are…"

"How's the brain pan?" Dad asks, filling in her silence.

Mom kicks him under the coffee table. It's like I'm still six years old and won't notice. Maybe they'll start spelling the words they don't want to say in front of me.

"Fine," I say. "I'm feeling better."

"Really?" Mom asks.

"Really," I say, which was true until I got here. It's easier not to think about your looming mental health issues when you're busy obsessing on the number of times a guy's hand brushes your sleeve. Adam didn't say much else, but just having him near me was plenty distracting.

"You look flushed," Mom says. "You should have taken the car."

"Cold air is still fresh air." I shrug. "I should go up. I have homework, and I'm getting a late start."

"Do you want some dinner?" Mom asks, practically turning herself inside out to keep her eyes on me as I walk behind the couch. "There's pad thai on the counter."

"I'll grab some later," I say, taking the stairs two at a time.

I don't want to eat.

I want to figure this out. Julien disappearing, my bizarre Blake repulsion and inappropriate Adam obsession, this whole hot mess with Mags—all of it.

My bedroom door clicks softly shut behind me. I flip on the radio on my alarm clock. I learned that trick through a *Psychology Today* article. Music buys privacy. Many people (read: parents) are less likely to pop in on you if you've got a radio on.

Helpful tip for when you don't want to be checked on.

I flip open my laptop and cringe at the new background picture. Blake and I, arms linked around shoulders and waists.

It's disturbing. I used to spend *hours* daydreaming about our wedding, doodling his name in my notebooks. Now everything about the guy makes my skin crawl.

Add it to the list of everything else that makes absolutely no sense right now.

I open a spreadsheet and my Internet browser and then check

Facebook and Twitter and a couple of other random sites. It's a little surreal seeing all the crap I've blathered on about. I don't even read it at first. Not really. It's like getting into a cold pool. I inch my way around it, dipping my toe into profile pictures and dates.

From the looks of things, I was a busy Internet beaver all summer. Until somewhere in the middle of September. After that…total radio silence.

It's creepy, really, looking through posts and status updates. Almost like I'm stalking myself. Though, I've got to admit, this is not quite the James Bond experience I was hoping for. And if all of my posts are as boring as these, I really need to get a life. Or make one up, at least.

I scroll through my last month of activity again, looking for anything scary. Or hell, even interesting.

08/02: Stalking my mailbox. Where are my scores?

08/06: Sixty days without coffee. I should get a spiffy coin.

08/17: Really? Still no scores! Gah.

08/20: New jeans + new boots = me actually looking forward to colder weather.

08/24: Blake bought me daisies. Just because. How sweet is that?

08/24: Okay, not that sweet. Blake got his SAT scores (ridiculously good). Flowers = preemptive apology for my potentially bad scores. If they ever show up.

08/25: They're here! They're here! They're here! And…I'm afraid to open them.

08/25: 2155 *dies*

09/09: Second week of senior year and still no coffee. Take that, doubters!

09/13: Wrapping up extra credit project number four. So far, so good. Let's hope university big shots agree.

09/18: I'm so excited about the party this weekend. I'll talk Blake into it, for sure!

I scroll over the list, feeling my face curdle like day-old milk. It's like I've been possessed by an academic pep rally. The last entry is the worst. When the hell did I start saying crap like "for sure"?

My cursor hovers over the two words, and I frown hard at it. I wouldn't say this. I don't care what's happened to me in the last six months. I can imagine myself saying some seriously stupid crap but not that. Not in any universe I can think of.

It's just…wrong. It's like someone I don't know at all—a stranger. The same stranger who smiles out at me from dozens of pictures I don't remember taking? Maybe.

But why nothing since September? I'm not a junkie about these social things, but it's not like me to go more than a few days. A week, tops. Now I'm going off grid?

If there's an answer, I have no clue what it is or where to find it. I rub my hands over my face and glance at the clock on my laptop. I've been at this two hours, and all I've seen is forty new Facebook friends and a crap-load of extra credit assignments I've turned in. And by a lot, I mean an insane *crap-ton* of assignments. I stopped counting after twenty-six.

I flip to my school website and find a little more there. I'm officially hot shit, academically speaking. I'm on the honor roll and in the peer tutoring club and blah, blah, blah. None of this tells me why I can't remember the last several months of my life. Or why I'm so convinced I have something to do with Julien Miller's disappearance. Other than the glaringly obvious fact that I need professional help.

God, I really need to let this go. I blow out a sigh and start shutting my programs down. I move to save one of my documents when something catches my attention. Another file—a text file—in my list of recently accessed items.

Julien.

I rub my eyes and lean forward in my chair, but I didn't read it wrong.

My skin goes ice-cold, my palm growing damp on the mouse as I hover over the six letters.

Maybe it's about someone else. A new friend. Someone I'm tutoring. Maybe it was something I did for her before she left. The excuses pour out of me so fast I can barely keep track of them, but it doesn't matter.

This file scares me, and it wouldn't scare me if there wasn't a reason. I knew something about Julien, and I'm about to find out exactly what that something is.

I double click and receive an error message informing me that the path is invalid. I try it again because it's got to be there. Everything I've touched since we bought this computer is still there.

No go. The file is gone.

Heart pounding, I click to my deleted items folder.

Empty.

The blank white box rattles me to the core. I rarely delete and never purge my deleted items folder. Maggie used to tease me mercilessly about it. She'd say if I didn't get this under control, I was going to be one of those creepy moms that kept my baby's teeth and their hair and every sock they ever wore, *just in case*.

No, this wasn't me. Which means, someone else has been cleaning up. Crazy, yeah. But less crazy than me suddenly deleting things out of my computer.

I drag my hands through my hair and take a shaky breath.

It's a start. Now I know what I'm looking for.

Things that are no longer there.

• • •

Someone taps on my door, and I jerk my head off my desk, blinking blearily. Three soda cans and an empty bag of spicy tortilla chips are lined up by my keyboard. The chips are probably responsible for the god-awful taste in my mouth.

Mom knocks again, and I see the pale promise of sunlight drifting around my curtains. Is it morning? Really?

"Chloe?" she asks.

"Yeah?" I click to bring up a half-finished paper on electromagnetism. I figured it'd be a good cover last night, but I didn't need it until now.

"Honey," she says, looking alarmed. "Did you sleep?"

"I napped on the QWERTY row I think." I manage a groggy grin, rubbing my forehead. "But not much. I'm probably going to crash for a couple of hours."

"Today? But it's Saturday, honey."

I blink at her. It's *way* too early for this. "Right. Ergo me not needing to rush off to school."

Mom laughs, shaking her head and wagging her finger at me. "Very funny. Blake's going to be here in ten minutes. I can put your tea in a travel mug if you want."

"Blake?"

She looks at me like I've lost my mind, but I'm pretty sure if anyone's crazy, it's her. It is oh-dark-thirty on a Saturday morning. I'm generally not even conscious on Saturdays for several more hours, so why in God's name would Blake be on his way?

"You're a regular comedian," she says. "You're lucky he isn't running early like he usually does."

"What time is it?" I search around my desk for my phone, shifting papers and knocking over an empty soda can.

"Seven fifteen. What are you looking for?"

"My phone. I need to text Blake. I can't go out right now. I've barely slept."

Mom crosses her arms and looks severe. "Chloe, your Saturday mornings with Blake aren't dates."

Wait a minute—I do this every Saturday? Voluntarily? I blink up at her, hoping she'll fill me in. I can tell by her face there's a full-force lecture on standby, so I try to look attentive.

"Those kids depend on you," she says, and then she waits, clearly expecting me to get with the program.

Which isn't going to happen since I don't even know the program. Instead, I revert to my current default mode. Faking it as pleasantly as possible.

"You're right. I'll get dressed. Ten minutes?"

She glances at her watch. "Seven. I'll get your tea."

I shuck off yesterday's clothes and tear through my closet, finding jeans and a baby-blue sweatshirt that's buttery soft against my skin. I've barely tossed my hair into a ponytail and brushed my teeth when I hear the doorbell ring, the sounds of cheerful morning-people greetings floating up the stairs.

When I get downstairs, Blake's standing with my mom, holding my tea. "Where's your binder?"

Binder? What binder? I don't even know where I'm going and now I have to bring props?

Mom sighs. "Honestly, Chloe. It's in the dining room. I put it on the hutch."

I find it easily enough, along with a helpful label that reads: EISENHOWER ELEMENTARY TUTOR PROGRAM. So that explains the kids counting on me. Wait a minute, can I *fake* tutoring? I mean, what if all this brainiac stuff didn't take?

It took.

An hour later, the boy across from me grins a gap-toothed smile, chin smudged with pencil marks. "How did you figure that out so fast?"

I shrug. "Trade secret."

Though, truthfully, I just have no idea. Last time I checked, I still counted on my fingers. I mean, I skated by without needing summer school or anything, but I wasn't exactly a human calculator. Now? Now, I can do triple-digit arithmetic in my head. Like the problem Tyler and I just finished.

"You must be a super genius or something," he says, squirming around on his chair.

"Not even close. But I have done a lot of extra homework this year."

"I hate homework," he says.

"Yeah, me too," I say, and then I wink. "But I like being a smarty-pants. How about number ten?"

"Do I have to?"

I tilt my head, playing at thinking this over. "Well, we could do a makeover instead. I could paint your nails. Braid your hair."

Tyler laughs, and it's that awesome no-holds-barred kind that everybody seems to lose when they hit puberty. I grin as he simmers down to a chuckle and then looks at me with resignation.

"I still hate math. Even if you're cool." He hunkers back down over his homework, and I scan the community center while he works.

I'd heard that they hold tutoring here, but I'd never really seen it. It's actually pretty cool. The parents can leave or wait in the lobby, though God knows why they'd want to stay. There's nothing out there but a coffee machine and enough old newspapers to papier-mâché a small city.

In this room, the gray walls offer signs for everything from AA meetings to senior yoga exercises. Six tables have been set up, but there are only three of us working. Blake, me, and Tina Stubbs—a girl I barely knew last year. Today she hugged me and blabbered on about some guy she desperately wants until Tyler arrived to save me.

Blake is sitting two tables away from me. He's supposedly reading Dr. Seuss with the kid in front of him. Too bad he's not looking at the book or at the poor second-grader who's stumbling his way over each word. He's staring at something under the table, I think. Something in his lap, maybe?

Ah, cell phone.

He's texting someone.

"Is that right?" Tyler asks.

I glance down at his work. 327 + 456 = 773. "Super close, Tyler. One number is off. Do you think you can find it?"

Damn, I'm good.

I look up again, and Blake's student is reading even slower, his voice growing small as he tries to labor through a word that's obviously stumping him. And my sweet-as-sugar boyfriend is apparently too busy texting the Gettysburg Address to care? Something's very wrong with this picture. He's the tutoring *coordinator*.

"I got it wrong again?" Tyler asks, sounding worried.

I realize I'm making a seriously ugly face, one that isn't aimed at Tyler at all. Too bad Blake is way too absorbed in his cell phone to notice I'm shooting it in his direction.

I check Tyler's work and shake my head.

"It's perfect. I knew you could do it," I say, forcing a wide smile. "You've just got to remember right to left. Opposite of reading, okay?"

"Yeah, I think I've got it."

"You're going to do awesome. Consider that test aced," I say, and then I snag him an extra pencil out of the treasure box at the back of the room as I walk him out.

I release Tyler to his parents in the waiting room. The door chimes open as we're exchanging waves and farewells. I have no idea if I have another student or what's going on, so I step over to the door to say hello.

And then I just about fall over.

"Adam," I say. I don't even really mean to say it, but it's like my mouth was just waiting for a chance to get it out.

"Hey." He looks up, a half smile on his lips. Lips I really have to stop looking at, especially when my *boyfriend* is in the other room. My belly feels tight and I can feel myself smiling and this is not good.

So not good.

"You tutoring today?" I ask, hoping that will be a safe bet.

Wrong answer.

Something dark flashes over his features. He doesn't answer me, just shakes his head like he can't believe I would go there.

Panicked, I turn to follow him as he moves farther into the room. It's only then that I see the white logo in the corner of his blue shirt and the giant rolling trash can he's pulling behind him. Yeah, he's here to clean the desks, not sit at them.

My heart twists in my chest.

Obviously the me without amnesia *knows* he's a janitor here, and that me wouldn't say something so horrible. Unless, of course, I wanted to make him feel completely shitty about being a janitor.

Fantastic.

I stand there, wishing I could go back in time, while he collects trash and runs the dust mop under the chairs. I have to say something. I can't let him think that I think…well, whatever awful thing he probably thinks I'm thinking.

I expect him to head into the tutoring room, but he doesn't. He cuts into a hallway off the waiting room, one that leads to restrooms and offices and all sorts of places I'm probably not allowed to explore.

I follow him anyway.

"Adam, wait!"

"Working here," he says, the bite in his tone as sharp and hard as teeth.

It would make more sense to head into the women's room first, but he moves right past it for the men's room instead. He shrugs his shoulders at me with a false apology in his eyes. The men's room door swings shut with a yellow "Restroom Being Cleaned" sign dangling from the handle. It's like a silent dare.

Yeah. Well, there's a reason I streaked Clementine Drive in my undies in the middle of February. I'm not the kind of girl who turns down a dare.

CHAPTER EIGHT

. . . .

I push the door open and slide into the world of urinals and general male restroom ickyness.

"You really don't take a hint, do you?" he asks, leaning back against the sink with his arms crossed. How anyone can look this hot in a polyester button-down with *Peachy Kleen!* emblazoned across the pocket is beyond me, but he's managing it.

He's more than managing it.

"I didn't mean that," I say. "I didn't think."

Well, technically I didn't know, but it's not like I can say that.

"Yeah, you've been doing a lot of that lately. Not thinking."

I take a step toward him. I'm not sure it's a good idea, but I'm not sure I can stop myself either. "I'm sorry."

"It's fine."

"No, it's not. It's not fine. And I'm sorry."

"Yeah, you've said that," he says, and then his brow furrows. "So is that it?"

I blink at him, stunned into silence.

He lifts his hands briefly, latex gloves stretched over his palms. "Apology received, Chloe. Consider your conscience clear."

I open my mouth, and God, why is it like this with him? I'm

completely defective with Blake, but I swear the whole room hums when I look at Adam's eyes.

He suddenly walks forward, coming close enough to steal the breath right out of me. Words continue to evade me, which is probably for the best. Nothing's coming out right anyway. And frankly, I'd rather stand here in silence than have him tell me to leave.

Adam clenches his fists at his sides and takes a sharp breath. His voice is low, with a pleading edge that doesn't match his hard expression. "I have work to do, Chloe."

"Adam, please." I reach for him instinctively, my fingers wrapping around the bare flesh of his wrist.

The memory rocks through me like a shock wave. Quick and powerful.

I see leaves. A red-gold carpet of them litters my lawn. My rake pushes them into piles, baring trails of green grass and the crisp, unmistakable smell of autumn in the air.

Beside me, Adam looks up from his own rake. "I can't believe you talked me into this."

I roll my eyes. "You're the one who kept me up until three in the morning for, what was it? Eight Halo *rematches last night? Remind me again how many of those you won?"*

Instead of replying, Adam tosses his rake and lunges for me.

I feel his hands on my waist and laughter bubbling out of me as he hauls me into the air and then tosses me into the pile. Leaves crunch beneath me as I laugh, pulling at his feet and knees until I bring him down beside me.

I smell the sweetness of October all around me as we lie there side by side, laughing until my cheeks ache with it. Adam rolls on his side to face me. His eyes are so blue I feel myself getting lost in them. I know I'm staring and I know it's obvious, and somehow it's so ridiculous that it only makes me laugh more.

My shoulders are shaking and I should stop, but it's just so crazy. Then Adam reaches for my face, and there's nothing funny about it.

His eyes go soft, and my insides curl like ribbons on a gift. I feel the ghost of his fingers on my hair. It only leaves me aching for more.

"I shouldn't even be here, you know," he says softly.

"I know," I say. But when he moves to leave, I take his hand. And he lets me.

"What's going on, Chloe?"

I jump away from Adam at the sound of Blake's voice. And there we are, Blake staring at me, Adam staring at Blake, and me staring at the wall, cheeks burning like someone lit them on fire.

"Chloe?" Blake prompts again.

"I called her a bitch," Adam says, with a shrug that says I'm making a big deal out of nothing.

Blake and I both look at him—me in shock, Blake with disbelief. Adam just crosses his long arms across his middle again and tries to look bored.

"You called her a bitch," Blake says.

Okay, I'm not sure what Blake's trying for, but if it's anger, he's missing the mark. Like *way* missing it, because if anything, he sounds amused. And maybe he is. I don't even care. All I care about is getting out of here. Like, now.

"Okay, I'll bite," Blake says, giving an exaggerated shrug. "Why would you say that?"

"She was spitting out your Goody Two-shoes crap. And God knows she can't let it go," Adam says, gesturing at me with something that I think is supposed to look like disgust.

Okay, everyone in this room needs acting lessons. None of us are buying *any* of this, but I don't see anything else for sale.

I cringe, desperate to break the awkward silence. "I wasn't—"

Blake turns toward me, face expectant.

"You weren't being a self-righteous bitch?" Adam asks, his snarly tone a complete contradiction to his tense expression. "*Sure* you weren't."

"Whatever. Can we just go now, Blake?"

Blake cuts his eyes to the urinal. "Well, if you're done here, I'd still like to use the restroom."

If I blush any harder at this point, I'll actually become a tomato. I cover my face, shaking my head. "Sorry. Here, I'll take your stuff and wait for you."

Blake gives me one more look and then hands me his binder and phone. I'm shooting for the door before he's even fully let go.

Once outside, I hear Blake speak again, his voice muffled by the door. "Don't forget yourself, big guy. Boyfriend is my job, not yours."

I stop short, somehow frozen by his words. Or maybe his tone. I mean, I know I'm his girlfriend. Even if I can't remember anything, I have about two hundred pictures to prove it. But there was something about his tone. Almost like he was joking.

Like us being together is a joke.

Stop it.

I shake my head because that kind of thinking really is crazy. Paranoid and neurotic and a thousand other things I should be medicated for. Blake doesn't have a malevolent bone in his body. Adam on the other hand…

But I can't think about all of his evil. I'm pretty fixated on the feel of his hand on my hair, the memory enough to make me shiver now. Yeah, if anybody's the bad guy in this relationship, it's not Blake. It's me.

As if on cue, Blake's phone buzzes in my hand. I glance at it and think about him slouched in the study room, texting under the table. Like texting a lot.

I chew the inside of my bottom lip, glancing at the lit screen out of the corner of my eye. It's absolutely wrong. An invasion of privacy and a breach of trust, not to mention how much of a stalker it makes me.

And, hell, I'm going to do it anyway.

The message is from a number I don't recognize.

Do your job and she won't figure anything out.

• • •

Riding home with a fake boyfriend sucks under normal circumstances. But now, said boyfriend isn't just fake. He's also hiding something from me. And it's not an early Christmas present.

77

I'm so relieved when he pulls up to the curb beside my house that I nearly fling my door open and leap onto the curb.

"Whoa, you in a rush?"

I offer the smile I've been flashing the entire ride home. So wide I'm probably showing molars and so fake it should come with a disclaimer.

"Sorry. I've got an appointment. I don't want to be late."

"An appointment?"

"Dentist."

"On a Saturday?"

"They're booked up because he's taking time off for Thanksgiving."

Of course they're not booked up and I'm not going to the dentist. But I can't tell him I'm going to my therapist. Where I'm going to proceed to tell even *more* lies. Seriously, I may want to ditch this whole psychology thing and go with a future as a con artist.

"See you Monday?" I ask, and then I force myself to lean in and kiss him. His lips are warm and soft, but I feel cold and hard all over.

Blake pulls back with a frown. "Why do I feel like you're giving me the brush-off?"

"I'm not," I say too quickly.

He looks at me, eyes sad. "That feels a little hard to believe. First I find you in the bathroom with Adam—"

"That was nothing, Blake. He was just being a jerk and I...I overreacted."

"C'mon, would you believe that if you caught me in the bathroom with Abbey? Or maybe Madison?"

The truth is, I'd pretty much expect to find Blake in the bathroom with either of those girls. They're bouncy in all the right places, and they probably know all the important lacrosse rules. They are *his* kind. And yeah, maybe I dreamed about being in this position for years, but the truth is, I don't belong here. There just isn't a bit of sense in it.

"Ever since that night you hit your head, you've been strange," he says, looking down. "I feel like you're hiding something from me."

I can't hold back my snort. "*I'm* hiding something? Okay. Sure."

"What's that supposed to mean?"

"Nothing. Just forget it." I turn, but his hand closes around my arm.

"What the hell, Chloe?" When I turn back, he doesn't look like a villain. He looks handsome and sweet and terribly hurt. "What did I do to make you so mad? Why won't you just tell me?"

I bite my lip, weighing my options. I've been over that text a thousand times, and I can't imagine it being anything but sinister. But it's not like I'm the poster child for objectivity here.

"Are you going to say anything?" he asks, and he doesn't look suspicious. He looks like a guy who deserves better than this. Hell, stray dogs probably deserve better than this.

"I saw something on your phone," I say.

He throws up his hands, clearly baffled. "My phone?"

"I didn't mean to. You have to believe that. It was a complete accident, but I saw a text on your phone."

Blake's hands come down into his lap slowly. For one second, his face looks fractured, like there's something cold and angry simmering just beneath his puzzled expression. When I blink, it's gone, and he's just an ordinary guy trying to calm down his obviously paranoid girlfriend.

"What text?" he asks. His voice is too low. Too quiet.

I look down at my hands in my lap, humiliated. "It buzzed while you were in the bathroom."

He cocks his head at that. "After you'd been with Adam, right?" His tone says it all.

Ouch. And he's totally right. He found me in the men's bathroom with my hand on another guy's arm, and I'm getting bent out of shape over a totally vague text message that I had no business looking at in the first place. Hello, Kettle, my name is Pot.

"Blake, I know what that probably looked like, but that wasn't what it was."

"And neither is this. What did the text say, Chloe?"

I feel my cheeks growing warm. "It said, 'Do your job and she won't figure anything out.'"

"That's all you read?" he says.

I nod, even though it seems like an odd thing to say. Was there something worse I could have read? Ugh, why can't I just stop?

"That's it?" he repeats, obviously waiting for me to say something.

"Yeah. Yeah, that's all."

He laughs then, like he thinks I'm completely ridiculous. And I have a bad feeling I'm about to agree with him. "Chloe, it's about Christmas. Dad bought Mom a bracelet for Christmas.

He's keeping it in my room in case she goes snooping in his usual hiding spots."

My cheeks go hotter, and I look down again. "Oh. Well, I…"

There isn't a thing I can say that will make this better, so I trail into silence. God, what is wrong with me? I finally get the guy of my dreams, and I'm going to lose him because I'm a neurotic whack job. Terrific.

Blake laughs again, which makes me flinch because I feel like I'm going to cry.

"Chloe, look at me," he says.

I feel his hand on my face, cooler than is exactly comfortable, but it is November I guess. I look at him, holding back my tears.

"I'm really sorry," I say. "I guess I was just feeling insecure."

"It's cute that you're jealous," he says, looking a little smug.

"No, it's not. It's obnoxious. I really wasn't trying to invade your privacy."

"I know that. We both have enough respect for each other not to do that."

I sigh in relief, and this time, when he leans into kiss me, I try to savor it. It's still harder than it should be. I don't remember kissing being a difficult thing before. Hell, maybe it's just one more thing I forgot.

When he pulls away, I zip my coat and ease open the passenger door.

"So I'll see you Monday?"

He grins, checking his collar in the rearview mirror. "I wouldn't miss it."

Blake's engine rumbles as he pulls away, and the front door creaks open behind me. I hear the hum of the vacuum cleaner before Dad closes it again. He's got a paper under his arm and keys in his hand.

"Back from tutoring?" he asks.

"Yeah, but I have an appointment with Dr. Kirkpatrick."

"I know. I, uh…I thought I could drive you."

Read: Mom wants me to drive you so I can try to figure out how nuts you are.

I take a breath, but to my credit, I don't sigh. It takes everything in me to hold it in. I can't blame him though. I know better than anybody that with my mother, sometimes it's easier to just give in.

"I'm hitting Rowdy's anyway," he says, and I smile.

Rowdy's Roasters. Otherwise known as the best coffee along the coast of Lake Erie. A steamy café mocha sounds amazing. Or it does until I think about the way my stomach turned itself inside out at one whiff of the pot the other day.

But this is Rowdy's. I can stomach that, right?

"Maybe you could grab me a mocha?"

He heads for the garage, eyeing me over his shoulder. "Thought you gave up the good stuff."

"Call it a relapse."

We climb into Dad's pickup, settling into an easy silence. The hum of talk radio and rumble of the engine keep the quiet comfortable as we cut our way through town. It's only a ten-minute drive to the office. If he doesn't get on it, he's not going to have any dirt for my mom.

Unless maybe this isn't about me at all.

"You and mom aren't fighting are you?" I ask.

He lifts his fingers from the steering wheel, halfheartedly waving that off. "No, Mom's deep cleaning. I'm looking for excuses."

He's still a bad liar, but I didn't expect anything about him would be different. It took him a year to get used to the idea of a weeping cherry tree in the front flower bed. The guy's not big on change. He's kind of like a glacier with hair. The steady, unflappable presence that keeps Mom from exploding and me from floating away on a whim.

He sighs, and I know he's going to confess. "All right, she wanted me to talk to you."

"Yeah, I figured."

"She's just scared, that's all. Scared that you're not telling us everything. Some of your stories don't match up."

I glance out the window, watch the town passing by in a blur of old houses and storefronts that need sprucing.

"Mom thinks maybe you're afraid to talk to us," he says.

"I'm not," I say.

"Because you can tell us what's going on. Even if you don't think we'll like it, we want to hear it."

I turn to the window again. This time, the tears in my eyes blur the images I see. "I'm not crazy, Dad."

Suddenly, I need him to believe it.

"Never thought you were."

"But, Mom…"

"Mom worries, Chlo. It's what she does."

I laugh. "Yeah, she worries that I'll let her down."

"She wants you to be happy."

"She wants me to make her proud, Dad. That's not the same."

He makes a face, and I think it's because he wants to defend her. In the end, he doesn't. He pulls up to the curb by my doctor's office and puts the car in park. "*I* want you to be happy."

I lean across the seat between us, squeezing him in a hug. I want to hold enough strength from his broad shoulders to make me believe things will work out fine, but when I pull back, it disappears. Steam vanishing into nothing.

CHAPTER NINE

. . . .

nside Dr. Kirkpatrick's office, I mentally prepare while she pours me a glass of ice water. She offers me hot tea first, top-notch imported stuff, she assures me. In the end, I opt for low-rent tap water because I'm too scatterbrained to pick flavors and sip carefully.

"It's hard to believe it's been almost a week since we spoke," Dr. Kirkpatrick says as she sets down my glass.

This is shrink speak for *Just how crazy have you been in the last few days?*

And my answer would be *pretty freaking crazy*, but I'm not here to give answers. If I'm forced to sit in this stupid office, I'm going to pick her brain until I find something that will help me get my memories back.

"I've been busy," I start. "But I think I'm starting to have things come back to me."

Blatant lie. If you add my new vanishing computer files, my list of missing items is actually expanding.

"That's terrific," she says. "Would you like to talk about some of those things?"

I bite my lip and glance over at her bookshelves. It's a calculated move. If I look too conflicted, she'll know I'm faking, so I do it fast, hoping to sell it just enough.

"I'm not sure. I might not be ready yet. Is that okay?"

"Do you feel that you need my permission?" she asks me with a smile.

"It's not that. It's just…I don't want to jinx it, you know? I want to be sure I'm really making progress."

More importantly, I haven't invented a memory to discuss today.

"All right, Chloe. Is there something else specific you'd like to talk about?"

And *that* is shrink speak for, *Obviously there's something specific you'd like to talk about.*

I stand up and head over to her bookcase, scanning the shelves. "I want to talk about psychology. I don't know if you remember, but I got really interested in it last year after that class I took."

"I do. I believe I provided a list of recommended books and some additional elective courses that I thought would be beneficial."

Okay, I didn't take the courses. After months of panic attacks and therapy sessions, I wasn't sure if I wanted to open that can of worms. No one needed another reminder of my Prozac Princess past, thanks.

I look down at my shoes and sigh. "I guess last year I was still tossing the idea around. Now, things are different. I'm a senior, and I'm applying to schools."

"You worked very hard this summer," she says, which almost makes me laugh. For all she probably knows, I spent my summer painting my toenails and watching *Tom and Jerry* reruns.

Still, I smile at her. "You're right. And now that I feel like I have a real shot at a future in psychology, I think it changes things. I'm pretty committed to this."

She leans back, looking proud. "Well, I think it's a terrific idea, Chloe. People are often called to help others who've experienced similar hardships to themselves."

"Exactly. And I guess that's what I want to talk about. I want to start with myself. I want to take control of my own recovery and be proactive."

I stop there because I'm out of fifty-cent words that I'm hoping will appeal to her.

She tilts her head, her too-black hair sliding over one cheek. "You know, even trained psychologists still need outside help sometimes. Going it alone isn't always possible or wise."

I resist the urge to roll my eyes. Barely. "I'm not trying to get out of therapy. But you always told me I will get as much out of therapy as I put into it. And I want to put my mind to work. I feel like I need a better understanding of how memory works."

She smiles, but it doesn't erase the tension from her eyes. "I'm happy to see you tackle this head-on, Chloe."

"Great."

Dr. Kirkpatrick purses her lips, and I can tell that we're not quite there yet. "But first, I'd like to talk here about memories. About what they are. These are fragile, subjective recordings of past events that change over time and evolve with your emotions."

I nod, leaning forward in my seat, ready to skip to the part where she tells me exactly how I can get these fragile, subjective recordings back.

Dr. Kirkpatrick leans forward too. There's something about the way she pauses that I've never seen. I can't help thinking she's rehearsing what she's about to say. Or maybe just second-guessing herself. Whatever it is, it creates a long pause before she speaks again.

"Chloe, during our last session I sensed you were reluctant to share the details of your memory loss with me. You know that this is a safe place, and I want you to feel comfortable with what you share, but I also feel it's important that I understand the extent of your impairment so we know how to proceed."

I should have expected this. I should have known at some point she'd want to know how serious this is. And I can't tell her. Something deep in my bones tells me to stay quiet.

It feels wrong, lying to her. Last year, when I could barely make it through a pep rally without feeling my throat close up, she's the one who told me how to cope, the one who told me to never doubt my own strength. She never once told me I was weak or overly dramatic or crazy.

I trusted her once, but I don't anymore.

"I guess I'm not sure how to answer that," I say, twisting my fingers. My stomach is knitting itself into a series of knots, each one a little tighter than the last. "I'm forgetting lots of little things. Deadlines. Bits of conversations. I feel sort of tuned out."

Dr. Kirkpatrick watches me very closely. I'm not sure if she believes me, so I focus on keeping my breathing even and my face serene. I force my hands to my knees and command them to stay loose and still. I take a breath since she is still silent. "Maybe it shouldn't bother me so much, but it really does. I feel like I'm missing pieces of my life."

Big, six-month-shaped pieces, but whatever.

"All right," she says at length, and I can tell by her tone that she's not buying this. She sits back in her chair anyway. "A good first step to reconnecting with the details of your life is to revisit recent events. Do you have any recent pictures?"

"My mom does," I say.

Luckily, I know this for sure. My mother is a rabid scrapbooker. Which sounds really loving and sweet, but actually means every moment of my life has been documented in ridiculous detail. She pulls out the camera for a good batch of lasagna, so I guarantee there's plenty of photographic evidence of the last six months.

And why in God's name didn't I think about this sooner? I probably could have filled myself in on all kinds of crap.

Dr. Kirkpatrick starts scribbling in her notebook as she talks. "I'd like you to look at some recent photographs and compare them to some of your older photographs."

"Older ones?"

"Yes. It's possible that revisiting an event you remember well will help you tap into more robust recollections of more recent events. Do you have any photographs from a school event? Prom maybe? Or a trip with friends?"

I nod, swallowing hard. "I have a scrapbook from art camp. A year and a half ago."

Maggie and I went together. Not because I have an ounce of talent, mind you. I don't. But Maggie *is* gifted. And I like to play with the pottery wheel. Plus, art camp has its share of good-looking boys—the kind with paint-spattered jeans and tortured souls.

Mom made me take her digital camera, demanding I take pictures of *everything*. We took this as literally as possible, snapping shots of the most inane details we could find. We had pictures of the bottom of people's shoes and wads of gum stuck to the underside of the tables.

I thought it would make Mom crazy. Instead, she was so happy she cried. She made Maggie and me matching scrapbooks. Truthfully, I flipped through mine only once, but it was sweet. And I did remember *everything* about that weekend.

"Terrific. I want you to go back and revisit that book. And I want you to find a few photographs that were taken more recently. Not portraits in a studio. Snapshots. I don't want you to just focus on what's happening in the picture. I want you to look at the background. Have you ever heard the saying 'The devil's in the details'?"

"Sure."

"I believe there's something to that. Not that there's evil in the details, but that they can sometimes be much more important pieces to the puzzle than we initially think. Consider the details in both photos. Write down some observations and see where that gets you."

• • •

I'll tell you where it's getting me. Absofreakinglutely nowhere. Unless depressed is a destination. I might as well be watching a documentary of butterflies dying in the rain.

I flip back to the cover of the art camp scrapbook, the one my mom painstakingly put together. A close-up of Maggie and me. My dark hair curling next to Maggie's fine, strawberry blond waves. Her eyes are brown and mine are pale, but our smiles are the same in this shot: wide and genuine.

The rest of the book is pretty standard scrapbook fodder. Me throwing clay. Maggie streaking dark ink across thick paper. Both of us offering gooey marshmallow smiles near a campfire.

I linger on that cover picture though, because I remember posing for this like it was yesterday. Every detail speaks to me. Maggie's cheeks and nose are pink, sunburned from swimming earlier that day. I can see turquoise paint spatters on my shirt and the orange-brown remnants of clay beneath my fingernails. And we're both wearing one of those ugly, hammered bracelets Maggie made.

Those things made their way straight to the metal box under the oak tree at the edge of Maggie's property. We call it our Not Treasure Box because there's no real reason to keep anything in it. It's an oddball collection of our history. Buttons from our matching coats in the third grade. A photograph of Maggie kissing Daniel Marcum in the school play. Those hideous bracelets are in there too.

This photograph says a thousand things to me, but not one of them help a damn bit.

I push the scrapbook away and turn back to the recent photographs I found, the ones that might as well be pictures of another Chloe, one from a different dimension. I'm not too sure I want to go through these again. They creeped me out enough the first time.

I need to get over it. I need to suck it up, put on my big girl panties—whatever it takes.

One deep breath later, I spread them out on the table. Picnics and parties and a steak dinner that I'm pretty sure commemorates my seventeenth birthday. I remember none of it. I don't remember having fried chicken and pink lemonade at a park. I don't remember watching fireworks with half of the varsity lacrosse team, Blake's arm curved around my waist like we were glued that way. I don't remember playing softball *ever*, and certainly not with this group of girls, girls who I would never—wait a minute—

Is that Julien?

My finger traces over her image. Shiny blond hair, almond-shaped eyes in a plain but pretty face.

I still can't imagine her gone. She was probably going to be principal someday. Hell, maybe the mayor. Even when we were little girls on the playground monkey bars, she used to talk about buying a house on Belmont, living right across the street from her mom and dad. She knew her future, and her future was Ridgeview.

Goose bumps rise on my arms, but no matter how hard I stare, the picture doesn't reveal any more secrets. I shift it away, refocusing on the one of Blake and me. I know I should focus on the details, but the basics are eerie enough. The way our heads are mashed together, his golden hair starkly pale against mine. I stare hard at the picture, trying to imagine feeling comfortable like this. Trying to imagine a world where Blake's arm around me would be easy and normal.

"You're like a couple from a movie," Mom says, announcing her entry into the kitchen. "Almost too beautiful to look at."

"You're delusional," I tell her, but really she's not. Not about Blake, at any rate. He does belong on a movie set. Blond hair, nice biceps, killer smile. And I'm...well, I'm me. I've got a great smile, but I'm not the kind of girl who makes homecoming queen. And I'm not the kind of girl who dates Blake.

"I just call it like I see it," Mom says, pouring herself a cup of coffee.

I watch the steam rise from her cup and frown. I'd managed about a third of my mocha from Rowdy's this morning, but it still tasted terrible to me.

"Mom?"

"Hmm?"

"Did you ever think it was weird that I had so many new friends?"

When she turns to look at me, I see the wariness in her eyes, like maybe she thinks this is the start of an I'm-too-depressed-and-damaged-for-friends speech.

"What do you mean?"

I bite my lip, thinking. "I mean, I'm practically a different person. The grades, the friends—everything, really. I just wondered if it surprised you."

"Of course not." She leans forward, putting her hand on mine. "Chloe, you have such a good head on your shoulders. Deep down, I always knew you'd do something with it. Once you joined the study group, you were surrounded by successful kids. It makes sense that you'd want to join in with that crowd."

"When have I ever been a crowd joiner? Don't you remember the fourth grade, when I refused to wear pink because all the girls in school said it was the thing to do?"

"But you're not in the fourth grade anymore, are you? And you're with Blake now. I guess I figured…"

She trails off with a shrug, and I feel a rush of irritation flood me. "You figured what? That I did this to become someone worthy of Blake?"

The shock registers on her face like a slap. "That's not what I meant."

"Isn't it? I know this is going to come as a surprise, Mom, but I didn't do any of this so I could be with Blake or so I could sit at the cool kids table in the cafeteria."

"Okay, fine. Then why *did* you do it, Chloe?"

That stops me cold because I don't have an answer. I was happy on the fringe. I wasn't some school pariah with no social life and no prospects for the big dances. But I wasn't popular either. And I was always fine with that.

I think of Maggie's face in the hallway, her eyes so flinty.

God, what did I do? Is she right? Am I suddenly desperate to be cool? Was my entire summer some sort of late-onset in-crowd fever?

Mom rinses her coffee down the sink and shakes her head. "Please don't misunderstand me. It's been a surprise, Chloe. The tutoring, the grades, all of it. But no one's happier about your recent choices than I am."

I laugh weakly. "Yeah, I'm finally becoming the daughter you've always hoped for."

"You're finally living up to your potential," she corrects without flinching. She checks the clock on the microwave and sighs. "I'd better go. I'm meeting your dad at the garden center."

I nod because God knows this is going nowhere. Mom stops on her way out, glancing at the picture on top of the stack.

Stacey Moss, Abbey Binns, Kayla Parkerson, me…and Julien Miller.

"You must miss her," Mom says.

I startle a little, surprised she hadn't already left.

"What do you mean?"

"Julien. You two were pretty close before she left. I was really worried about you when she moved. You were…torn up about it."

I shrug and hide my hands under the table. I don't want her to see me shaking.

Mom seems a little lost in her own memories. "You never told me what you were working on that night."

"What do you mean?"

"The night she left. I tried not to pry. I know Julien had some…issues. You didn't ever want to talk about it. But I was scared that night."

"Scared?"

"Yes, Chloe, scared. You locked yourself in your room and worked on your computer all night long."

My blood runs cold in my veins. This was all news to me. I clear my throat to make sure my voice doesn't shake like my hands.

"I just needed to work through some things," I say. "I'm better now."

She kisses my forehead and leaves, happy to believe me. Happy to accept anything that will convince her I am still the new, perfect girl wants me to be.

CHAPTER TEN

. . . .

I hate the bench outside the principal's office. Nothing good ever comes from sitting here. The first time I perched my fanny on this slab of wood, I was waiting for my mom to pick me up when my granddad died. The second time was when Maggie and I got nailed at Starbucks during school hours and had to wait for detention slips. Today, I'm waiting so I can lie to the secretary.

Mrs. Love is a thin blond who was the prom queen, the head cheerleader, and the girl everyone thought would end up in Hollywood twenty years ago. Now, she's the school secretary. I'm never quite sure whether or not I should feel sorry for her for that.

"Chloe? Chloe Spinnaker?" she calls, as if the office is swarming with Chloes and she has to be sure she has the right one.

I approach the tall desk, tipping my head. "I'm so sorry to bother you, Mrs. Love, but I had something special I thought you might be able to help with."

"Well, things are pretty busy. Thanksgiving's coming."

Mrs. Love has a serious commitment to things like pasting paper turkeys and pilgrim hats and other seasonal stuff around the school. "I know," I say, feigning empathy. "But it's my senior year and you know my summer study group?"

She brightens at that. "Of course I do. I was the one who framed that newspaper article about your scores. Have you seen it?"

I wince, feeling kind of guilty. "I'm sorry, I haven't."

"Well, it's right in the trophy case," she says, looking a little put off. Does she really think that anyone who isn't wearing a letterman's jacket ever checks the trophy case? I've never looked at it, unless you count using the reflection from the glass to check my teeth after lunch.

I smile anyway. "That's sweet of you. I'll check it out."

"So what can I help you with?"

"I'd like to send the SAT group a Christmas card," I tell her. "Something handmade and special. But I want to make sure I don't leave anyone out or spell anyone's name wrong."

"Okay," she says, blinking up at me with vacant eyes.

"Well, I was hoping you might have a list here at the office."

Mrs. Love's mouth forms a perfect pink *o* and then she looks around. "Now, Chloe, you really should have this information from last year, shouldn't you?"

"I know I should. I just went a little crazy deleting emails, and I thought I had a copy, and I don't."

God, I'm laying it on thick. Apparently, she's buying it though, because she gives me a tight smile and hits a few keys on her computer. Next thing I know, two sheets of paper churn out of the printer. "I think it's good to stay connected with your school friends. You'll never have this time again, so cherish it."

"I promise I will," I say, biting back the urge to tell her that it might be okay for her to stop cherishing.

"Well, good luck with it," she says.

I thank her with the first genuine smile I've worn today. I don't even give the paper a glance until I'm out of the office and away from the windows where she might see me.

The hallway clock tells me I have twelve minutes of my lunch period left, so I scan the list of names quickly. There's more than a dozen. Maybe eighteen. I remember seeing some of them when I signed up for the group last spring. Blake, of course. Back then, he was still like a Greek god to me. Seeing his name near mine on a list was enough to make my palms sweaty.

Another name jumps out at me, though I already knew I'd see it here. Julien Miller. I find Adam's name too, to my surprise.

I fold the papers and tuck them into my purse and head inside. I've got government next, which is almost as interesting as watching paint dry. I thought I was supposed to be a super study girl now, but Mr. Morris still talks like a grown-up on the Charlie Brown specials. Everything is "mwah-mwah-mwah" and I just can't focus.

Especially when I start thinking about the names on that list.

Adam doesn't need a study group. Blake either.

For that matter, neither did Julien, but I could kind of buy it with her. She's a Miller for God's sake. If there's a committee in Ridgeview, a Miller is on it. Going to pointless meetings is in their DNA. And Blake's always been one to go the extra mile.

But Adam? No way. His name was an inside joke on every dean's list for the past three years. You can see the slow simmer of resentment in the teachers' eyes when they call on him, wishing just once he'd give the wrong answer. But he never does. He never misses a beat and he never mouths off. Just delivers his response in that low, I-couldn't-give-two-shits voice of his.

I bite my lip, thinking about the way his dark hair tends to slide into his blue eyes. God, I have it so bad for this guy. I seriously have to get my crap together.

The final bell rings. I dodge at least six people that want to discuss the weather, my hair, the truth about fair trade coffee—anything. I've been popular for like ten minutes, and I think I'm starting to hate it.

I'm trying to get to the bathroom when Blake rounds the corner, sporting a wide grin as he reaches for me. "There you are, babe. I was beginning to think you were avoiding me."

Yeah, probably because I *am* avoiding him.

"I know," I say. "I'm sorry."

"No big deal," he says, taking my books and then pulling me in.

There's no getting out of this kiss. I've avoided too many and stiff-lipped him through at least as many more.

I tip up my head, letting him catch my lips. It's soft and warm and so damn *weird*. I feel my shoulders tense, my hands like dead weights at the end of my arms.

God, this is ridiculous! This is Blake. I would have given a kidney to kiss him in any one of the last several years. Memory loss or not, this shouldn't be a chore.

Blake pulls back, and my tension is reflected in his eyes. "What's going on, Chloe? You seem…"

"Distracted?" I guess, trying for a lopsided grin.

He returns the smile, but he still looks wary, like he doesn't quite believe that's it.

"I know." I sigh. "I started in on college applications, and it's just so much work."

His hand comes down on my shoulder, giving me a little squeeze. "I thought we already talked about this. Emory, Brown, Notre Dame, right?"

"Huh?"

"Just focus on your top three. Your scores alone should be enough to get you into most of the others," he says, giving my shoulder another squeeze. "I don't think Vassar's going to happen, babe. You just don't have the history of extracurricular work they look for."

I flinch. I'm not crazy about the squeezing or the *babes* or the fact that he's delving out advice about my college prospects. Like this is all old news and we've decided together what's best for me.

"Did you need any help with the essays?" he asks. "You know I'd be happy to look at them."

My eye twitches. It really shouldn't. This is a perfectly altruistic offer. Blake is a good student and an obviously sweet boyfriend, and I really need to back off the bitch factor by about a thousand percent.

"Thanks, but I'm good," I say, just barely keeping the bite out of my tone.

"So dinner tonight?"

"I can't. Gotta look back over my Notre Dame stuff."

I even manage a regretful little sigh. Lies are getting easier than the truth.

One of his hands kneads at my waist. "Well, I'm craving some quality time, so try to fit me in soon."

He reels me in, leaning down to kiss me again. It makes my stomach hurt to feel his lips against mine, but I force myself through it, hands fisted at my sides and spine like a steel rod. The kiss is just one more lie to add to my stack.

If there is a hell, I am going there. Do Not Pass go; do not collect two-hundred dollars.

Blake pulls back with a little humming sound. "Tomorrow. Breakfast. I'll pick you up, and this time, I want to go somewhere and eat at a table. Thirty whole minutes with my girlfriend. Not too much to ask, is it?"

He cocks his head, giving me a million-dollar smile. I remind myself he is the guy I've always wanted. And if I don't resolve my crazy memory stuff, I'm going to push him away right about the time I realize how and why we ended up together.

I squeeze his hand. "No, it's not. Breakfast sounds perfect."

"Seven thirty."

"I'll be ready. Promise."

He nods and steps away, saluting me before he heads past me and out the doors. I see Adam leaning against the lockers, watching him go. Watching maybe everything that just happened.

I try to leave, but I feel frozen to the floor. Adam's eyes find mine across the hall, and there's a name for the look he's wearing. I'd call it jealous as hell.

• • •

It wasn't easy finding Adam Reed's address. I don't know what I expected, but whatever the image I dreamed up in my head was, it wasn't this. I once told Mags that Adam was probably a spoiled little rich boy, playing the bad kid to get daddy's attention. Looking at the sad, cramped town house in front of me makes me feel cruel and stupid for saying that.

This isn't one of those swanky apartments you see on CW dramas—slick, modern lofts with community pools and weekly scandals. We don't have those kinds of complexes in Ridgeview. We hardly have apartments at all, and the ones we do have are the kind nobody wants to think about.

This row of town houses sits behind the abandoned strip mall two blocks from Maggie's house. There are no welcome mats or fitness centers. Or grass, for that matter. The entire place looks tired, from the peeling paint on the identical front doors to the rusting Buick in the corner of the parking lot.

I put my keys in my pocket and step over the cracks in the pavement on my way to his front door. I hate this place already. It pulls at the fabric of my comfort, tearing the seams until I can see slivers of a life I didn't think was possible in my cute little town.

I square my shoulders and lift my fist, knocking three times. Inside, someone hollers Adam's name. I hear a cough next, a horrible, wet rattle. Two doors down, a young mother heads for her car with a crying baby in tow.

I glance down at the cigarette butts on the edge of the sidewalk because I don't want to look. I feel like a spoiled, ungrateful brat who doesn't belong here.

The door swings open, and there he is, this darkly beautiful and apparently tragic boy. He doesn't look happy to see me.

"What do you want, Chloe?"

"I need to talk to you."

"Talk to Blake," he says.

Holy crap, he *was* jealous. And I don't get it. I just don't. But I like it. Some very twisted part of me wants him to be jealous.

I want him to want me. Because some part of me clearly wants him.

"Can I come in?" I ask, my voice too high and small.

"In here?" he asks, like I'm completely crazy for asking.

"Or we could walk," I say, though my voice trails off when I glance around at the broken bottles and total absence of pretty.

"It's cold, Chloe."

"I know. I know that, but I really need to talk to you."

And I do. I've got questions burning up in my throat. I can feel them wanting to bubble out of me. Questions about the list. About the study group. About me and him and this thing that is so obviously happening between us.

He slides out of the doorway, close enough that I'm forced to look up to keep my eyes on his face. He's wearing a guarded look now, tilting his head at me.

"You think Blake would really want you here, Chloe?"

I feel breathless. Like something's squeezing hard around my ribs. He looks so angry. And even guilty in a way.

I can't take seeing him like this. I have to do something.

Adam scoffs at my silence and backs up. I snatch his sleeve, pulling on him.

"Adam—"

"Let go, Chloe."

He's shaking me off and moving back, and I feel a little frantic as his sleeve slips out of my grasp. I need him to stay here with me because I feel *right* with him. And I remember things with him. And I need to know why. But I don't say any of those things as he steps back into his house.

It's like my tongue is paralyzed.

"Go home," he says, and the door shuts in my face.

"I can't remember anything!" I shout.

My breath steams in the darkness as I wait one heartbeat. Then another. And then Adam opens the door.

I feel my shoulders sag with relief. He might as well have taken a thousand pounds off me. Whoever is inside his apartment coughs again, breaking the spell, reminding me that I'm still outside. Unwelcome.

Adam closes the door behind himself when he comes out again, his dark gray sweatshirt unzipped over an old T-shirt. He hasn't shaved. It lends a cold edge to his features, but he still looks like a slice of heaven to me—safe and warm and true.

"What are you talking about?" he asks.

I hesitate because I know I can't come back from this. I can't unsay these words once they're out.

"Chloe," he says, pressing me to go on.

"I can't remember," I say. "I can't remember anything since

May. And I know it sounds crazy, and it *is* crazy, but I'm not insane. Something happened to me. I fell asleep in study hall. I drifted off for a second, and then it was winter and my entire universe was different."

My words are tumbling out so fast, I can barely catch my breath. "Now, I'm this perfect person with these perfect grades and Blake and—and then you and me and I don't know what any of it means and how any of it happened or how I lost Maggie—"

"Slow down," he says, cutting me off midsentence.

"I can't slow down, Adam! I'm six freaking months behind, okay? I can't remember anything that happened to me! That night in the school? When you said I called you? I don't remember calling you. I don't *ever* remember speaking with you until that moment."

"You don't remember calling me," he says, brow furrowed. "That night at the school—you don't remember that?"

"I'm trying to tell you I don't remember anything! I have pictures that I don't even understand, and before you even ask me, yes, I've been to a doctor and my brain is just fine. Which means that the doctors and my family think I'm totally unhinged, and they don't even know how—"

"Hell, Chloe," he says, voice gruff.

His arms lock around me, and he hauls me into an embrace, burying my face in his T-shirt. I promptly burst into tears, my arms going around him like they were grown on my body for this purpose. I feel the press of his strong hands on my shoulder blades as he whispers soft, hushing noises into my hair. I inhale a shuddery breath, taking in his warmth and feeling right for the first time since I can remember.

And just like that, I *know*.

This is how it should be with Blake. Tingly and warm and bigger than any words I can think of.

"You're not insane," he says. Plain as day. Like it's not even a possibility worth pursuing.

I nod against his chest and close my eyes. His hands are in my hair now, and every single part of my body is intensely aware of every part of his. It's wrong to want him this much.

He seems to realize it too, and we separate. I don't want to let go of him. The truth is harder, colder outside his arms.

I look up at him, and he thumbs my chin, narrowing his eyes at me. "You said you don't remember anything before that night. But you remember everything up to May?"

"Yeah."

He believes me. I thought it would be harder to convince him, but he doesn't even look shocked. It's like people tell him they've lost enormous chunks of their lives every day.

He palms my cheek with his hand, and I close my eyes, pretending to think. But I'm not thinking. I'm soaking in the feel of his skin against mine. The familiarity of his hug. The way he smells. I exhale slowly and a memory comes.

Pizza. A cheesy, gooey piece. And chemistry notes spread out all around my plate. I'm reciting something about sodium chloride, and Adam nods and flips to the next card in his stack.

I pull back, shaking myself from the past. Right now I need to be present.

"Okay, step me through it because I'm a little lost," he says.

"I don't remember anything that happened between May and that night. The whole summer and fall are just…missing." I pause and swallow hard before I admit the rest of it. "Except for a few things about you. When you…touch me, I sometimes get flashes of things that happened between us."

I open my eyes, knowing my cheeks are red. Adam doesn't seem to notice. There's a smile on his lips, like he loves hearing this. But there's something else too. A shadow of sadness in his eyes.

"When I touch you?" he asks softly, stepping a little closer.

And then I take a little half step toward him. We're going to run out of personal space quick if we keep this up, but I don't care. No matter how much I should, I just don't.

"You've touched my hands," I say, and then I take his hand, sliding my palm against his.

I see flashes from before. Him looking up from a book. And then I hear his laughter. And then that pizza place. In my memory, he pushes a red, fizzy drink toward me with a smirk, and I scoot my chemistry notes out of the way.

"We ate at the Pizza Palace while we studied chemistry. You gave me something red to drink."

"Red pop," he says, nodding.

"It's just little things." I sigh, too embarrassed to admit the scene with the leaves in my yard. I release his fingers with a laugh. "Pretty pathetic, right?"

He looks at me for a minute then. I wish I could read whatever's going on behind those beautiful eyes.

"All right, lead the way."

"Huh?" I can feel myself gaping at him, mouth moving open and closed goldfish-style. He finally nudges me with his shoulder.

"Your house, Einstein. Let's go figure this out."

CHAPTER ELEVEN

. . . .

It is 10:38 on a school night, and a juvenile delinquent is preparing to sneak into my house. This is not my life.

"I am bushed," I tell my parents as I hang up my coat.

Bushed? Seriously? I'm a much better liar than this. Haven't I proved as much with Blake?

But Mom and Dad are engrossed in some World War II documentary they got from the library, so they don't seem to notice my decades-old slang or my long sigh.

"We can turn it down if you want, honey," Mom says, stealing popcorn from the bowl on my dad's stomach.

"No, that's okay."

We exchange good-nights, and then I slink up my stairs feeling like a criminal. I close my door and lock it. Not convinced it's safe enough, I move my desk chair over to the door, wedging it as quietly as I can under the door handle.

"Might want to look up *paranoia* while we're at it," Adam says, and I nearly jump out of my skin.

I clamp a hand over my mouth and spin to see him straddling my window frame, one denim-clad leg already inside my room.

I flip on the radio and cross the floor in two strides. "Are you insane? I was supposed to get the fire ladder. How did you even get up here?"

"I did use a ladder. Borrowed it from your shed out back."

"Oh. Well."

Adam slides the rest of the way in, and I stand there, crossing my arms over my chest as he moves quietly around my room.

Adam is tall. I mean, I've always known he's tall. But seeing him here somehow makes my whole room look so small.

"Cute bear," he says, picking up my rag teddy, Phillipe, from the dresser. I snatch him back and do everything short of wringing my hands while I watch Adam walk around my room, silently inspecting my posters and the miscellaneous earrings and perfume bottles on my dresser.

God, it's like that awful moment at the end of a first date. You're making painful small talk on the porch or in the car. Of course, you both know why you're stalling, but it's weird until someone moves—oh my God, this is *not* like that! We are not here to make out.

Are we?

I ignore the flutter in my belly and pull my laptop out of my nightstand. Research tools. Because we are here to research.

I tug two or three notebooks out of my backpack and dump at least ten pens and highlighters on top of them.

Adam laughs at me, cocking a brow. "How many people did you invite to help out tonight?"

I put some of the pens away and blush so fiercely my hair is probably turning red.

Adam turns to my bookshelf, running his long fingers over the spines. He pulls out three or four, and I turn my radio up a little louder.

He makes himself comfortable on my floor between the bed and the window. Back against the wall and knees against my box springs. It doesn't look terribly comfortable, but it's a smart spot. If, God forbid, my mom decides to pound her way through my reinforced bedroom door, he'll have plenty of time to climb out the window. Or at least slide under the bed.

"You want these?" he asks softly, offering me two books.

Right. I should start researching now. Read things. Write things. Stop staring at Adam.

I walk over to the bed and sit down, taking the two he's handing up to me. I'm familiar enough with the titles, but I haven't read much of them. At least not that I can remember.

"Um, what exactly should we be looking for?" I ask, sitting down and feeling really awkward.

"Memory stuff," he says, already nose-deep in a pretty dense-looking tome. "Something had to trigger this. Maybe if we can find it, it'll help."

"I don't think I'm going to find a chapter titled 'Recovering the Six Months You Lost,' you know."

Adam smirks but doesn't look up from his book.

"You know, you could fill me in," I say softly.

He does look up then, eyes catching mine above the pages.

I shrug halfheartedly. "You could give me a *Reader's Digest* version."

His smile is mischievous. "What makes you think I'd know? We're *strangers*, remember?"

I'm tempted to ask more, but he turns a page and furrows his brow, the very picture of focus.

I open my book with a huff and thumb through the pages aimlessly. This is stupid. I mean, maybe there is a book that might explain some of this, but I doubt I own it. I only own the basics— and whatever the hell is wrong with me is as far from basic as it gets. And why won't he tell me anything? Obviously we weren't strangers. We studied together. Raked leaves together. Did things that feel precariously close to cheating on my boyfriend together.

Maybe it's better if I don't know all the details.

I frown, slouching down against my headboard. I scan a couple of chapters in my child psychology book. Unless I'm concerned about the impact of potty training on my future offspring, this is useless.

I flip forward, and my fingers catch on something between the pages. Wait a minute. I find a yellow slip of notebook paper tucked in the middle of the book.

The chapter it's marking is titled "Memory: Safe Box and Minefield." There are a few things underlined in the chapter, but nothing that seems very pertinent. No how-to sections on recovering repressed memories or the kinds of traumas that cause them.

I pull out the paper and unfold it, and the scrawl on the front is immediately recognizable. Because it's mine. The three words seem innocuous enough, but they send a chill from the roots of my hair through the soles of my feet.

Maggie was right.

But right about what?

• • •

My clock reads 7:24 a.m., and I'm staring myself down in the mirror like I'm preparing for battle. My combat gear includes a white sweater, dark denim jeans, and just enough time on my hair and makeup to make it clear I'm actually excited to see Blake.

I'm not excited.

I don't think there's any thesaurus out there that lists *dread* and *apprehension* as synonyms of *excitement.*

I stayed in bed for ten minutes this morning trying to think of an excuse to call off. From breakfast with Blake. From school too, really. Or hell, from life in general. In the end, I decided to get on with it.

The truth is I'm being a lousy girlfriend. And it's not because my memory's wonky or my study group is suspicious. It's because I'm completely hung up on another guy.

I sigh and tell myself for the thousandth time how Adam couldn't be further than my type. Ridiculously gorgeous? Yes. Nice? Actually, yes. Smart choice? Um, no. I can just imagine me introducing him to my dad. Or even better, my *mother*. No. No times infinity.

But, God, I can't get him out of my head.

I'm still sitting next to my front door resolving to get over it when I hear the Mustang pull up in front of my house.

Showtime.

I take a breath and pull on my coat, sliding out the door with a smile plastered on my face. Fake it till you make it, right?

I bound down the steps, tossing my hair because I *will* be happy today. I will force myself to share muffins and to talk about the weather. I will be the best girlfriend Blake's ever had.

"You look just about perfect," Blake says, opening my door and sliding me into the car.

"You don't look too bad yourself," I say.

And it's no stretch. Button-down shirt, faded jeans, hair tousled in a way that probably took longer than mine. He should be in a Gap ad selling polo shirts with that million-dollar smile.

"How about Trixie's?" he asks.

"Fine by me."

Trixie's is five minutes from my house. Even I can come up with enough small talk to fill six minutes. And I don't really have to because Blake turns up the radio and we listen until we pull into the parking lot.

The diner has seen better days, but it's clean and familiar. The white counters are pristine, and the stainless steel trim around the chairs and tables gleams.

Conversation rises from the booths and tables as the blond, busty hostess seats us. She sends an extra smile to Blake, and he returns it but keeps his hand on my back. And then he waits to sit until I do because he's chivalry personified and I'm an idiot to have strayed. Even mentally.

"I'm starving," I say, picking up my menu. "I could eat ten pancakes."

Blake chuckles. "You'll definitely need to watch your carbs if you don't want to pick up the freshman fifteen next fall."

I laugh and look at him, but he doesn't look like he's joking. Seriously? I'm not a size 0 or anything, but I'm sure the heck not tipping the scales. I lower my menu to check his expression again, but Blake seems transfixed with the selection of eggs and bacon.

Okay, roll with it. He probably winked when I was blinking or something.

The waitress returns for our order, and I'm just opening my mouth to request a double Belgian waffle when Blake orders first.

"We'll both have the number one, eggs scrambled, with turkey sausage and wheat toast."

I blink so rapidly that someone walking past would probably think I've got something in my eye.

Apparently the time jump thing has happened again, but this time it sent me backward to the 1940s, or whatever year it was when boyfriends ordered food for you after commenting on your weight. Gee golly, maybe he'll let me wear his letterman sweater at the soda shop after school.

I need to count to ten or something because this is supposed to be a nice breakfast and right now all I can think about is chucking a saltshaker at his head.

"So how are those applications coming?" he asks me.

"I didn't do too much. I was pretty wiped last night after dinner," I say.

"Slacker," he teases. "Two of mine are already done."

"Yeah? Which ones?"

"Brown and Notre Dame," he says.

"Huh, those are two of my schools," I say, wiping a little condensation off my water glass.

Blake laughs. "Uh, yeah. That was the point, remember? Getting into the same school."

No, I don't remember. I have no idea which colleges he's applying to, and I sure the hell don't remember planning out the next *four years* of my life based on a guy I've been dating for what? Three months?

Okay, I'm freaking out. I don't want to watch my carbs or go to Notre Dame. I don't want to be here at all.

Our waitress sets down our plates, and I stare at the scrambled eggs and wheat toast I never would have ordered. I have a sweet tooth in the morning. Eggs or meat this early just gives me a stomachache.

Blake watches me closely as I pick up my fork, and it's pretty clear he can tell something's up. His look turns cool and detached, and I put my fork down, feeling like something in a petri dish. My stomach squirms, and I feel a cold sweat slick the palms of my hands.

I sit back in the booth. "Blake, I'm sorry, but I'm really not feeling well."

"Maybe some hot tea will help. Chamomile is supposed to be soothing," he says, looking around for our waitress.

"No." The word comes out a little louder and harsher than I intend. I feel bad enough to bite my lip and look down.

"What is it, Chloe?" he asks, and there it is again. That almost clinical expression that makes me think he should be holding a clip-board. If this were biology class, I'd be the thing in the metal tray with the pins holding my skin apart. And I don't want to be dissected.

"It's my stomach," I say, and for once it's the God's honest truth. "I think I need to head home."

"Let me get the check. I'll drive you."

"I appreciate that, but I don't want to puke in your car."

For a minute I can tell he's not a fan of that possibility either. But he covers it up fast with a worried frown. "Chloe, don't be crazy. You can't walk. It's got to be two or three miles."

"If you cut through the neighborhood, it's nothing. I used to walk here with Maggie for pancakes every Saturday morning."

Saying her name sends another kind of pain through my middle. I might cry if I stay here. I can feel it, and I don't want to do it in front of him.

I stand up, pushing my plate away. "I'm sorry. I really am."

"Well, feel better. Call me if you need me."

I barely manage to nod before I rush out the door and into the too-bright morning. The air is crisp and dry, clearing my head and unknotting my nerves.

I should head straight home, but I don't. I feel pulled back to Belmont Street. My feet know all the shortcuts by heart, so I follow without thinking. Across Mound Street, then through the newer development to Belmont. I follow the elm trees that line the street, proving just how long these houses have been here. Before I even understand why I'm here, I'm standing in front of Julien's house.

I try to remember Mrs. Miller in the flower bed or Julien on the porch swing, but I don't even know if she liked to sit out here. She was practically a stranger to me before. Now, she's like a ghost in my mind, a hazy silhouette of girl I never really knew. And never will, because she's gone.

I close my eyes and try to picture her. Maybe hear her voice. She is just a set of vague features. Blond hair, small nose. Shy smile. It could describe half the girls in my school.

"You're sad that she's not coming back, aren't you?" a young voice says.

I look down at the girl in front of me, coat half-zipped and cheeks red from the cold. She can't be more than eight or nine.

"What?" I ask, though I'm sure I heard her right.

"Julie," she says. I've never heard anyone call her that, but I doubt she's referring to someone else.

I bite my lip, realizing this little girl probably saw her like an idol, the beautiful princess from the biggest castle on the street. I smile down at her. "I'll bet she misses you."

"Yeah, maybe. She made snowmen with me sometimes. I don't think you can do that in California," the little girl reasons, wiping her nose with the sleeve of her coat. She looks up and must not like the pity she finds in my eyes. She crosses her arms and tries to look tough. "But it's not like I stand here crying because she's gone."

"I'm not crying."

The little girl blinks up at me. "Maybe not now, but you did then. I saw you crying here. The night she left."

Goose bumps rise on my arms, but I try to chuckle, as if I can laugh them away. "I'm sorry, you must be thinking of somebody else."

"Nuh-uh. You were wearing that same red coat. You stood out there for a long time. You know, my mom was going to call the cops."

"The cops? Why?"

She shrugs and makes a circle on the sidewalk with her boot. "I don't know. Maybe she thought you were going to do something bad."

"I wasn't," I say, but I don't know that. I don't even remember *being* here, so I sure the hell don't know what I was doing. Or why I was crying.

"Well, I gotta go. Don't be sad about Julie. You can send her letters. She likes my glitter paper, so you can borrow some if you want."

I try to thank her, but there's no voice left in me. Instead, I watch her leave, a ribbon of dark hair flapping above her pink coat as she runs. I wish I could run too, hard and fast until my lungs burned and my eyes watered.

But I know it would never be fast enough. I'm sure my past would still catch up with me.

CHAPTER TWELVE

. . . .

I've covered all my bases. I called school and my parents and even changed back into pajamas. As if I'm actually going to sleep. I'm a million miles from sleep.

I double check my phone for the thousandth time, making sure my text message to Maggie actually sent. I can't imagine her ignoring a message like this, no matter how terrible things between us have gotten.

I look at it again, wondering if maybe I wasn't clear.

> I need your help, Mags. I'm really in trouble. Please, please call.

No, I'd say that's pretty freaking clear. But she hasn't called, and I can't sit here waiting around for her to do it. As much as I wish things were different, they obviously aren't. I'm on my own.

I sigh and toss my quilt back over my bed, shuffling into a pair of fuzzy bear-feet slippers before I settle in at my desk. I catch a glimpse of my reflection in the mirror. I look like an advertisement for depression medication, all thin lips and dark circles under my eyes.

Okay, enough. I don't care what the hell happened in the last six months, I'm not going to turn into one of those girls who writes bad poetry about endless suffering in solitude.

I stick my tongue out at myself in the mirror and cross my eyes. Better. I'll pick goofy over whiny any day of the week. And twice on Sundays.

I clear my throat and open my laptop because I've got the whole Internet at my fingertips. Surely some study group secrets are out there. There were eighteen of us, for God's sake. Someone had to say something. I just need to find it.

By lunchtime, the most exciting thing I've found is knitting instructions on Cally Baron's blog. I'm not even kidding. I've practically surfed my way into a coma because this is the most pathetic stalking adventure ever.

These people aren't just clean. It's like I type in their names and get routed directly to the definition of Goody Two-shoes. There isn't a single current reference to any study group member that isn't good-grades this and another-success that, and it's all so boring I could just die.

It's also mostly useless for anything other than filling me in on a few gaps about the group itself. The Ridgeview SAT Study Group lasted the entire summer, and it was a crazy success. God knows exactly what worked, because from what I can tell from everyone's posts and tweets, we basically just hung out a lot.

Once a week, we'd get together officially to do outlines and flash cards and—meditation and tea? I guess it's studying with a side of Zen or yoga or whatever. And somehow we're now all born-again Einsteins? This is ridiculous.

I mean, really. This does not make sense.

Frowning, I flip screens back to the study group website, sure I'm missing something in the fine print. There's a knock at my bedroom door, and my dad appears, looking a little worn out.

"Hey. Aren't you home early?" I say.

"I'm coming down with something too," he says, sniffling. "Figured I'd check in on you."

"Oh, I just had a stomach thing," I say, which isn't entirely untrue. "I feel better now, but I figured I was already in my jammies."

Dad's face tightens briefly, but in the end he relaxes. I don't tend to skip school, and he doesn't tend to play the heavy. Or maybe he's just tired. His nose and eyes are a little red.

"Do you want me to heat up a can of soup for you?" I offer.

He shakes his head and produces a tissue, blowing his nose trumpet-style. Then he nods at my computer. "Did they ever update that website?"

I glance back at the study group with a frown. "Uh, I guess not."

My father crosses his arms, looking a little haughty. "I figured he'd be all over getting his corporate sponsor stuff front and center. I still can't believe they're planning on charging for that next year."

"Charging?"

"For the study group," he says, then he narrows his eyes at me. "Don't tell me you changed your mind. You were halfway ready to write the school board when I told you about it."

"Right. Sorry." I wave my hand over a stack of miscellaneous papers. "I'm all wrapped up in this history paper."

"Well, I'll leave you to it. There's some ginger ale in the fridge if you want it."

"Already had one. You look like you could use some sleep."

He grunts and turns around, closing my door behind him.

And I stare at it, more confused than ever. The whole thing is turning into a *Scooby-Doo* episode. Who'd be all over this? And what corporate sponsor? Why in the world would I care about any of it?

My phone buzzes, and I glance over, seeing an incoming call. My phone screen goes bright with light, and Maggie's picture dances across the screen. Every cell in my body does a little jump for joy.

I dive for my phone as if I'll blow up if I miss the call. I just might.

"Hello?" I ask, trying not to sound too eager. And failing miserably.

"Hey."

The sound of her voice alone is enough to make me feel better.

"I'm so glad you called," I say, closing my eyes as relief washes over me.

"I'm n-not sure I should have. But you seem pretty freaked out. Though I'm not sure what you think I'm going to d-do about it."

"I am freaked out. And I'm not expecting—"

I cut myself off, taking a deep breath and leaning back in my chair. The piece of paper I found in the book stares up at me.

Maggie was right.

"You were right," I tell her.

"It's known to happen."

I grin at that, wishing things were still easy between us. Losing Mags feels like losing a sister. Or maybe a limb.

"Maggie, I have to tell you something, and I know it's going to sound crazy."

"I doubt you can t-top the last four months of crap you've spit out."

"The last four months feel like a blur," I say softly. "A really bad blur that I can barely remember. Or remember at all. And I know this is going to sound completely paranoid, but I think there was something really weird about that SAT study group I was in."

"Gee, you think?" she asks, and there's no missing the sarcasm in her tone. I can even picture her face, pale brows arched in mock surprise. "How many times did I t-tell you that, Chlo? A d-dozen? A hundred? And every t-time you threw your New Age crap back in my face, yammering on about your perfect boyfriend and eating healthy and your meditation horseshit—"

"Meditation?"

"Why d-did you call me, Chloe?" she asks, sounding irritable.

"Because I want to know what happened to Julien Miller. And I think you might have an idea."

It's a hunch but not a crazy one. That note in my book and the things she's saying—it means something. I hear her sigh on the other end of the line, and I know she doesn't want to tell me anything. Maggie doesn't trust me anymore. It's impossible but true.

"Why don't you j-just ask Blake?"

"I don't want to ask Blake. I'm asking you, Mags. Not him. You."

She waits awhile, and I can hear her adjust her phone. Switching ears or something. When she speaks again, her voice is very soft. "I don't know if I want t-to talk to you about any of that. I don't know if I want t-to talk to you at all."

"I know. And I know I probably deserve that," I say, because the truth is, Maggie is damn near impossible to piss off. I don't know what I've done, but the hatred she's spewing at me has to be warranted in some way.

"There's no *probably* about it," she says.

"Will you think about it? About talking to me? I know there's something going on with this group, but the details are all fuzzy now. I can't explain it, but it's almost like the whole summer was a bad dream."

She's quiet again. I know I should stop myself from getting too hopeful, but I don't. I go on, careful to keep my voice light. "I want to pick up the pieces, but I don't know where to start."

"I already t-told you where to start," she says. "Dr. Kirkpatrick."

The world screeches to a halt, my body's rhythm's hitting an awkward pause. I want to say something, but nothing comes out. Maggie doesn't wait long thankfully.

"Look, Chloe, I know she called it monitoring, b-but there was something way creepy about that. Is it normal to have a psychologist sit in on a study group? I mean, it wasn't a study group for the mentally disturbed, so what g-gives?"

"I don't know," I say, swallowing thickly, feeling the hot fingers of adrenaline needling up my spine. I think about Dr. Kirkpatrick's comments about how hard I'd worked over the summer. She wasn't blowing sunshine—she knew because she was there.

"It's a place t-to start," she says with another sigh. "Look, I gotta go, but, Chloe…"

"Yeah?"

"Get some help. Someone you trust."

"I trust you," I half whisper.

"I c-can't get involved," she says, but I can hear a little bit of regret in her words. Or maybe I'm making it up, but either way, I'll take it. Anything is better than the silence she gave me before.

"I'm glad you called, Maggie. It means a lot."

She doesn't say anything else, but I still smile when she hangs up.

• • •

Adam doesn't look thrilled to see me at his house. Again. He wedges his shoulder in the door and glances at his shoes.

"I'm sorry to come over, but I need to talk to you," I say.

"You couldn't talk to me at school?"

"I wasn't in school today."

His eyes shoot up then, a concerned look softening his face. "I figured you just skipped our classes together. Are you sick?"

"No, I'm—"

How the heck am I going to finish that? No, Adam, I'm not sick. I'm dodging my boyfriend because he gives me the creeps. And also because I'm completely infatuated with you.

Yeah, I don't think so.

"I just had a lot going on," I say, "but I really need to talk to you. Can I come in?"

He gives me that hard look again, and suddenly it isn't so unreadable. He's embarrassed. He doesn't want me to see his house.

The stranger inside chokes out that same rattling cough, and I force myself not to flinch.

"Look, I get it," I say. "I can tell that you don't really want me checking out your space, but I don't care about that. Unless you've got a goat-sacrificing ritual going on in the living room or something, it's cool, okay?"

He doesn't answer that, just cuts his eyes sideways. It's hard not to stare at him, even now. It's hard to imagine anyone this perfect-looking living in such an ugly space.

"I don't have anywhere else to go," I say, and then I drop my voice low. "Not with this."

It's completely quiet for a second. Then he pushes open the door, and I force the surprise off my face as I follow him inside.

It's not dirty. I mean, it's not lick-the-floors clean, but the tiny dinette right inside the door isn't sporting piles of dirty plates, and the kitchen counters seem freshly wiped. It is tiny though. Just this little kitchen and dinette and a set of stairs across from a door I'm guessing leads to the bathroom. And another room I can't see well in the back.

A pale blue light spills out from that back area. A television, I guess. I hear the coughing again, coming from the unseen room. It's the kind of noise I imagine when people say "death rattle."

Adam stays right in front of me on our way to the stairs. We are so close I can smell him. Six inches and we'd have full body contact. I feel hot and cold at once, and then he stops abruptly, one foot on the stairs.

He stares me down, eyes glittering. It's like he's daring me to say something. Or maybe to chicken out. He's going to have to stand there a long time if he thinks a little icky coughing is going to scare me out of here. I'm actually not sure an army of opera-singing roaches would change my mind. I'm beyond desperate.

"Adam?" someone calls. A woman. I'd guess grandmother by the sound of her voice. But somehow the row of liquor bottles I saw on the back of the counter tells me she's not the type to bake cookies and start college funds.

"Adam!"

"I'm here!" he shouts back, and then arches a brow at me, dropping his voice low.

"I need a drink," she says, slurring each word.

His face grows even darker as he smiles at me. "Do you want one too, Chloe?"

Test. I can see it in the half sneer in his eyes. He's testing me. I'd bet a thousand dollars right now that he never touches those liquor bottles. The disgust in his eyes is a little too obvious.

Inside the living room, the woman begins to snore.

I reach forward, spanning the distance between us to take his hand. "Thank you for letting me in."

I only meant to reassure him, but something serious flickers over his face, something that makes my heart skip three beats. It skips three more when he laces his fingers through mine and pulls me toward the stairs.

I step through the classroom door and look around. It's only half-full, maybe twelve of us or so. Cally glances up from her phone, giving me a little wave, and Kyle and Seth nod from their desks. Adam looks up too, but the smile on his mouth doesn't reach his eyes. I feel a hand—Blake's hand—on the small of my back. We make our way to our seats, and then I feel something else. Adam's eyes burning into me as we pass.

He releases my hand once we're upstairs. I look around the narrow hallway and then follow him through his open bedroom door. I blink in the sudden brightness, and I feel like I've stepped onto another planet.

I never thought about Adam's room before, but if I had, I would have guessed death metal posters and clothing strewn all over the floor. Maybe a stolen street sign nailed to the wall next to a spray-painted quote about anarchy.

This room is so clean it belongs on a sitcom. No, maybe on one of those crime shows, where murders seem to occur in only meticulously tidy houses. As if serial killers all share a rule about freshly scoured sinks and bedroom floors that are never, ever littered with yesterday's dirty socks. His room is like that, so Spartan it almost looks like pretend.

The bed is neatly made. Two bookshelves above it are filled with a variety of fiction, and I'm not talking about X-Men comic books. Tolstoy, Nietzsche. Serious stuff. Stuff I'd probably only read if I were ordered to do so at gunpoint.

A tiny desk sits by the window, home to a computer so old I find myself searching for a floppy disk drive. The monitor is one of those huge boxy deals, some leftover from a computer era long past. That said, I could eat off the keyboard. It practically gleams. I think of my own smudgy laptop, one with all the bells and whistles, and wince.

I turn around, getting ready to comment on how pristine everything is, and that's when I see the back wall, a wall that is covered top to bottom with photographs. Black and white, mostly, but a few colored ones are mixed in.

I stare at the densely packed collage, photos of bridges and skyscrapers and that famous opera house in Australia. There are close-ups too. The detail on a soffit. An angular porch. There's so much to look at, I could be here all day.

Adam must see me gaping because he sinks into the chair by his computer and shrugs. "I like architecture."

"Understatement," I say, exhaling slowly as I spot another narrow bookshelf crammed with books on that very subject. A sleek black-and-gray skyscraper made of Legos perches on the top.

"Did you make that?"

He nods, looking fidgety. "In the third grade."

"You made that in the third grade?"

I was probably still eating paste in the third grade.

I take a breath and turn to face him. On the desk beside him, I see a stack of envelopes like mine. Even from here, I can see that one is from Yale.

Adam must see me looking because he flips it over and rolls his chair in front of the stack. "What did you need, Chlo?"

"Okay, brace yourself, because I know how this is going to

sound." I wipe my palms down the sides of my jeans and take a breath. "I think all of my lost memories have something to do with our SAT study group."

Adam glances up sharply from his desk.

"The SAT group?" he asks, and his voice sounds pinched. "That ended months ago."

"Yeah, I know, but there's something weird about it. I mean, do you know how many of us have scores over two thousand?"

Adam shrugs as if the idea of this doesn't seem so very crazy to him. But it is. Completely crazy.

"Look, we're not all MIT material like you," I say, sweeping my arm around the room. "I don't know what that group did, but I'm not that smart."

"Yes, you are, Chloe. You're as smart as anyone on the dean's list. We've been over this."

We have? Man, I wish I could remember that because that look he's giving me almost makes me believe it's true.

"I know I'm not stupid," I say, "but I'm not a star student. I've slacked for three years, Adam. I don't even think three months of solo tutoring with a Harvard professor would land me the kind of score I've got."

"This year, you've got a 3.9 GPA," he says.

I do? Not important right now. I shake my head, moving closer to him. "Look, if the scores aren't weird enough for you, what about Dr. Kirkpatrick?"

"What about her?" he asks, frowning at me.

Maybe I'm too close. I step back, feeling suddenly uneasy. This is…I don't know what this is. All I know is, this isn't going right. He's suddenly jittery and distracted. Shuffling papers and checking his phone.

"She *monitored* our study group," I say.

He checks the window and then his phone again, and it's like he has absolutely no opinion on any of this. What the hell?

"Doesn't that strike you as a little weird?" I ask, hoping to get some sort of reaction.

"She was there to help us with some relaxation techniques. Easing test anxiety or whatever. I don't think it's a big deal."

As soon as he says it, I have a flash. *Dr. Kirkpatrick at the head of the class, looking serene and composed. She tells us to take a deep breath. I close my eyes and obey.*

Here and now, Adam is watching me with a stony expression. And can I blame him? I come here with some bizarre theory, one I have no evidence to back. I look like a complete whack job.

"Forget it," I say. "I shouldn't have come here."

I take a step toward the door, and a muscle in Adam's jaw jumps. Why did I think I could trust him? What, because I harbor some sort of hormonal fascination with him?

I feel completely stupid.

"I'm sorry I bugged you," I say, reaching for the door handle. The moment my fingers graze the knob, he's off his chair and moving toward me.

This room has about the same square footage as a postage stamp, so when he steps in front of me, there is nowhere to go unless I dive into his closet or throw open the door. So I stand there and wait, forced to look up to meet his eyes because we are *that* close.

"You're not bugging me," he says, fingers resting on my shoulders. I sink into his touch. "This is going to be all right, Chloe. *You're* going to be all right."

I shake my head because he's wrong. My entire world is inside out and upside down, but right now with his hands on my arms and his smell all around me, I don't even care.

And there's nothing all right about that.

CHAPTER THIRTEEN

. . . .

D r. Kirkpatrick sits in her pale green armchair wearing a practiced expression of serenity. She spent years in school training herself to spot signs of deception. I figure my chances of pulling this off without her figuring me out are about one in a billion. But I'm out of options. The only lead I have in this mess is sitting across from me, and I'm not leaving this office until she tells me something.

This time she waits ten minutes before speaking. Maybe she wants me a little nervous today.

"So how did your exercise go?"

Exercise? Oh crap. I rush through our last meeting in my mind, remembering her little assignment. The scrapbooks.

"I think it helped," I lie. Testing the waters. Given the way her eyes just narrowed a little, I'd say those waters look muddy as hell.

"Would you care to tell me a little about it?"

"Well, to be honest, the details in the old stuff felt more real," I say, hoping that little nugget of honesty will throw her off enough to buy my next line. "But just looking at the newer pictures gave me better perspective."

"Perspective?"

"Yeah," I say, tipping my head back and forth, like I'm searching for the word. "Like I can remember things better."

"Good," she says, and she looks strangely relieved by this. "How does it make you feel, remembering these moments more clearly?"

I square my shoulders and look her right in the eyes. "I feel like I miss Julien."

She flinches.

She hides it fast, sliding on that calm smile. But it's there. A tiny crack in her smooth facade. I see it. And that little frisson of tension in her face goes through me like a blade of ice. I resist the urge to fidget, holding my fingers steady in my lap.

"You remember Julien, right?" I ask. "From our study group?"

She smiles, but I can tell she's uneasy. Maybe even sad. Apparently even trained clinical therapists aren't immune to the clenched jaw and tight smiles that give the rest of us away.

"I believe I remember Julien," she says softly. "As you remember, my time with your study group was very limited. Just a few minutes here and there. I sadly didn't have the opportunity to know you very well as individuals."

Is she making excuses? It sounds like excuses. And the way she's playing with her pen looks like guilt.

Oh God, Maggie was right. Something happened to Julien, and Dr. Kirkpatrick knows what it is.

"I don't think Julien wanted to move to California." I say it before I can stop myself.

"Sometimes families make decisions that will upset some of the parts of the whole."

"Maybe. Or maybe none of them wanted to go."

This time there's no mistaking the way her cheeks go pale. She is nervous. Maybe even scared.

"It doesn't make any sense," I say, chewing my lip before the accusation I'm feeling shows. "The Millers have been here forever. Mr. Miller was on the Chamber of Commerce. And Julien loved it here. They all did. And now, she's just gone."

She uncrosses and recrosses her legs and glances down at her notebook. "You know, Chloe, I believe our lives should be examined and explored until some sort of understanding is reached."

"Well, you *are* a therapist. Wouldn't it be weird if you didn't think that?"

She smiles then, the corners of her eyes crinkling. "That's probably true. But despite believing that, I also know that some things in life don't have answers. Some things must just be accepted."

"Are you telling me it's not important for me to understand why she's gone?"

I'm hoping it will rattle her, but it doesn't. Her smile softens with her eyes, telling me that I'm playing right into her hand.

"What I think is *most* important here is that you miss her," Dr. Kirkpatrick says. Her ultracalm mask has descended, the little notepad she uses held easily in her palm. "I think the real lesson to be learned is how to deal with that loss."

I shrug and slouch back in my chair in defeat. The clock ticks by and I let it. I need a minute to get myself together. I should have known I wasn't going to lead this whole conversation. Her whole job is to take the reins in here.

"Maybe it isn't just Julien that I miss," I say at length.

"Is there something else you're missing, Chloe?"

"Nothing obvious. I mean, I have the perfect life right now, like every little thing has been laid out exactly like it should be."

"You don't sound pleased by that."

I glance up at her, letting a bit of the accusation I'm feeling show. "Well, maybe I didn't want the perfect life. Maybe I liked the life I had just fine."

I watch her closely now, but her face is remarkably still. I see her hands though, her knuckles going white in her lap. It's more than enough proof for me.

She knows things. If she didn't, she wouldn't be on edge like this, her face as smooth and hard as stone.

Her eyes flick up to the clock and her jaw unclenches. "I'm afraid we're running short on time today. I'd like to talk more about your feelings on this next week. Can you prepare for that?"

"I'll be ready," I say, knowing my smile is bordering on predatory.

Which is exactly how I want it to be. I'm not some mute seventeen-year-old who's going to be terrified into silence because this woman's got a few degrees on her wall. I have every right to know what's happened to me, whether or not she wants to tell me.

I let the door close behind me, leaving Dr. Kirkpatrick alone. The lobby is empty, which is typical since I'm the last appointment of the day. I pull on my coat and look at the empty receptionist's desk.

I look at it for a long time.

No. I'm a lot of things, but I'm not a snoop.

Still, no matter how many times I say it in my head, I still frown at the motion sensor above the main door as I push it open. The door chimes, indicating my exit. Except I'm not exiting. I'm wedging my purse in the door and walking back toward Dr. Kirkpatrick's office.

Not my proudest moment.

My cheeks are burning with shame as I lean closer to her door.

It's totally silent. Okay, not *totally*, but the paper shuffling and the soft tap of keys are the only things I'm hearing. And it's not exactly a sinister sound track.

Any minute now, she's going to come out here with her lipstick refreshed and her briefcase in hand and I'm going to be standing here, looking obvious and creepy.

Still, it's a little concerning how easily I can hear through this door. Normally, there's some soft elevator music out here, but apparently the receptionist turned that off on her way out.

Ugh, I need to go. This is just too slimy.

"It's me."

My head perks up at the sound of Dr. Kirkpatrick's voice. This is not her therapy voice. This voice is tired, a little wary maybe.

"I know you don't want to talk, Daniel, but my career is on the line here," she says.

Great. I'm stalking my own therapist so I can listen to her fight with her husband? Clearly, I do need therapy. Probably for the rest of my life if I don't get my crap together and get out of here.

"Well, if everything's so fine, why is Chloe Spinnaker asking me about Julien?"

Everything goes cold and still, inside and out. I don't blink or breathe. I stand there, legs turning to jelly, wishing I could hear whatever's being said on the other end of the line.

She's talking quieter now, or maybe she's turned so that she's facing the other way.

The phone rattles into the cradle, and I bolt like a horse out of the gate. I dance sideways through the waiting room, trying not to knock into the magazine stand between the chairs.

My heart is drumming so loud I can feel it behind my ears. I slink over to my purse, tugging it free of the door as I step outside.

• • •

The light from my front door looks like heaven. I feel myself deflate like a balloon as I turn off the car, my shoulders finally relaxing.

I still know nothing. Tomorrow I'll still wake up with a gaping hole in my memory and a best friend who won't speak to me. Plus, I have no idea who the hell this Daniel person is or how he fits into all of this.

But I'm one piece closer, and that's something.

Outside, the air is frigid, and I find myself cursing my missed summer again. I climb the steps to my porch with visions of a hot shower and fleece pajama pants in my future.

I toss my keys on the end table and chuck my coat on the hook by the door. And then I hear someone laughing in the kitchen. No, not someone. Some*ones.*

"Chloe?"

It's my mom who calls out, and I'm about to answer when another figure appears in the kitchen doorway. Blake. Blake is standing in my kitchen, sock-footed and holding a mug of something steamy.

I see my mom and my dad and everyone's smiling and this is supposed to be normal, but my teeth are starting to chatter again and then he's kissing me. Right in front of my parents. He just leans in and kisses me, letting it linger just long enough so that it feels like he's proving a point.

"Hey, babe," he says.

I return his embrace like a puppet, invisible strings lifting my arms and placing them around his middle. Over his shoulder I can see my delighted parents. Or my delighted mother at least. My dad's smile looks just a little too tight around the edges to totally convince me.

"Your hands are freezing," he says when I pull back, rubbing my fingers between his palms.

"I didn't know you were coming. I didn't see your car," I say stupidly, and then I look to my mom and dad for help because, really, aren't boys supposed to call first?

Apparently not when the boy is Blake Tanner, because he's exactly the guy you want your daughter to date. He's one of the good guys. A Boy Scout. An athlete. Hell, he's been on the Ridgeview Good Citizens' list so many times they should practically name it after him.

"I took my dad's car," he says, nodding out the window where I can see a shiny, black Audi parked on the street. "Mine's in the shop for a tune-up."

"Oh," I say. "Okay. Did you need something?"

He laughs and waggles his chemistry book at me. "Um, chemistry? Midterm's tomorrow?"

"Right," I echo, wishing to God I could just warm up enough to keep my chin from trembling.

I imagine the rest of my night studying with Blake. Which makes me think of Adam folded into that narrow space between my window and bed. Which makes me think of slamming my head into the nearest wall—seriously, what am I going to do here?

"I figured you might want to run over the review," he says. "Like we always do."

I nod and smile because everyone else seems to be happy about this plan.

"So…" he says, trailing off and jerking his head just a little toward the kitchen. Or my bedroom. It could be either.

Please let it be the kitchen. Please.

I glance around because, hell, I've never had a boy come over to study. Not a boy I'm dating at any rate. I have no idea what the parent rules are in this situation.

"Let me go get my book," I say dumbly, heading for the stairs.

"Or I can come up there," he says, shifting his own book in his arms. "I actually dropped my stuff in your room earlier."

He was in my room. Presumably alone. I feel icky all over at this.

"There's more room in the dining room," Dad says, and I can tell by his face that he'd prefer us there, a mere ten feet away without a doorway in sight.

But Mom frowns at him pointedly. "We're getting ready to watch a movie, George. They'll never be able to focus. Plus, there's no Internet in there."

"They need Internet to study?" Dad asks, emphasizing *Internet* and *study* as if they're code names for something much dirtier.

"Don't be obtuse, George. They always study in Chloe's room."

Do we? Or is my dad closer to the truth? Do we do something else? I feel my throat going dry as I realize exactly what we really might *do* in my room.

"I'm sorry," Mom says, waving us toward the stairs with a roll of her eyes like she's completely cool with all of this.

I am not cool with this. My ribs feel tight, and my knees are wobbly.

"The dining room would be fine," Blake says, but I'm not buying his tone. This has brown-nose-the-parents all over it.

"Don't be silly," Mom says, clearly eating right out of his hand. "We'll be down here if you need anything."

"*Right* down here," my dad adds.

I storm up the stairs, catching a glimpse of my crimson face in a decorative mirror on the wall. None of this seems to bother Blake, who follows me like a Labrador retriever, closing my bedroom door very quietly behind us.

I immediately scan every inch of my bedroom for signs of Adam. Ridiculous, I know. It's not like he left a trail of clothes or anything. God, don't think about Adam stripping off clothes. Not when Blake might be expecting me to strip off clothes.

Better yet, maybe I can just not think at all.

"What's the test on?" I ask, the words squeaky.

Blake just laughs and crosses the floor between us, threading his fingers in the back of my hair. He pulls me in and all I can smell is his cologne. It's too much, too strong, and all I can think is, *Mom would die if she knew how this guy had snowed her over.*

I have maybe a half second to process that this is going to happen, and then his lips close over mine.

I've been kissed enough to know when someone's doing it right. And Blake is technically doing it right, tilting my head just a little. Urging my mouth to open for him. And he's pressing into me just enough to make things interesting, without mashing his kibbles and bits against my thigh or anything.

My heart is hammering for all of the wrong reasons. I fumble under his kisses, feeling like there's no right speed for my lips, no comfortable perch for my hands. And I really need to stop overthinking this before he starts thinking something is up with me.

Trouble is, something *is* up with me.

Namely, I can't stop thinking about Adam.

This is wrong. Guilt is tearing through me, my every instinct commanding me to pull away from him. I can't do this. I just can't.

I pull away, and Blake gazes down on me, eyes dark with hunger. "What's wrong?"

"Nothing," I say, forcing myself to touch his shoulders. "School is just…"

"Hm…" he says, cutting me off with another long, slow kiss.

It's even worse than before. All I can think about is Adam. And

God, it's wrongity-wrong-wrong, but for one second, I close my eyes tight and pretend I'm with him. I think of blue eyes and a low laugh and all the things I should never think of now.

Blake gives me a little appreciative moan, and the sound of his voice is so startling and so foreign, that I pull away, wiping a shaking hand over my mouth.

"I'm sorry," I say, stepping back to my desk. "I'm really sorry."

Blake watches me in a very cool, detached way. The same way he looked at me that morning at Trixie's. As if he's about to pick me apart and label all the gooey bits he finds.

"You know, I thought we were done with this," he says.

"Done with what? I'm just tense, Blake."

"Yeah, I got that memo. You've been *tense* ever since that night at my house."

I don't have to ask to know what night he means. The night I hit my head. The night I forgot. Or remembered. Hell, I don't even know what to call it.

You could tell him.

I toss the idea almost as soon as I think it. Something as deep as the marrow of my bones tells me I can't tell Blake about this. Not any of it. And I'm definitely a girl who believes in going with her gut.

"I'm sorry," I say again. A broken record. "I think the pressure of the applications and senior year—it's a little more intense than I thought."

"Are you doing your meditations?"

"Yeah," I lie, turning away so he won't see the irritation on my face.

But it's there, burning through me. A strange mix of fear and discomfort. I don't like him acting like my mother. Trying to *fix* me.

"You know you should think about coming with me to the gym. It might help you burn off a lot of that anxiety."

"Thanks, I just don't…" I trail into silence because it hits me like a ton of bricks. I don't want to be with Blake. I just don't. Even if Adam didn't exist at all, I still wouldn't.

Despite everything I felt, all the long afternoons I spent gazing at him on the lacrosse field, this isn't right. Not for me.

"Blake," I say, but then I pause because I can't believe I'm about to do this. "I think I might need a little bit of time. A little… time off."

"Time off," he repeats, and while it's crystal clear he knows where I'm going with this, he's not angry. Not angry or shocked or even particularly hurt.

"A break," I tell him. "Just to sort out my head."

I turn back to him, and he's very still and calm. After a while, he comes forward, touching my face with soft fingers. The touch is tender, but somehow his face isn't. God, it's so confusing.

"Do you mean break for now or break forever?" he asks.

I don't know. I don't know what I mean or what I'm doing. Walking away from Blake is counter to everything I've ever wanted. I keep hearing Maggie's words in my mind. Am I running away? Is that what this is?

"I don't know," I say honestly. "I just know I need some time to sort it out."

"Of course, Chloe. Take your time. You know I'll be here."

The words are the stuff of movies, but his face is flat. He's like a very bad actor reciting even worse lines.

And I'd like to know who the hell wrote them.

We file back down the stairs. He is all easy civility as he offers me a sideways hug at the door.

"Leaving already?" Mom asks. Her eyes flick nervously between us. Sensing trouble in paradise? Maybe. Dreading said trouble? Definitely.

"Yeah," he says, scratching the back of his head. He looks more upset now, and somehow I feel like that's for show too. Like it's all for her benefit. "I'm suddenly pretty tired."

"Well, be careful driving," she says. "Tell Daniel we said hello."

My eyes go wide as I turn to her, blood running through me like ice water. "Daniel?"

"His father," she says. "Honestly, Chloe, where is your head these days?"

Stunned by my slipup, I say nothing. Blake's slipping too, that thin veneer of sadness sliding away to reveal the first expression I've believed all night.

Suspicion.

CHAPTER FOURTEEN

. . . .

I pound on the door this time. No delicate knock. No mill-
ing around on the welcome mat. Or the place where there
would be a welcome mat if this place were in any way welcoming.
I just spilled out the biggest whopper of a lie I've ever laid on my
parents to get here at eleven o'clock on a school night, and my
patience has run seriously thin.

I'm just about to shout Adam's name or throw a rock at the
window when the door flings open, an old woman appearing in
the entrance. Damn.

She's wearing a floral polyester shirt, one that hasn't seen a
washing machine in far too long. Her thin white hair is pinned
sloppily away from her wide and wrinkled face. This woman
doesn't share a single feature with Adam. From her watery green
eyes to her skin, which is so white it's almost pink, she is the
absolute opposite of Adam, who is all sharp, dark lines and pierc-
ing eyes.

I finally find my voice. "I'm sorry to disturb you."

She doesn't say a thing, just blinks up at me like she can't even
imagine what I want. Or maybe like she doesn't understand a
word I'm saying. Which is possible if the smell of booze coming
off her is any indication of how she's spent her evening.

"Is Adam here?"

He slides into view then, still tugging a shirt down over his torso. I catch a sliver of damp, golden flesh above his jeans and force my eyes to his face.

His hair is still wet from the shower, his feet bare on the carpet.

"I've got it, Grandma," he says.

"Gloria?" she says, looking up at Adam with an expression that's much sweeter than the one she offered me.

"No, Grandma, it's me. Adam."

"Adam," she says, touching his arm.

"Yes," he says, turning her gently back toward the house. "You should go in. It's cold."

Her face puckers up, lines folding in on lines until she looks like a raisin leached of its color. "Son of a bitch! Son of a bitch!"

My mouth drops at her sudden hostility. Her shouts dissolve into a coughing fit, and then she walks away, still swearing as she hobbles deeper into the apartment. Adam watches her for a moment, and then turns to me, looking wholly unaffected.

I must look desperate because Adam holds up a hand and grabs his jacket from a hook by the door. I watch him jam his bare feet into his half-laced boots, and then he's following me into the night, his breath steaming in the darkness.

"You can't be here," Adam says, and God, I thought I was paranoid, but he's redefining it tonight. He's searching the parking lot, pacing back and forth on the tiny slab of cement outside his door. "Have you ever heard of a phone?"

Is he looking for a girl? Oh God, he just got out of the

shower. He could be getting ready for a date, and I just showed up here.

I feel sick to my stomach. Sick just about everywhere, really.

"I'm sorry," I say. "I couldn't—I needed—" I can't even make words anymore. I'm looking around too, dreading the arrival of a girl I never even considered existed. But I should have.

"Just tell me why you're here. And make it fast, Chloe. It's not…" He doesn't finish, just sighs and looks at me expectantly.

I don't know how to condense all the things that brought me to his door tonight. My call with Maggie? What I overheard Dr. Kirkpatrick say? The fact that I think somehow whatever happened to me wasn't an accident or a sickness and the fact that I think Blake's dad, maybe even Blake himself, is in on it?

I have a million reasons to be here tonight.

"I think I broke up with Blake," I say. Moronically. Because that fact isn't anywhere on the list of relevant crap I need to say to him.

Except that it obviously is, because Adam stops with the looking around. He looks right at me, until I know beyond a single doubt there isn't a girl coming. There isn't a girl at all. Not one that isn't standing right in front of him.

The air between us feels hot and cold together. Charged the way I'd imagine it would be before lightning strikes.

"You said that'd be a huge mistake," he says, taking a step toward me.

His eyes flick down to my lips, and God help me, but I feel that look in my knees. Maybe right down into my bones. "I did?"

My voice is breathy, and I'm moving in too. Adam nods, those gorgeous kaleidoscope eyes of his drinking me in like he's been starved to do it.

It's wrong. Every part of me knows that you don't slide into a new guy's arms a pitiful three hours after breaking up with your boyfriend.

Still, I can't help this. Or maybe I just don't want to.

My hands flutter up to his chest, and he's leaning in so close I can feel the dampness from his hair against my forehead. He closes his eyes, and I curl my fingers in his shirt.

"You have to go," he says, and there's this broken twist to his words, like he's forcing them out.

"I don't want to go. And I don't think you want me to either."

"You have to," he says, and the words sound like torture, but he pulls back from me. My fingers drop away from his shirt, and he starts looking around again. Checks his phone.

My chest feels too tight, my heart too big. Whatever I'm feeling for him is too much. I hate it. It eclipses everything I've ever felt before, and I don't think I'm ready for that. I don't know how I got to this place with him.

Probably because someone stole the memory of it from me.

Tears spill hot and slick down my cheeks, but there's nothing I can do to stop them. "Someone did this to me, Adam. Someone made me forget things, and I know it had something to do with the study group. And with Dr. Kirkpatrick—"

"Chloe, I can't do this," he says. I can see the pain in his eyes, but he's shaking his head and taking a step back. He looks bound and tied. He stands mute, checking the street with a furtive glance.

"Fine, then don't. But give me something, Adam! At least tell me what happened between us."

"Nothing," he says, but the look of anguish on his face tells me otherwise.

"Liar," I say, and then I rush him, taking both of his hands and pulling him closer to me.

I can smell clean water and soap and cinnamon, and I can see his body go tense beneath my touch. "Not one of the moments I've remembered is *nothing,* and I think you know it."

His eyes drift closed and he swallows hard. I have never, ever wanted to kiss someone so much in my life. Except it's more than that.

"Go home, Chloe," he says, gritting each word out like it's physically painful. "Please just…go."

• • •

I stare at the pictures on the fridge across from me and push the oatmeal around in my bowl. Mom offers me a mug of something steaming, and I shake my head.

She sighs and slouches into the seat across from me. "Did you work it out with Blake last night?"

Work what out? Oh. Right. My ruse for getting out of the house was rushing after my devastated boyfriend.

I shake my head again. It's about the only move I've got this morning.

"Maybe he just needs some time," she says, assuming Blake was the initiator of the breakup.

The whole thing with Adam last night has me totally on edge, so her comment pisses me off endlessly. My head snaps up like a cocking pistol. "Blake isn't the one who needed time off. I do."

"You?" she says, looking faintly horrified. "You broke up with him?"

I scrub my hands over my face because the whole thing is ridiculous. How am I even having this conversation? How can I break up with someone I don't even remember dating? "I don't know. I said I needed space. We're taking some time."

"Time? From Blake? Honey, have you thought this through?"

"Yes."

"But you've loved him since you were a freshman."

"Well, I'm not a freshman anymore!"

Her face goes tight and hard. "Watch your tone, young lady. I'm perfectly aware that you're not a freshman. It's just a little shocking. The two of you have been so happy."

"Have we, Mom? What do we do together that makes me so happy?"

She pushes back from the table, looking startled.

"I grabbed some pictures from your scrapbook room," I tell her. "The ones by the book you're working on for this year."

"That was supposed to be a surprise," she says weakly.

"Mom, you give me one every Christmas. You leave them on the table in the basement for months leading up to it."

Her face twitches a little, her gaze drifting to the table.

"I love them," I tell her. It's a stretch, but she seems to need to hear it. "It's sweet and thoughtful, but it's not really a surprise, okay?"

She shrugs. "Fine, but what does it has to do with Blake and you?"

"I don't see how I was happy with Blake," I tell her. "Every picture showed me at places I never liked to be. Most are at school. Some are at games. There was a *bowling alley* page."

"You had a double date that night," she says defensively. "What's the big deal?"

"The big deal is that I *hate* bowling, Mom. I don't really like school, and I've never, not once, been to a baseball game."

"Well, Blake's an alternate on the team, isn't he? It's different when you're dating an athlete."

"Yeah? Well, who is *he* dating? Because the girl in those pictures isn't me, Mom. It just isn't."

I can tell this is too much for her to process. She collects my untouched bowl and the mug of tea she'd offered and rinses them in the sink.

"Your supportive silence is touching," I say.

"What do you want me to say, Chloe? You think leaving Blake will make you happy? I'll believe that when I see it."

"What's that supposed to mean?"

"Some people choose unhappiness, you know."

"No, I don't know."

"Yes, you do. Somehow, right around the time you turned sixteen, you decided your life was just too miserable."

"When I was—"

When I was sixteen. When the panic attacks started. I feel my face blanch. My hands go into fists as I force myself to silence.

"I don't know what to do with you. You've been in therapy.

We've bought every book, tried every strategy. We've given you freedom, and then we've pulled in the reins, but nothing works. Sometimes I'm just not sure you want to be happy."

I stand up, a bitter laugh rising out of me. "Forget I ever said anything. I was happier with Blake. Gee, maybe I'll call him this afternoon so that we can go Putt-Putting. Or, hey, maybe he can take me to the batting cages."

I shove my chair in too hard, and Mom whirls on me, eyes cold. "Keep it up and I'll take your car."

I cross my arms and stare right back until she looks away, drying her hands on a dish towel. "I'm not the enemy, Chloe. I want to help you, but at this point, I have no idea what it is you need."

Yeah? Well, she can join the club.

The doorbell rings, and I head for it without another word, grateful for the distraction.

I swing it wide and suck in a tight breath, shocked at the slim, strawberry blond I find on the other side of the door.

"Maggie?"

CHAPTER FIFTEEN

· ·

I don't ask her why she came. I honestly don't care.

I just yank her inside before she changes her mind and pull her into a hug.

"Your timing is impeccable," I whisper into her hair, momentarily forgetting that things are different between us.

I don't forget for long. The stiffness in her shoulders and the way she pulls back reminds me that Maggie and I are not like we were before.

"It's been a long time, Maggie," my mom says.

"Good to see you, Mrs. Spinnaker," Maggie replies.

"Well, I'll leave you two to catch up." Mom leans down to peck my cheek as if we're the perfect little family and have not just been holding verbal Armageddon over the dining table.

She slips out the front door, and Maggie takes a step away from me.

"I j-just came to bring you this," she says, handing me a sweatshirt she borrowed at least a year ago. I can't think of a single reason she'd return it now, unless she's here to talk. My hope is short-lived when she scowls and turns toward the door.

"Wait, Maggie, don't go."

She sighs, turning a little away from the door but still not enough to really look at me. "It's really early, Chlo. I've got t-to get to school."

"I know, and I know you've got every reason to not be speaking to me, but I *need* to talk to you."

The quiet is so painful that I search for noise. I hear the hum of the fridge and the soft rumble of a car on the next street over. Finally, I give up on her response, filling the silence with my own words.

"I'm desperate, Maggie. You're the only one I trust."

She studies me for a long moment and then jerks her head back toward her car. "You c-can ride with me if you want."

"Great," I say, grabbing my coat and my backpack from the rack. I'm moving fast, wanting to seal the deal before she changes her mind.

"This doesn't mean we're okay," she says, and I ratchet down the smile that's threatening to split my face in two.

"I know. I know that."

"Okay."

We don't say anything else as we get in the truck. Maggie drives an ancient pickup with like a hundred and sixty thousand miles on it. Her uncle used it for his electrical contracting business over a decade ago, back when money was really tight. Which means there are no bells and whistles. Crank windows, vinyl seats, and a standard transmission.

Maggie taught me to drive stick shift in this truck. Or tried to, anyway. I've never been much of a driver. One of the many reasons why I've logged so many hours in the passenger seat of this hunk of junk.

I listen to the familiar sounds of Maggie's keys in the ignition and the engine coming to life. I know it's ridiculous being so giddy over a six-minute ride in a rust bucket, but for the first time since this started, my morning feels right. Normal.

I expect her to back out, but she pauses, hand on the gearshift.

"So what d-do you need to talk to me about?"

I take a breath and brace myself. "When I tell you this, you will think I'm crazy."

"I already think you're crazy," she says, and there isn't any humor in her eyes.

"This will take it further," I tell her, "which is why I haven't told anyone."

Except Adam. But I can't talk about Adam. Every time I even think about Adam, I feel my throat close up and my eyes get teary and I just can't go there. Not right now.

She backs out and sets an easy pace through the neighborhood. And I fall silent, watching the bare branches of the trees slip by my window.

"Are you going to t-tell me?"

"I think someone's been messing with my memory." I glance sideways, but Maggie's focus is on the road.

She looks a little pinched around the lips but not astonished. And not amused.

The truck rolls to a stop at Beecher, and she turns left instead of right. This way will add three minutes to our trip. She is buying me time to talk.

I go on in a rush, letting the words tumble out as quickly as my lips and tongue will form them. I don't just tell her that I can't remember. I tell her about the CT scan and the therapy sessions and the stack of college applications that paralyze me with fear. I tell her about the strangeness of Blake's kisses and Dr. Kirkpatrick's phone call and about Daniel. I even talk about Adam, though it's a fleeting mention that I rush right over.

When I look up, I realize we're in the historic neighborhood. One street over from Belmont Street. We are also late for school, something that doesn't concern me half as much as it probably should.

Maggie parks the truck on the side of the road and palms her keys, turning sideways in her seat.

"We're n-not friends anymore."

This isn't exactly shocking, but hearing it doesn't feel good. I push away that aching hollow in my chest and try to find words. "I know that. I just don't know why."

"I think I believe you," she says. "But it doesn't change anything. I c-can't get into all the things that you did, b-but you made choices, Chloe. Maybe you don't remember them now, but you made them."

"And that's just that? We're not friends. And that's forever?"

"I thought so," Maggie says, and for the first time I can see the pain behind her eyes. Reddish blotches appear on the pale skin beneath her eyes. It is a telltale sign that she is upset.

She shakes her head then, and her face goes hard once more. "I d-don't want to get into all of that right now. I'm n-not ready."

I nod, but I'm not ready to let it go. Everything in me is clinging at this tendril of possibility now. "But maybe someday?"

My voice sounds pitiful, even to me. She turns away from me, looking out the window. I can see the backs of the Belmont Beauties even from here.

"All of that c-can wait," she says. "But I need to show you something. And I d-don't think it can wait."

Mags and I have done a lot of crazy things together, but not in my wildest dreams did I ever think we would skip school to sneak into the Millers' house. Mainly because I could never imagine the place being empty. Not reliably empty at any rate.

Now, we slink quietly along the hedges at the back of the house, the back door and windows strangely curtain-free.

"Watch the street," she says as we step onto the back porch.

She pulls out a large circle of keys from her purse and starts flipping through them.

"What are you, a cat burglar now?"

"They're my uncle's. He's fixing a problem in the k-kitchen. L-lighting or something."

"He won't miss his work keys?"

"He's hunting today."

Terrific. We're using stolen keys from a guy who owns six hunting rifles and a couple of crossbows to boot. I'm just about to tell her this is a bad idea when she finds the right key, the door opening with a soft creak.

"Get in," she says, and I follow her command, slipping into the dim kitchen.

I've only been in the Millers' house for a few parties. It was completely different then. The kitchen used to look like the after picture on a home decorating show, with pitchers of fresh flowers and color-coordinated dish towels hanging from antique hooks. Every nook and cranny had some sort of homey, artsy touch. And now it's just…blank.

The shuffle of my sneakers across the wood floor seems to echo off the walls. Even the air feels different, cold and dry and empty.

Maggie doesn't allow me much time to dwell. She rushes through the kitchen and dining room, to the wide, oak-railed staircase. We climb the stairs, and my palm grows slick on the banister. I know where she's taking me. And something inside me doesn't want to go.

We open the six-paneled door at the end of the hallway, and I feel as if I've stepped through a curtain of ice. The barren room gapes at us through the open doorway. Pink walls and a wooden floor. It is stark and terrible, nothing but dry bones stripped of their living, breathing parts.

I want to leave.

I can see a dark rectangle in the floor, the space where Julien's bed must have rested, protecting the wood planks from the sunlight that must have poured through her three windows on clear days.

"Over here," Maggie says, and I jump a little.

She's standing inside the empty closet, crouched low to the ground. She looks up, wrinkling her nose. "I came with him when he b-bid on the house. Had to get my allergy shots afterward."

"Why were you up here?" I ask, rubbing my arms.

"Bored. Curious. I don't know. I don't even know why I opened the closet, but when I d-did, I found this."

I move closer, rubbing my arms where goose bumps have sprouted. I can see the pale lines of pencil mark even before I crouch down near Maggie to read what has been written on the wall.

I wasn't crazy before.
Someone did this.
Chloe knows.

Three rows of neat, girly print whispering secrets that were never meant to be seen. But all that bleeds away from my vision, leaving two words burned into my mind. *Chloe knows.*

• • •

School has been a special version of hell since I walked through the door. The bell rings, and I nearly jump out of my skin. Again. I've really got to get a grip. I've spent the entire day tensing at every slammed locker, going cold every time someone mentions something I can't remember. Which in my present condition happens about every twelve seconds.

A sophomore darts past me, and I clutch my books to my chest and try not to yelp. What period is it, anyway? I squint at the clock and the rapidly emptying hallway. Usually someone chats with me all the way to my next class, but today I'm a social leper.

Then again, yesterday I broke up with Blake. Popularity is a fickle thing, I guess.

Kristen Simpson stops at a door up the way and gives me a wave that says, *Hurry up*. Mind you, last year, Kristen wouldn't have spit on me if I was on fire, but today any friendly face is welcome. I smile at her and start in that direction. Computer lab.

Also known as the one class I share with Blake and Adam. I stop short in the hallway and wave Kristen along. I can just imagine how great that class would be, them shooting each other hateful glares. Me wishing I could disappear into the cracks in the floor.

I can't deal with seeing them right now. Hell, I can barely deal with walking today because my mind has one track, one subject, one single line of repetition.

What do I know about Julien?

Is she hurt? Did her parents force her to leave to protect her? Or did someone else force her? And why would I know anything about any of it?

The bell rings, and I duck into the nearest bathroom and drop my backpack onto the floor. I brace my hands on a sink and stare at my reflection. My eyes look empty, but I think they should be full—full of all the things I've seen but can't remember. Things about Julien.

A new thought forces my hands to go tighter on the sink. What else am I hiding? And does anyone know?

I think of Dr. Kirkpatrick's phone call to Daniel, whoever he is. I know it's crazy to think it's Blake's dad, but I keep going back to it. Even as neurotic as I am, I can't seriously believe that my boyfriend and his dad are *both* involved in a memory-altering conspiracy that somehow forced Julien and her family out of town.

I stop cold as the facts ricochet around my head like bullets. My name on Julien's wall. My therapist's phone call. The missing file on my computer. The text on Blake's phone.

My stomach rolls, my palms going slick against the porcelain.

All these crazy things are hinged to a single axis, the six months I can't remember.

The door bangs open, and I nearly jump out of my skin.

"Hey, you," Abbey says, but her bright smile vanishes almost instantly. "Oh, Chloe, you look like you've seen a ghost."

I try for a smile, but it's a sad imitation at best. "I've been sick. I think maybe I tried to come back too soon."

"Do you want me to help you down to the nurse's station? You poor thing!"

"No, I'm fine," I say. "I think I'll just get a drink of water and head back to class."

"Are you sure?"

I nod and give her a cheery salute as I head out the door. And I do get a drink. I get a drink right before I slip into the parking lot. I made it through three periods. That's got to count for something, right?

The winter sun is gleaming with brute force today, warming my skin despite the chilly breeze. I zip my coat and plunge my hands into my pockets, knowing it's going to be a long walk home.

And maybe home isn't the best plan. Now that I'm thinking about that missing file again, I doubt my computer is safe at all. If Blake has been in my room, messing with my computer, I have no idea what kind of tracking software he could have installed.

I could call Dad; he wouldn't make a big deal out of skipping out a few periods early. Maybe he'd even take me back to his office and I could snag one of the spare computers there. But then what? Dad tells Mom, and Mom forces me back to the doctor for a battery of tests since I'm not feeling well.

No. I need answers that a doctor isn't going to have. A block later, a plan forms in my mind and my pace quickens. I cut across Parkview and then take a left on Jenner Street. The small brick building peeks out at the end of the road.

There used to be a sign at the edge of the parking lot. Most of it blew away in a windstorm a few years ago. And apparently our town's economy is still in the crapper because it hasn't been replaced yet. All that's left to read are the letters BRARY followed by a very 1980s graphic of a stack of books.

I pull open the doors and breathe in the smell of old copies and older books. I can't remember the last time I came to the library, but I love this place. I always have. When I was little, Mom would bring me here. I'd curl into one of the leather armchairs at the ends of the aisles to read picture books, and she'd browse the cooking section. Everything looks older now. Faded and worn down like the sign out front.

It's sad, really. The library is a relic of a time long gone, a time when the Ridgeview mayor believed new books were as important as putting pretty planters down the main drag every April.

I wipe my shoes on the mat and peer around. The place looks utterly deserted. A sign on the desk informs me that Mrs. Nesbit, the librarian, is filing in the reference section if I need her.

I don't.

I need a computer.

A pair of reasonably new Macs are stationed across from two study tables. I remember Mrs. Nesbit came to the high school to meet with the technology club last year when they were installed. I saw them all talking in the computer lab once, and it was crazy. I mean, she's got to be like a hundred and thirty years old, but I'm telling you, she can talk downloads and upgrades like a pro.

I settle myself behind the desktop. The computers are fine, but the connection is molasses in January. Even bringing up a search engine takes a full minute. I sigh and stretch my neck, willing the computer to move faster. Wondering if I'll actually be able to search and find anything or if I'll just end up sitting here waiting until sometime after graduation. Maybe I could check the microfiche copies of our newspaper for information on the Millers instead.

Or I could abandon all of this private eye crap and ask one of the gossip hags, like Abbey Binns. Surely I could pry a little more information out of her.

The search engine pops up, so I type four words into the box. Daniel Tanner Ridgeview Ohio.

The machine grinds miserably for thirty seconds. A whole minute. I could send a telegraph faster than this. *Come on, already!*

A list of links finally pops up, and to my frustration, I don't see anything incriminating. It's all pretty standard rich-guy stuff. Social mentions, charity donations, reelection to the school board: your basic high society crap. High society for Ridgeview anyway. The Tanners are definitely A-listers. I mean, they aren't the Millers. They don't live in one of the Beaumont Beauties. They actually live in one of the cookie-cutter mansions in the newer development on the south side of town. I think they own some sort of medical research company or something.

I scroll through the links, spotting one that clears it up. Tanner Technologies. The news article is from seven or eight months ago. At that point, Mr. Tanner's company had lost some sort of pharmaceutical bid and was in jeopardy of closing down.

Great. I may not be an ace detective, but I've watched enough prime-time cop dramas to know that a total financial meltdown motivates people to do really awful things.

Like manipulating the memories of a run of the mill seventeen-year-old?

God, this is pointless.

"Oh, Ms. Spinnaker, it's so good to see you."

I whirl around, thinking she has to be talking to another Ms. Spinnaker, even though there are no other Spinnakers in this town.

I finally meet Mrs. Nesbit's gaze. She's smiling down at me over a stack of hardback books in her arms.

"Hello," I say.

"It's been almost a month since you've been in!" she says, sounding genuinely surprised by this. As far as I know, I haven't stepped foot in this library since elementary school.

So apparently I get to add mystery library visits to my list of things I can't remember.

"Where is that handsome friend of yours?" she asks.

Blake? Blake came here with me? This is just...I can't even. I open and close my mouth a few times before giving up on speech and offering a shrug.

"Well, I can't believe he'd leave you to your studying alone," she says, getting that wistful look that old women sometimes do when waxing on about young love.

"Oh, Blake and I are actually just friends now," I say, trying to let her down easy. She looks startled, shaking her head.

"Blake? The Tanner boy? Why, I haven't seen him in a couple of years at least. I was talking about Adam."

Now she's looking at me with something akin to reproach, like I'm a brazen little hussy with two boys in my pocket. She's got no idea how close she is, but I don't have time for that. I need to find out what in the heck I was doing here with Adam.

I minimize my search window and laugh nervously. "Right, I'm sorry. I'm so distracted with all of my college application essays."

I have no idea where I pulled that from, but she hums with a mournful look, like she knows just what I mean.

"You know, I'm sure Adam could help you with that. Of course, you were in that study group of Daniel Tanner's, so—"

"I'm sorry, what?"

It's rude to interrupt. I know that. But I also know my pulse just jumped to warp speed.

"The study group," she repeats, looking a little put off. "You were in that group, weren't you?"

"Yes. I'm sorry, I just didn't realize Mr. Tanner was behind it."

"Oh, yes. He was the major corporate sponsor. From what he

tells me, things will be expanding next year. They may even need use of our facilities here."

She's practically beaming, and I'm about to throw up all over her Mac. This can't be happening. It just can't. Because this means the phone call was real. My breath seems to freeze into something solid in my lungs.

I stand up abruptly, feeling like I don't have an ounce of blood left in my face. "I'm so sorry, Mrs. Nesbit. I completely forgot I'm meeting my mother today."

"Oh, well. You know I still have that book on reserve for you," she says with a frown. "*Fundamentals of Hypnosis.* You're actually a week or two past our standard hold time, Ms. Spinnaker."

"I'll have to come back for it. My mom's probably in a dead panic."

I eye the door hungrily, but follow her to the circulation desk, where I hand over my library card and wait what feels like three hours for her to check out the book.

Finally, I stumble toward the door, feeling shaky as a leaf. Hypnosis? I mean...

CHAPTER SIXTEEN

• •

I stumble into the library parking lot, skidding to a cartoonlike halt when a familiar Mustang pulls in. Déjà vu washes over me as I watch the car track through the parking lot, headed straight for me.

Just like it did that first night at the school. The night I woke up.

I blink as he parks the car, my feet turning to lead weights at the ends of my legs. How? How did he know I was here? Because it has to be me. No way did Blake just happen to decide to visit the library for the first time in *years* today.

I think of the text on his phone, the books in my room, and most of all, the way he looked at me at Trixie's Diner. None of that would mean much of anything if his dad didn't have his hands in all of this. The engine turns off, and I feel adrenaline pumping through me as the truth hits with bone-rattling force. Blake is following me.

The car door opens, and I clench my hands into tight fists. I can't run. If I run, he'll know I figured him out. And I don't want him to know that yet.

Blake is just stepping out when another car pulls into the parking lot. It's a really old black Camaro, engine grumbling in a menacing way. The paint is beyond dull, almost gray instead of black, and that almost makes it more intimidating.

It grinds to a halt in the spot next to the Mustang. I see Blake's face turn dark just seconds before Adam opens the door.

Oh my God, they both knew. They both somehow knew I'd be here, and they're here and I'm trapped.

Adam pulls a book bag and a stack of library books out of the passenger seat, and I manage a breath. Okay. Okay, stop being paranoid. Adam happens to be at the library. And Blake—

Yeah, no, Blake is stalking me.

My thoughts cut off into nothingness as Adam looks up, meeting my eyes with surprise and then noticing Blake moving toward me. I try to convey how uncomfortable—screw uncomfortable, how *terrified*—I am with my eyes.

And I watch, holding my breath as Adam shoulders his pack… and heads right past me.

"Chloe, we should talk," Blake says, sparing a final glance at Adam's form.

I shake my head, swallowing hard. "I don't want to talk."

I can still see Adam making his way toward the door. He's just going to leave me here when it's clear as day I'm a damsel in some pretty freaking serious distress! Unbelievable.

"I could drive you home," Blake says, voice sweet but eyes hard. "Just give me ten minutes."

"I really don't want to talk," I say, voice cracking. "I told you I need some time."

Adam's almost at the door. Maybe he's moving slower or maybe

I'm just wishing for that. But if he doesn't stop moving altogether, I'm going to be alone out here in about two seconds.

"Be reasonable, Chloe. It's not safe to walk all the way home," Blake says, and he's closing the distance between us.

"It's Ridgeview, not Harlem," I say breezily. Inside, I'm screaming. I know why cornered dogs bite now. I'd be snapping like a maniac if I had sharp teeth.

"Chloe," Blake says, and it almost sounds condescending. Then he touches my arm, curling fingers over my sleeve. I yank myself free.

I can't help it any more than I can explain it. It's like recoiling at a roach or maggots. I don't know why, but I know I need him away from me.

"How about I call you?" he asks.

"She said she needs time, man."

Adam.

I feel my whole body relax. I don't know when he turned around or why I didn't hear him walking back, but he's right here now, book bag still slung over one shoulder and eyes narrowed to dangerous slits.

Blake sneers at him. "How about you mind your own business?"

"No, he's right," I interject. "I do want some time, Blake."

"And I'm happy to give it. This isn't some effort to win you back," he says, as if the idea is completely ridiculous. "I'm just concerned. As your friend. Skipping classes and leaving school early. I'm worried you're jeopardizing your future."

He doesn't look concerned. If I didn't know better, I'd say he looks determined. He's wearing a face that reminds me a whole lot of my mother's my-way-or-the-highway stance.

Blake takes another step toward me, and I flinch just before Adam slides in between us, facing Blake.

"Let it rest."

"She could need help," Blake grits out.

"She said she's fine."

"This *isn't* your gig, Reed."

"Not yours either anymore," Adam says, bringing me back to the present.

This doesn't feel like it's about me. I mean, I hear the words, but there's something way bigger than jealousy in their eyes. Maybe this whole situation just gave them a reason and any second now someone's going to throw a punch.

Blake juts toward him, but then catches my eye over Adam's shoulder. His face molds into something that feels plastic. Counterfeit.

He seems to shut out Adam then, speaking only to me. "I'm sorry if this came off wrong. I just wanted you to know I'm here if you need me."

I manage a nod, and he smiles in a way that doesn't reach his eyes. I watch him turn to head for his car. The Mustang purrs to life, and I command my heart to stop running a hundred miles an hour.

Adam doesn't even look at me. He just walks back to the library as if nothing happened at all.

"Is he following me?" I shout after him, the adrenaline still coursing hard enough to make my hands shake and my teeth chatter.

"Sorry?" Adam asks, looking for all the world like a guy who wasn't about to throw down in the library parking lot twenty seconds ago.

"How did he know I was here, Adam?"

He looks away from me, his jaw a hard, beautiful line above his collar. And what did I expect? Why would he know? Still, despite the books and the backpack, something tells me Adam followed Blake to the library.

Maybe he's studying now, but somehow, I'm sure he came for Blake. Or maybe even for me.

"You should get out of here," he finally says. "You'll be safer at home."

• • •

Home my ass. I'm staying in this parking lot until he comes out and explains what the heck is going on. Which sounds a lot more committed than it really is since the library closes at four o'clock on Fridays.

Still. It's cold, and there's a distinct look of rain in the clouds gathering overhead. Rain in November in northern Ohio is every bit as unpleasant as it sounds.

The library lights go dim, and a few moments after, Adam emerges. He's got a couple of books under one arm and his jacket slung over a shoulder with his backpack. As if he's impervious to the cold that has me shivering to my bones beside his car.

He wrangles his keys free of his pocket, and I clear my throat.

His eyes go wide as he takes me in. "Are you serious with this?"

"As a freaking heart attack," I say, lifting my chin.

"I don't know why Blake knew you were here. Maybe he followed you."

"Maybe you followed him."

He waggles the books at me. "No, I come here to *study*. Why the hell would I follow Blake?"

"You tell me."

I step back from his door, which I probably shouldn't. But I'm not going to physically force him to stay here. He wrenches his car door open and throws his books inside. I half expect him to just get in and drive away, but then he slams it again and glares at me.

"What is this even about? Now you're pissed that I interrupted you with Blake?"

I roll my eyes. "Yes, that's exactly it, Adam. I was obviously chomping at the bit for some alone time there."

"Then what?" He's loud now, not quite shouting but close enough that I flinch when he moves closer to me. "What the hell is this, Chlo? One minute you and I are—"

"What? What are we, Adam? Because I already told you I can't remember anything, and you refuse to fill me in."

"There's nothing to be filled in," he says, convincing no one.

"I don't believe you." I'm so cold, my teeth are starting to rattle, my breath steaming around me like a cloud. "I can still feel it, Adam. Whatever I forgot? It's still in there. Every time you look at me, every time you walk past me in the stupid hall I feel…"

"You feel what?"

I can see the impatience in his eyes. And something else too.

"This," I say, reaching forward to take his hands. "*Us*, Adam."

His fingers, blissfully warm, curl around mine, and his face tenses with worry. "You're freezing, Chlo. You shouldn't be out here in this cold. I'll take you home."

"Don't you dare. Don't you dare put me in this car and turn on the radio and pretend nothing's going on here."

"Why are you so sure something *is* going on?" he asks, and he sounds tense and miserable and just a little bit desperate.

I don't have an answer I can put into words. So I curl my hands in his and breathe in his scent, soapy and clean with that soft tang of cinnamon. I let my eyes close.

"I remember things when I touch you," I say. "I remember studying with you. Raking leaves with you."

"Yeah, Chlo, it happened. But it obviously didn't mean anything."

I open my eyes and swallow my fear. "No, Adam. I think it might have meant *everything*."

He jerks his hands free of mine, and I flinch. He plows his hands into his hair, breathing hard and stepping back from me. I feel colder than cold, as if something crucial has been torn from my grasp.

He shakes his head, letting out a bitter laugh. "You don't get it. We *can't* do this," he says. "We can't go here, Chloe. Not now. Not ever."

He's looking left and right, and then he's going for his car. God, he's going to go. He's just going to leave me standing here after I said that.

He doesn't leave, but he goes still and tense. I hear him let out a shuddery breath, his feet shifting on the pavement.

"Damn it," he says, shaking his head once.

He turns back to me, and I don't even have time to blink or breathe or anything before his hands are on my face, in my hair—and then, he's kissing me.

His lips are soft and hard together, sending electric shocks through every inch of me. I'm heavy and trembling under his kiss, my half-frozen hands fisting in the front of his shirt, soaking in his warmth.

My mouth slides open with a sigh, and the kiss goes on and on until I no longer think about the cold or the danger or any of the million questions I want to ask. I can't think about a single thing outside of the feel of his arms and the taste of his mouth against mine.

We separate in a steaming rush of breath, our foreheads pressed together and my hands threaded into his hair.

"Tell me we haven't done that yet," I breathe.

He pulls back, mouth swollen and eyes flashing in a way that makes me want to kiss him again.

I bite my lip. "Please tell me I didn't forget that too."

"No," he says, grinning. He strokes warm lines down my face with his thumbs. And then his mouth dips into a frown. "You really don't remember, do you?"

I shake my head. He pulls me into his arms, still breathing fast into my hair. "We can't talk here, and we need to get you warmed up. Can I take you somewhere?"

I close my eyes and burrow into his chest with a smile. "Lead the way."

CHAPTER SEVENTEEN

· ·

W e drive to his house first, and he drops his backpack inside. I call my parents while he's gone, claiming a study session with some of my SAT friends. He slides back into the car around the time I hang the phone up, and then he's watching me. Holy crap, I'm not sure I'll ever look at this guy without thinking of kissing him.

"Are they cool with it?" he asks.

"Yeah, why?"

"Good. Turn off your phone."

I open my mouth to argue, and he frowns at his hands on the steering wheel. "What do you think the chances are that Blake won't call or text you in the next couple of hours?"

"Hours?" I ask, feeling my brows arch.

He looks sideways at me with a smile that makes me blush. "You in a rush?"

"No," I say, powering down my phone with trembling fingers. "So where are we going?"

"It's a surprise."

"I love surprises," I say, grinning.

He grins right back, reaching over to take my hand. "Yeah, I thought you might."

We drive twenty miles south of Ridgeview, and I don't feel desperate to fill the silence. Instead, I revel in the peace of it, watching the stark beauty of the winter landscape roll past my window.

Before I know it, we're in the heart of Corbin, a town about the same size as ours without the benefits that come with being on the lake. I have no idea why he's brought me here, especially after five, when the few shops and businesses are closed.

Adam pulls into a gravel lot near the center of town, a construction zone if the fencing and rubble is any indicator. I crane my head, spotting a large building, or the bones of what will someday be a building. The first few floors seem roughed in, but the ones above that are all steel beams and sky.

Adam parks the car, and we both get out, staring up at it. "I come here once a week. Things are slow now that it's winter, but it's still coming along."

I nod, moving next to him, sliding my hand into his palm. He squeezes my fingers and kisses the top of my head.

"So can we get in?" I ask.

He cocks a brow at me, that bad boy smirk curling his lips. "Legally?"

I return his smirk and look back at the building. "C'mon. I'll race you."

I have no hope of outrunning Adam, but lucky for me, he has no interest in winning. He follows me through the bare floors, around support beams, and up a flight of cement steps. The second level is just like the first, floors and beams, but there's open air above us. I tip back my head, gazing at the crisscross of the beams in the waning sunlight.

There's something about this place or maybe just about Adam that makes me buzz with energy. I feel like anything is possible. I pace around while Adam checks something on the other side of the floor. I can almost hear his mind working, gears and chains clicking as he runs his thumb along a concrete ledge.

I watch him from a distance, touching poles and scuffing my sneakers on the floor. And then, on a whim, I decide I want to go higher.

It's easier than I thought it would be. I find footholds and corners, and before I know it, I'm another floor up. And then another.

The wind whips through my hair, making my eyes water as I stare out over the roll of unfamiliar neighborhoods and houses. The beam in front of me is ice-cold, but I hold it anyway, terrified and exhilarated.

I laugh, despite myself, and then I hear Adam approaching behind me. I squeeze the steel in front of me even tighter as his arms wrap around my waist from behind.

"You weren't supposed to climb up the beam work," he says into my hair.

I shrug. "I've always been a monkey. Mom says I crawled out of my crib on my first birthday."

"I can see that about you," he says.

God, he smells good. And he's so warm. I'm pretty sure this is what heaven would be like. If I could choose everything about heaven.

"So what is this place?" I ask.

"The county's new government offices," he says. "Or that's what it will be next spring when they finish it up. Simple design, but they've got an incredible arch planned for the entry. You can see the structure of it there." He points down to a section way too close to the ground for me to want to focus on.

"Have you seen planning pictures or something?"

"I saw blueprints," he says. "They're better."

"Architect porn," I muse, and he murmurs affirmatively before resting his chin on my shoulder.

My smile just keeps getting wider. I'm sure I look like a lunatic—wind-chapped and grinning like the Cheshire cat. "You're going to build stuff like this one day, aren't you?"

"I want to build stuff twice as beautiful as this," he says.

I turn around in his arms, careful to keep my feet on the beam before I steady my hands on his waist.

He lifts his brows at me. "You are a fearless little thing."

"I used to be."

"Used to be? Not very many people would climb up here. Not sure I would have if I wasn't coming after you."

"I'm not afraid of things like this," I say, and then I sigh and tilt my head. "But whoever did this to me…I'm scared of them."

He leans in, kissing me once, long and soft and deep enough that I almost forget where I am. When he pulls pack, I wish I could just freeze everything about this moment so I could keep it with me.

"No one's going to hurt you, Chloe," he says softly.

"You going to protect me?" I ask, leaning in to kiss the underside of his jaw.

He groans a little. "As long as I make it off this building alive, I am."

We climb down and settle into his car. There's nothing open, so we make do with gas station fare: a pack of Twinkies and two tall, steaming cups of coffee. Mine goes down like heaven without a single nauseous afterthought.

"I thought I'd never drink coffee again," I say, cradling the paper cup to me like an old friend.

"I'm a bad influence."

"Yeah, I'm glad you brought that up," I say. "You're supposed to be this bad boy, so what gives?"

"What gives?"

"Yeah, you're like…like Clark Kent."

"Clark Kent?" He looks less than pleased at the comparison.

"Well, you did come to my rescue in the library."

"Right, that." He shrugs. "I figured it'd be a good way to get around to kissing you."

"Making me freeze to death while you studied for another hour *after* rescuing me? Interesting strategy."

He smirks again, and I think I understand why girls go for the bad boy. Or at least, the guys who appear to be bad boys.

"I think it's all an act," I say, licking Twinkie filling off my finger. "This bad boy thing. You do it to pick up girls."

"Is it working?" he asks, leaning closer.

"Jury's still out," I say, but when he kisses the side of my neck, I'm pretty sure the verdict is in.

• • •

It's eight o'clock at night when the waitress drops off our pancake platters. I pour what must be a half gallon of syrup over the top, and Adam laughs.

For ten minutes, I pick at my food while I talk. Adam listens to me outline all of the weird things I've pieced together, from my missing Julien file right down to the mystery Daniel/Dr. Kirkpatrick phone call. I even mention the hypnosis research, though I still can't imagine how that would factor in.

I take a break to dig into my now lukewarm stack, and Adam leans back thoughtfully, his plate mostly clean.

"So how does it tie together? Did Dr. Kirkpatrick somehow hypnotize you into forgetting all about the last six months? Why?"

"I have no idea."

Adam's brow furrows. "I don't know, Chlo. She did relaxation stuff but nothing like what you're talking about. And I can't figure a motive. Something like this would destroy her career."

"Maybe she's being blackmailed? Maybe she wants more money? Who knows what drives people to crime?"

"Typically, what drives people is pretty transparent. I mean, I've met the lady. She doesn't really have an evil vibe."

He's got a point, but I've got more than a point. I have freaking evidence. Sort of.

"Adam, she was talking to someone about Julien. Someone named Daniel. As in possibly Daniel Tanner, one of the sponsors of our little study group."

"Or as in Daniel Smith down at the post office or Daniel Starinsky who runs the gas station by the school. Do you know how many Daniels are in Ridgeview? For all we know, Julien has another doctor named Daniel and she was talking to him."

I push a piece of pancake slowly through a river of syrup. "You think I'm grasping at straws."

Adam reaches across the table, fingers covering my hand. "You want to know what happened to you, and I get that."

"But?"

"But you're too ready to point the finger. Maybe at people who didn't do anything wrong."

"She sounded nervous, Adam. Why would she be nervous about me talking about Julien if she hadn't done anything wrong?"

"Maybe she was upset. Julien was in our group, Chlo. Maybe she got attached to her, and she's worried about how upset she thinks you are about it."

His points feel like they're picking mine apart. And not doing a bad job of it either. "Fine," I say with a sigh. "I'll let it go."

Adam smiles, but there's something a little wary in his eyes when he shakes his head. "No, I don't think you will. I'm pretty sure you don't let much of anything go."

"Careful. Being this smart can't be good for your bad boy rep," I say.

He steals one of the sausage links beside my pancakes, and the conversation shifts. He points out the beams in the ceilings, and I talk about an article I read on the mood impacts of decor like this, with vintage photographs and household items displayed as artwork. It's the first time I've felt normal since I woke up in the classroom.

The drive home is long and quiet. He keeps the radio low, and I use the seat belt in the middle so I can curl up under his arm. I find a jagged scar, just above his wrist, tracing it with my fingers while I watch the road unfold before us.

For a while I think of what I should call this. Is he my boyfriend? It feels like such a small, childish word for the way I feel. And some part of me knows I should be afraid of this, this feeling of absolute rightness I have being pressed up against him.

But then he kisses the top of my head, and I smile. After that I don't think much at all.

I'm half-asleep when I speak again, a sudden thought stirring me from my drowsiness. "I haven't remembered anything."

"What's that?" he asks, his voice rumbling through his chest next to my cheek.

"All the times we kissed today, I didn't remember anything. I usually remember things when you touch me."

"Only me?"

"Only you," I say. "But today I didn't. I didn't remember anything."

"Maybe the wrong part of your mind was engaged tonight," he says, tickling my side until I laugh out loud and smack his arm.

But he's got a point. With his lips against mine, my mind definitely doesn't function at its highest level.

He walks me to my door but hesitates when I lean in for another kiss.

"Did you turn into a pumpkin?" I tease.

"Cute," he says. "I just haven't met your parents yet. Seems a little rude to make out with you on the doorstep."

He's smiling, but that same tight look is back on his features. He looks around the road and then back at me before pressing a quick kiss to my lips.

"Sweet dreams, Chloe."

I nod through a yawn then snag his hand as he's turning away. "You're still going to help me get to the bottom of this, right?"

"How can I resist an offer like that?"

I kiss him again, lingering a little before I draw back. "You can't. I won't let you. I'll see you soon?"

"Not soon enough."

I'm not sure my feet even hit the ground as I walk inside. I'm floating on a bubble of hormonal giddiness. I swear, I should have chirping birds trailing behind me.

I glide into the kitchen, smile so wide my cheeks hurt. It dies on my lips when I flip on the overhead light, illuminating my mother leaned against the sink.

"I think we need to have a little talk."

CHAPTER EIGHTEEN

. . . .

There are no little talks with my mother, and this one is no exception. It's like sitting through a eulogy or a recitation of the local phone book. Except I'd prefer either of those things over this.

She doesn't yell either. Just drones on and on about the endless depths of her disappointment and my failure to live up to my potential.

"Are you even listening to me?" she asks.

Not really.

"Yes."

She shakes her head, signaling the move into act three. The Guilt Effect. "Chloe, when you tell me you're out with friends to study, I believe you. That trust is broken now."

"I said I'm sorry," I say, pressing my still-tender lips together. "I'm not sure what else you want me to tell you."

"Well, I'd ask you where you've been, but I'm not even sure I want to know."

I look up then, and there's no mistaking the way she's looking at me. I haven't checked a mirror to be sure, but I know there's no chance my hair and lip gloss are anywhere close to being intact.

"It's not as bad as you're obviously thinking," I tell her, hoping it will appease her.

It doesn't.

"You know, did you ever stop tonight to think about how Blake would feel if he knew you were out with another boy?"

"Mom, please." This is *so* not a conversation I want to have with her.

"Don't *please* me," she says. "I thought I raised you better than this. That boy cares about you. And he could provide you with a hell of a lot better future than Adam Reed."

I stand up then, chair legs scraping on the hardwood floor. "You were spying on me?"

"I was worried about you. When Blake called tonight, I had no idea where you were."

"Wait a minute, Blake called here?"

"Isn't that what I just said?"

"He called here *tonight*?"

"Yes, tonight. He said he was out with most of the SAT group and wanted to see if you were interested in joining them. Which was really interesting news to me, since you were supposedly already with them."

Fear moves through me as cold as the air I just walked out of. "What did you say to him?"

Her eyes go dark with anger. "Don't worry, Chloe. At that point I didn't know, so I didn't spill your little secret. But I can't tell you how deeply it disappoints me that all you're worried about is hiding your liaison with *that boy*."

"No, Mom, I'm not thinking about my *liaison*. And I'm not thinking about *Adam* either, who, by the way, has an academic record that makes me look like a trained chimp. Right now I'm thinking about Blake, who's been practically stalking me since I broke up with him."

Mom crosses her arms and rolls her eyes. "Don't you think that's a bit dramatic?"

"I think you see whatever the hell you want to see. With me. With Blake. Even with Adam, who you don't know anything about at all."

"I know he's got a criminal record, and I'm not talking about a string of parking tickets. Did he tell you about that, Chloe? Did he tell you about the time he got arrested? Because I was on shift at the hospital that night. I stitched up his arm while the officers read him his rights."

● ● ●

Mr. Chow moves in the front of the class, holding a stack of papers. I glance around. The faces around me are getting familiar. Julien grins at me, and I return it, glad I've hit it off with someone so quickly. Almost as glad as I am that I get to spend every Tuesday and Thursday evening in the same room with Blake Tanner.

"This is a timed math test," Mr. Chow says, passing out the papers. "The objective is to move as quickly as you can to keep your mind sharp and prepared for change."

"What's the catch?" Blake asks, motioning at the desks that have been set up in pairs.

189

"Trading," Mr. Chow says, smiling. "Every sixty seconds you will trade papers with your partner. This will keep you from looking ahead, a common mental pattern that can leave you anxious for future questions. Anxiety is like kryptonite to peak performance."

"Sounds easy enough," Julien says, and we smile at each other pointedly. She knows darned well math is a strong suit for me.

Mr. Chow shakes his head at this, chuckling. "I don't think so, girls. I'll be assigning the partners. Blake, you're with Raul. Julien, with Tanja. Chloe, you'll be with Adam."

I force myself not to grimace. I've avoided him since the fire alarm incident, and really, I think that's preferable. We sit down across from each other, papers facedown and timers set.

I look at my cuticles and check for split ends while Mr. Chow fiddles with a malfunctioning timer at another table.

"Pull any fire alarms lately?" Adam asks.

I roll my eyes. "You just couldn't let it go, could you?"

Adam grins up at me. "I really didn't think you'd have the guts to go through with it."

"I'm full of surprises, I guess."

"Good," he says. "I like surprises."

• • •

The sound of my phone pulls me from my dream. Not my cell phone, but my house phone, a corded pink concoction that I almost forgot I still had. I grope blindly for the handle, lifting it clumsily to my ear.

"Hello?"

"So d-do you need a ride t-to a school or what?"

I bolt upright, clutching the blankets to my chest and grinning like a loon. "Yes! I mean, yeah. If it's not too much trouble."

"I'll b-be there in twenty," Maggie says. "By the way, your cell phone's off."

"Okay. See you soon."

It's better than Christmas. I practically dance out of my bed and to my bathroom. Then I rush back, finding my phone in the jeans I shucked off last night before falling into bed. I find a five-dollar bill in one of the pockets. Change from the Twinkies I bought.

I trace the red squares Adam doodled in the corner of the receipt to demonstrate some basics of structural stability or something. I think of my mother's comments last night and then of the scar I felt on his arm.

So what? He's not a bad person. Whatever my mom *thinks* she knows is obviously wrong.

I pick out clothes and head into the bathroom, glancing at the time on the clock.

Time. Timers. What a minute.

I stop, one foot into the hallway, and remember the dream I woke up from. Except it wasn't a dream. It was a *memory*. Holy crap, it's finally starting to come back.

I'm showered, dressed, and ready ten minutes before Maggie said she'd arrive. And it's worse than a first date because I'm pacing in front of the door and chewing my lip. I'm half-convinced she's never going to show. That she'll stand me up and leave us right back where we were a couple of weeks ago.

The ragged putter of the pickup's engine is heaven to my ears. I adjust my backpack and pick up both of the to-go coffee mugs I prepped. It's almost like every other morning I can remember before all of this happened.

I head for the truck and hand her the coffee.

"You still drink it with cream?"

"You're drinking it again?" she asks, obviously surprised.

I drop my bag on the floor with a smirk. "I haven't changed that much."

Mags takes a sip of her coffee, and I see her smile for the first time in what feels like forever. Okay. Yeah, it's going to be okay.

I drink my coffee and listen to Maggie's latest punk obsession, and I promise myself I will treasure this moment. I promise I won't think about Blake's dad or Adam's scarred wrist or any of the stuff that's happening. I don't quite manage, but I'm close.

• • •

My day has taken a steep nosedive. Maggie barely said boo on the way to school. And I managed to tank not one but *two* quizzes in my first three periods. What the hell happened to my superpower brain?

I slide through the lunch line, grabbing a tuna sandwich that looks as pale and lifeless as I feel. I snag an apple and set it on my tray with a sigh.

"Bad morning?"

I try to bite back a smile, but it's impossible. I feel the press of Adam's arm against my shoulder, and my face practically blooms.

"I thought you might have bailed today," I say.

"I never skip school."

I frown up at him, furrowing my brows. "Why on earth not? You've got a godlike GPA. I'd probably only show up on Tuesdays."

He just laughs and pushes his way down the line, paying for both of our lunches.

"So do I actually get to eat with you or is this a drive-by flirt?" I ask.

"Drive-by," he says, then he looks over his shoulder at a table where Blake is glaring in our direction. "I think it's too early to stir the waters."

"Since when do you care what he thinks?"

"I don't. But I think you still might."

I feel like a balloon that lost its air. "So yesterday…"

"Was a *very* good day," he fills in with another shoulder bump.

"But it was just a day," I say, hating the hollow ache in my middle.

"Hm, I think I need to be more clear." A wicked smile curves on his face as he leans close, his breath tickling the side of my neck. "I'm not going to kiss you in front of him. But you'd better believe I'm thinking about it."

He backs away again, and I'm pretty sure he takes all the oxygen in the room with him because every breath I take feels thinner than the last.

"So this weekend," he says. "Study date? We've got that pre-calc final."

"I just tanked my quizzes in chemistry and English. You might need to trade me up for a better model."

"Hell no. Math's *your* subject. You're not getting out of helping me because of a bad mood."

He dumps his tray by the cafeteria door, keeping only the apple he stole from my plate. I can't help but call across to him.

"You're not even eating?"

"I paid for the company," he says. He gives me one last grin, one that makes my whole middle squeeze in on itself, and then he's gone.

Blake's expression wipes the smile right off my face. I see him whip out his cell phone, texting something almost violently.

"Okay, I'm officially wanting t-to know what the hell you're up to."

I whirl with my tray, tuna sandwich almost sliding off. "Maggie?"

I don't know whether to do cartwheels at the fact that she's speaking to me in public or to be terrified of the bald accusation in her eyes.

"Yeah, we need t-to talk," she says. "Back steps?"

"Definitely."

We make our way out of the cafeteria to the back stairs of the school. During freshman year, I got in trouble once for being too loud in the cafeteria. When it became perfectly clear I was never going to learn to keep my trap shut, we found the back stairs. Right across from the girls' bathroom, we could always claim feminine issues if the teachers asked.

I glance at the bathroom door, listening to the squeal of under-classmen inside. I remember those days, poised in front of the mirror, lip-glossing myself into a shimmery concoction for a boy that probably didn't even know I existed.

We nibble our sandwiches in quiet for a while before Maggie puts hers down and brushes off her hands. "So what's going on with you?"

"What do you mean?

"I mean your sudden g-guy switch. You're t-trading in Blake f-for Adam?"

"It's not like that," I say, but really it's sort of exactly like that.

"Are you sure you know what you're doing?"

I put down my uneaten half sandwich. "No. I'm not."

Maggie seems satisfied with this until she frowns. "I never got it, you know. The hot factor."

"With Adam?" I ask.

She waves a hand dismissively. "No, not Adam. He's g-got that whole tragic but beautiful thing happening, though I never thought you noticed."

"I didn't," I admit, dropping my voice to a whisper. "But I do now. I can barely go an hour without noticing."

"I was t-talking about Blake."

I feel my nose wrinkle. "You didn't get why I'd like Blake? Who doesn't like Blake? He's Mr. Nice Guy," I say, though I'm sarcastic as hell.

Mags pushes her plate away and looks across the hall, shaking her head. "Maybe. Or maybe that's what he wants everyone to think. I could never t-tell."

"You never said anything to me."

"I never thought your crush would come t-to anything." She turns sideways on the step to face me.

It stings like a barbed hook, and I lean back, recoiling. "So you thought I never had a chance with him?"

"No. But I d-didn't think he'd have a chance with you either. Not if you really knew him."

I don't know what to think then. I nod once, and Maggie picks at her sneaker.

"Did you look into Dr. Kirkpatrick?" she asks.

"I did. I thought I had something, but it might be a dead end."

"Keep digging. I'm t-telling you, there's something there."

"What about Mr. Chow? Is he even still here this year?"

Maggie shakes her head. "I heard he got a teaching gig b-back in China. I don't know—he seemed p-pretty harmless."

"And my mild-mannered therapist didn't?"

Maggie's face pinches off. "Maybe. But she wasn't."

"Then I guess I'll have to keep looking."

"You don't have to d-do anything." She shrugs, sliding her disinterest back into place.

"Yes, I do. Julien said I know what happened to her. Do you think I can just let that be?"

"I d-don't know how long you can *let it be*. Lately you haven't exactly b-been the person I thought you were."

"I'm *still* the same person. I haven't changed." Mags looks unconvinced, so I reach for her hand, giving her fingers a squeeze. "I know you don't believe me."

She pulls free from my grip. "You're right."
"Then I'll prove it to you. And I'll start with Julien."

CHAPTER NINETEEN

• •

I t's one o'clock in the morning, and I'm hiding in my kitchen using the Internet on my dad's cell phone. It's not my finest moment. But I'm grounded from everything except going to school and using the bathroom, so I don't have much of a choice—unless I want to risk the possibility that someone is tracking my phone or laptop and will see what I'm up to, which I seriously don't. Yeah, I am totally that paranoid now. And determined, thanks to Maggie's little challenge on the stairwell.

Sadly, Julien's cyber trail is pure as driven snow. There are dozens of news clips from her life in Ridgeview. Her volunteer work at the senior center and a bunch of stuff on different academic awards she's won over the years, but, funny enough, not a single thing from San Francisco. It's like she fell headfirst into the San Andreas Fault.

My own phone buzzes in my pocket, and I pull it up, surprised to see Maggie's number and a text message.

You asleep?

Nope. I'm researching.

A second passes, and my cell phone rings. I answer it with a laugh.

"Me too," Maggie says.

I grin and wait her out. She wouldn't be calling if she wasn't helping. "I found an address for the M-Millers."

"The PO box, right?"

"No, a real one. And guess what? It's not in San Francisco. It's in San Diego. I mean, it could be someone else, b-but with the initials *I* and *Q*?"

Iona and Quentin. Miller is a common enough name, so I never even thought to try. Maggie gives me the address and the name of the nearest high school. I shake my head, amazed.

"I don't know how you found it, but you're a genius. I've got to call Adam."

Maggie takes a breath on the other end of the line. I hesitate, frowning. "What's the sudden silence? You want to say something, don't you?" I ask.

"No. Yeah. M-maybe."

I sigh, dropping onto one of the kitchen stools. "So what's stopping you?"

"Nothing. I j-just think you should be careful."

"Careful with Adam."

Her silence confirms it. I roll my eyes. "You know, you're starting to sound like my mother. The guy isn't Hannibal Lecter, okay? I mean, maybe he's had some trouble—"

"It's pretty big t-trouble," Maggie says, interrupting me. "Has he ever talked t-to you about it?"

"No. But I've never asked. So what if he made some mistakes? Haven't we all?"

Maggie's quiet for a moment, and I can tell she's treading carefully. "Just ask him, all right?"

"Will do."

"I need to g-get some sleep."

"Mags, wait," I say, before she can hang up.

"What?"

"Thank you. It's been…really good to talk to you."

She pauses before she hangs up. I know she's not ready to say the same. But she's thinking about it, and that's something.

I put down my phone and stare at the browser on my dad's phone, wondering about Adam's so-called crimes. But juvenile records aren't public record.

He's been nothing but good to me. Good and honest and there. I don't have a single reason not to trust him.

Except for Maggie's advice.

I chew on my bottom lip and think long and hard about calling him. I could just ask. It wouldn't hurt to ask, would it?

In the end, I snap my dad's phone back on the charger on my way up to bed.

• • •

Adam finds me in the lunch line again. He must actually be hungry today because he grabs an orange and a club sandwich and sets them on my tray. "Exactly how long are you grounded?" he starts.

"Until my thirtieth birthday," I say. "You gathering more food to dump into a trash can?"

"Not this time. I've got a hot date."

I take a granola bar, feigning disinterest. "In the Ridgeview High cafeteria. You're secretly a player, aren't you?"

"I just ooze cool," he says, handing over another ten-dollar bill to pay for our lunches.

I open my mouth because I don't need him to do this. I've seen where he lives. And somehow I doubt working as a part-time janitor has him rolling in extra cash.

"It should be my treat this time," I say.

His face pinches a little, but he covers it with a smile. "Don't judge a book by its shit-hole apartment."

"I'm sorry. I didn't mean anything by it."

He shrugs it off, but I feel like a schmuck. I nudge him with my elbow, looking up at him. "Am I really in the doghouse already?"

"Nah," he says. "Unless of course, you're going to try to get out of our date."

"No chance."

"Then your chariot awaits," he says. He puts the tray in the return area and tucks the sandwich and orange into his coat pockets.

I follow suit, grateful I went with granola and yogurt instead of the massive salad I was eyeing.

Then he slips out of the cafeteria without looking to see if I'll follow. We're allowed off campus for lunch, so I don't get his secrecy. But I follow him anyway, slipping through the parking lot until we're hunkered down in the front seat of his old Camaro.

We eat lunch with the radio playing as softly as the snow that's drifting down around the car. After I push my empty granola wrapper into my yogurt cup, Adam pulls my feet into his lap and starts fiddling with the laces on my shoes.

I have no idea how that's sending goose bumps up my legs, but it is.

"Did you get your pre-calc review back?" I ask, trying to act casual as I lean against the passenger window.

He shrugs. "Yeah. I did all right. You?"

"A minus. And I hate to break it to you, but you don't really understand the meaning of *all right*."

"I don't?"

"Nope. *All right* indicates an average score, and you don't do average *anything*."

His hands are climbing up to my ankles now. And I don't know if it's the way he's looking at me from under those dark lashes or some secret drug coming out of his fingertips, but he's making me dizzy.

"I'm average at plenty of things."

"Oh, please," I say, pulling my feet off his lap with a smirk. "Let me guess. You probably mean you got like a ninety-seven."

"Ninety-six," he corrects me.

I gasp, hand at my throat as I scoot closer on my knees. "You *are* slipping."

"I must be distracted," he says.

He grabs my legs, right under my knees, and pulls me toward him on the bench seat. And then his lips are trailing along my jaw and I couldn't spell *distracted* if someone paid me it feels so good. We kiss until we're running dangerously close to second base during school hours. We ease up with a glance at the clock on his dashboard and the school in the distance.

"We're awfully good at this for being so new at it," I say, scooting back to my own seat.

"You're only surprised because you can't remember how we looked at each other for the last several months."

I make a face at my wild reflection in the mirror, trying to finger comb my hair.

"It's no use," he says. "You're going to look hot no matter what."

"I do rock the kissed-senseless look," I say. "So there were heated looks between us, huh?"

"Left scorch marks on our flash cards."

"So tell me already. When did this all start?"

He thumbs his chin, looking pensive. "October. Mrs. Malley's class."

I feel my face scrunch in confusion. "Mrs. Malley? She was my fourth-grade teacher."

"*Our* fourth-grade teacher," he says.

I shake my head, laughing. I barely remember him being in my class. He was just a dark-haired boy, always carrying a skateboard and lost in a series of faded T-shirts. Adam tucks some of my hair behind my ear and gives me a little smile that promises more to the story.

"You punched Ryan McCort on the playground. Do you remember?"

I nod. I can still practically *feel* that moment; the sharp, shocking pain in my knuckles and the sickening feeling that went through me when Ryan's nose spurted blood. I can still hear Ryan mocking Maggie. *"M-m-miss m-m-me, M-m-maggie?"* He'd laughed. Mags cried. I punched.

"He had it coming," I say.

Adam nods. "He did. Hell, Ryan usually has something coming, but that day he picked on the wrong girl."

"It's a simple speech disfluency. She's not stupid," I say, unable to shake the defensive edge in my voice.

"You don't have to tell me. Maggie stomped my ass in AP English last year," he says, smiling wider. "But who knew you'd lay him out next to the swing set. He had six inches and forty pounds on you, easy."

"I guess I've always been a fan of justice."

"I guess I've always been a fan of you," he says.

And there isn't a thing I can say to that. Not a single thing. I brace my hands on his shoulders and lean in until our foreheads are together.

"Are you honestly telling me you've had a crush on me since the fourth grade?"

"Scout's honor."

I laugh. "You were never a Boy Scout."

He laughs back, and I kiss away any reply he might be tempted to give. And any questions I ever meant to ask.

• • •

When I arrive home from school, the house is empty. Not surprising. Mom works a lot of overtime for Christmas money and it's November. She's got the Thanksgiving grocery list on the fridge and everything.

I'm halfway through a slice of Colby jack when I see Mom's note on the table. My name flows across the top in her pretty, slanting hand.

Chloe,

I thought you should see this. This isn't a judgment. It's information. I know you'll make the right choice.

Behind the note is a copy of a newspaper clipping. I check the date in the corner. Two years ago. The crime beat.

I feel a rush of rage so strong I'm surprised I don't crumple the soda can in my hand. But as much as I hate it, it's not just anger running through me. It's curiosity too. I want to know.

I scan the copy, spotting a penned circle around one section.

I close my eyes and let out a long sigh. I think about Adam in the car today, his long fingers on my shoelaces, his smile so easy and comfortable I could curl up in it for a nap. I don't want to give that up.

But I don't want to be in the dark. Not ever again.

I square my shoulders and start reading.

Youth injured while breaking into a local pharmacy. The perpetrator escaped on foot but was arrested later. Police confirm that the investigation is still ongoing, but the pharmacy owner states that stolen medications have yet to be recovered.

I set the paper down, placing my note on top. I turn it just as it was turned before, as if I never read it. As if I never even saw it lying here.

But I did see it. And I remember the rumors anyway. The halls were wild with crazy talk about Adam robbing a bank or killing a guy or whatever, but I never thought anything of it. I mean, I knew he got arrested, but he was back in school pretty fast, so how bad could it be? I always figured it was a fistfight. Or maybe street racing. The idea of breaking and entering never crossed my mind.

And he didn't rob a bank. He robbed a pharmacy. For *drugs*.

I push out mental images of him counting out pills or—God—reeling out of his mind on some nameless high. It doesn't feel possible.

I back out of the kitchen, wishing I'd never come in here, wishing I could turn back time and somehow unsee what I just read.

But I can't.

CHAPTER TWENTY

● ●

I switch the phone to my other ear, sure I couldn't have heard what I thought I heard. "Wait a minute, what?"

"I want to plan a reconciliation trip," Maggie says. "Are you even listening?"

"Yes," I say, because I am trying to listen. I can't stop thinking about Adam. "I'm just confused."

She sighs. "I d-don't still hate you, okay? B-but I'm not ready to go sing 'Kumbaya' or whatever either."

I drop my chin into my hand, staring blankly out my window. "All right, then why are you proposing I go with you to California?"

"Okay, you *weren't* listening," she says. "My mom was invited to be a part of some big d-deal Thanksgiving dinner in L.A.— she's doing all the breads."

"Right," I say.

"And we could go with her t-to reconcile our friendship or whatever."

"But you said you didn't—"

"We'd be going to find Julien, Chloe. God, are you sleepwalking?"

I wish. I wish I could go to sleep right this second and not wake up until my entire universe is normal again. Though at this point, what the hell would be normal?

"I'm sorry, I'm listening. Just tell me the plan again."

"We go with my mom to L.A. We convince her t-to let us take a day trip to San Diego to rekindle our friendship."

"No way they'll let us drive around California unsupervised. My parents watch way too many documentaries for that crap."

"There's a train. What's more wholesome and trustworthy than Amtrak?"

I bite my lip, staring at the dust on my windowsill.

"I'll give it a try," I say, "but I'm grounded for the rest of my life right now."

"I think you should let me try. I've already g-got my mom convinced."

It's not a bad idea. My mom has always loved Mags. "You want to stop by today?"

"We're going out for lunch. We'll come b-by after."

"Okay. I guess I'll see you then."

I change my outfit four times and my hair twice while I'm waiting. I have to find the perfect mix of happy, normal teenager and contrite, refocused daughter. Lip gloss? Yes. Mascara? No. I make a succession of similar choices until I'm pretty sure I look right.

Now comes the hard part. I head outside and slip down the hallway, careful not to bump the laundry chute or step on the creaky part of the floor. I hover at the top of the stairs, listening for my parents.

I hear the TV, but it's down too low to be of any serious interest.

I head down the stairs and find them in the kitchen, Dad leaned into the fridge and Mom peeling carrots at the sink.

"Are we eating at home tonight?" I ask.

Mom gives me a passing smile. "I thought I'd do vegetable soup. It feels like a soup kind of day."

Feels kind of like a plotting and scheming day to me, but I'll keep that to myself.

I look through the window above the sink where wind is sending fallen leaves skittering against our fence. And of course, the leaves make me think of Adam, which makes my head hurt.

"I could peel potatoes if you want," I say.

Mom looks up, clearly surprised. Dad closes the fridge and pops the tab off a Samuel Adams. "I think that's a terrific idea."

"Of course you do," Mom says, arching a brow at him. "It was your job until she showed up."

I've got the potatoes peeled and cubed when I hear the doorbell. It takes crazy willpower to stay at the table—to pretend I'm still reading the magazine I've been blindly thumbing through.

Mom looks up from the stove with a frown. "Who could that be?"

I just shrug, turning the page without looking up. In the living room, I hear my dad's jolly greeting. And then I hear Mrs. Campbell. And Maggie.

"Well, that sounds like—"

"Virginia," Dad says. "Why don't you and Chloe come out here for a minute?"

I stand up, exchanging a clueless look with my mom that she

swallows hook, line, and sinker. She wipes her hands on a dish towel, and I follow her out of the kitchen, praying my knees will stay strong and that I will not start trembling like the nervous wreck I am.

And I shouldn't be nervous. This is just Maggie.

Maggie here to hatch the biggest plot we've ever dreamed up, that is.

Mom gasps, and I force surprise onto my face.

"Mrs. Campbell," I say, and then, more softly, "Maggie."

Maggie looks up at me, eyes and nose red. Has she been crying? What happened? She wasn't crying on the phone. Did her mom figure her out? Oh God, she figured it out, and I am about to be busted. Again.

I'm going to be grounded until I have grandchildren.

Maggie hesitates for a second and then rushes across the room. I feel her arms around me and hear her half sob into my hair.

"I'm sorry," she says.

I don't know if it's part of the plan. I don't know why she'd go to these lengths to be convincing, but I don't care. When I hug her back, I don't have to force my own tears to come. They just do.

• • •

Maggie and I are side by side at the top of the stairs. She hasn't said a thing about the crying, and I haven't asked. I'm not sure I want to know. Her reasons might not be as sweet as the ones I've dreamed up.

It's like we've regressed to our twelve-year-old selves, spying on the grown-ups from the top of the stairs. A plate of gingersnaps sits between us, and occasionally one of us will grab one and take a nibble. Mostly, though, we listen.

Without a whole lot of success, because all three parental units are obnoxiously staying put in the kitchen, where it's only possible to hear every third or fourth word.

"Do you have any idea what they're saying?" I ask in a whisper.

Maggie holds up a hand to quiet me. She's always had the better hearing of the two of us. She says it's a side effect of her crap vision. There's been no celebration in our history that has yet to live up to The Day Maggie Got Contacts.

I eat another gingersnap and watch her brow furrow as she listens hard. I'm only hearing bits and pieces. "So much pressure" and "terrible seeing them apart" and things like that.

Then she looks at me, clearly shocked. "I think it's working."

"You're kidding."

Just then, I hear chairs and feet in the kitchen. We scuttle back to my bedroom in record time.

Barely a minute passes before we hear the call.

"Girls, can you come down here for a minute?"

My mother. She sounds happy. Which means…we won. Maggie and I exchange a smirk, waiting just long enough before we open the door to not be completely obvious.

Maggie goes ahead of me, moving down the stairs with a bounce in her step that I try to mirror in my own.

"You know holidays are a special time," my mother starts. "Under normal circumstances, I'd want you home with us, Chloe."

211

My dad huffs and cuts in. "Oh, stop torturing them. You're going."

My mother looks irritated briefly, but her anger relents when Dad kisses the top of her head. Maggie leaps up with a squeal, and we hug and dance around in circles like we're ten years old and we've just been given concert tickets to see the biggest boy band around.

It's almost like we aren't faking it at all.

"But you'd better not come back here without one of those snow globe things or a keychain or something," Dad says.

"Thank you, Dad," I say, kissing his cheek. And then I turn to my mother and hug her tight. "Thank you."

Mom hugs me back, and I feel the strength in her hands as much as I hear the sniffle in her voice. "Don't thank me. It's Mrs. Campbell who agreed to take on the two of you. I hope you'll make sure she won't regret her generosity."

"She's never been a bit of trouble," Mrs. Campbell says. She slings an arm around my shoulder, and I smell yeast and cinnamon and of course that makes me think of Adam.

How am I going to explain this to him?

"Chloe?" Mrs. Campbell asks. "Is that okay?"

Crap, I wasn't paying attention. I shake my head to clear the thoughts and smile widely. "Yeah, it's great."

Maggie knows me better and frowns. "So we'll pick you up tomorrow right after school."

"That's what I just said," her mom says, chuckling.

"Tomorrow's great. I guess I'd better go start thinking about what to pack."

We exchange our good-byes and I head upstairs to my room. After ten minutes pulling out a few outfits, I can't resist any longer.

I have to at least tell him I'm leaving.

Adam answers on the third ring, and I can hear music in the background. "Are you finally not grounded?"

"Sadly, I think that sentence has a couple more years on it," I say. "But I do have some good news."

"What's that?"

"Maggie and I sort of mended the fences or whatever."

"Hell of a feat when you can't even leave the house," he says. I can hear the smile in his voice.

"Well, Mom is fine with Maggie coming by."

I wince as the silence on the other end of the line stretches. Damn it. That came out completely wrong.

"I'll take it your mom disapproves of the company you were keeping as much as the lie."

I sigh, sinking onto the foot of my bed beside a pile of tank tops. "She's upset that I lied, but yeah, she's concerned about you too."

"But not about Blake," he guesses, his laugh so low and bitter I feel my stomach clench at the sound. "That's rich."

"Look, she doesn't know you, okay?"

"But she wasn't exactly ready to give me the benefit of the doubt, was she?"

"It's not—" I cut myself off and press my free hand to my forehead. "My mom works at the hospital. She was on shift the night you hurt your arm."

Silence greets me on the other end of the line. It stretches out long enough for me to wonder if the call dropped or if maybe he's not planning on responding. And then he does.

"So I suppose she gave you the whole story then."

"She told me what she knows of it. Or what she *thinks* she knows. She's just worried, Adam. All moms worry."

He laughs, and it's so caustic, I'm surprised my ear doesn't sting. "No, Chloe, not all moms worry. So now you're worried too, right?"

"I'm not."

"Then why is this bothering you, because it obviously is?"

"Look, just because I pulled a damn fire alarm and snuck around a construction site doesn't mean I'm cool with *felony*, okay?"

A beat passes, and I imagine my words spraying at him like bullets.

When he speaks, he's quieter. "You think I stole drugs. That I was dealing maybe."

"You broke into a pharmacy. Am I supposed to think you did it for the free measuring spoons?"

"Why I did it doesn't really matter to you, does it, Chloe?" he says, and I hear him scoff.

The thing is, it does matter, and I want to tell him, but I'm somehow frozen. All I can think of is that newspaper article and sitting my parents down to explain why dating a thief is a smart choice. And I can't. I just can't imagine it.

Not any more than I can imagine Adam breaking into a pharmacy.

"I think your silence is a pretty good answer," he says.

The line goes dead while my mouth is still opening to speak.

My throat is hot and swollen, and my eyes itch like crazy. I swipe at the tears that find their way out with the heel of my palm and tell myself that I will figure this out. I will calm down and call him back and everything will be fine.

Except that deep down inside, there's a scared part of me that doesn't think it will.

CHAPTER TWENTY-ONE

The airport distracts me from the Adam angst. I've always enjoyed the airport on holidays. Yes, the lines are long and cancellations can cause riots, but if things run smoothly, it's the happiest place on earth.

I cross my legs to make room for a family of four moving past me. They trail by with an endless stream of chatter and video games and brightly colored kid luggage.

"I remember when you two were that little," Mrs. Campbell says wistfully.

On my right, Maggie props her chin in her hand and gazes at them. "I wonder where they're going."

"Home, I guess," I say.

In a way, that's where I'm headed too. I glance at Maggie, and we exchange a tentative smile before I take a sip of the Starbucks she bought me. At the boarding call, we stand up and pull up our luggage, and it's all as simple as it's ever been between us. It's crazy ironic that I'm flying two thousand miles, hoping to God to end up right back where I started.

Maggie and I buckle into two seats by the window. Mrs. Campbell ends up across the aisle from us, headphones in and a crossword puzzle out before we've even taxied down the runway.

"So how much of this do you have planned out?" I ask Maggie as Cleveland shrinks into a quilt of freeways and lights outside my window.

She snorts indelicately and pulls out a notebook. There are two pages filled with inconspicuous academic stuff. Notes on some science theory or whatever. She flips right past those, opening the book to another section. I see a listing of train departure times and directions to an unfamiliar address in San Diego.

"Yeah, what's up with that? Everyone else said it was San Francisco."

"Yeah, well, the p-post office called it an address forwarding error." Maggie makes little air quotes around *address forwarding error* like she doesn't believe that for a second.

"Wait a minute, are you saying they didn't even admit to the right city?"

Realizing my volume, I glance over at Mrs. Campbell, who's dozing off, her pen slack in her hand. I drop my voice to a whisper anyway. "Why would they lie about that?"

"Technically, they d-didn't," she says. "The Millers were really vague about the whole thing, remember?"

I give her a pointed look, and Mags waves, looking contrite. "Right. Sorry. They said they were moving t-to California for some great business opportunity and didn't have a permanent address, but everyone knew it was about Julien. She'd b-been a mess all summer. They never let her out of their sight."

I feel my eyes growing wide. "So other people are suspicious too."

"Hell, no. Ridgeview's t-too small-town. They just thought the p-perfect little Miller girl had cracked." She shrugs. "It happens. It was still freaky though."

"Yeah?"

Maggie puts up her hands. "It's the *Millers*. Moving across the entire damn country!"

"Thank you!" I say, glad someone has seen the pertinence of this fact. I chew the inside of my lip, still trying to work it out. "And it's even weirder that they don't let Julien keep in touch. It's like they cut her off completely. Do you think her parents did something illegal?"

Mags gives me a disbelieving look. "Mrs. Miller was a choir director. *Literally.*"

"Okay, fine, but what about her dad? My parents never could stand the guy. I've heard my dad talking about him."

"Well, if they up and left for no reason, maybe, b-but they had a reason. A bat-shit crazy d-daughter they wanted to hide."

I swallow hard, shocked at the idea of it, but a little afraid to ask whether or not she's joking. Because if all of this happened to Julien, it might still happen to me.

The flight attendant arrives offering drinks, saving me from my total lack of response. I sip my ginger ale and pretend to be mesmerized by the scenery outside my window.

Mom and Dad took me to New York once, and I remember flying over the city with my nose pressed to the glass. My eyes had to be the size of dinner plates. I couldn't even conceive of a city so immense, of so many buildings clustered around the brilliant green rectangle of Central Park.

Landing in Los Angeles is totally not like that. It's kind of like landing in Cleveland. Except I spot the Hollywood sign just before I hear the landing gear grinding down.

Maggie's mom must be even better in the kitchen than I think because we're whisked to the hotel by a chauffeured car. Granted, it's not a limo, but still. A sleek black town car with leather seats and television screens in the backs of the seats is a far cry from my decrepit Toyota.

Everything is green and alive in California, as if November doesn't even exist here. After spending every winter of my life in northern Ohio, I feel like I'm on another planet.

"Wow," I say, gazing out at the seemingly endless stream of palm trees and slick cars. "It really is kind of like the movies."

Mags grins at me. "First, we check out the beach."

"First, we check in to the hotel," Mrs. Campbell corrects us, slinging one arm around each of us as our driver unloads our luggage.

If this was my mother, we'd spend the next two hours inspecting the room and discussing safety precautions. But Mrs. Campbell's way more relaxed, so I know we'll see the ocean before we hit the sack.

Two hours later, the three of us make our way to Venice Beach. We try fish tacos and ice cream and laugh the whole way there. Maggie's mom heads into a coffee shop and we wander off to a bench for the best people watching.

I always kind of figured the wildness was exaggerated, but I was dead wrong. The boardwalk is like a giant, scrolling circus sideshow. An enormous guy with the smallest dog I've ever seen rides past on a bright green bicycle, almost bumping a girl who's juggling at least five oranges. A couple of long-haired kids veer around them, speaking to each other in full-on Shakespearian.

Maggie and I shake our heads and trade our cones to try the other's flavor. It's maybe the most perfect day I've had. Unless you count the one I had with Adam, and I can't count that. I can't even think about that unless I want to cry.

I see Maggie out of the corner of my eye, her red-gold hair shining like a penny in the setting sun.

"Maggie?" I say, staring out to sea.

"Mm?"

"Are you ever going to tell me what happened between us?"

Her nose wrinkles, and I wish at once I hadn't said it.

"I'm n-not sure," she says.

I watch the long waves curling in, wishing my memory would come back like the tide. But in the end, maybe I don't want to remember. Maybe it's best to let it stay hidden in dark places.

"Whatever it is, I'm sorry for it," I tell her.

"Yeah. I know that now."

• • •

The train speeds forward, cutting down the California coast. I wring my hands and try not to think about where we're going. Or what we're going to see when we get there.

"This is why we're here, Chlo," Maggie says, reading my mind.

"How much longer am I going to be stuck in this train freaking out?"

"Not long now. But I'm sure you'll spaz in the cab too."

The train pulls into the station, and Maggie navigates us to a taxi without any fuss. Maybe it isn't such a big deal for her, but I'm freaking out a little about seeing Julien. If she's gone crazy now, am I next?

Still, the sunshine is positively balmy here. I peel off the sweater I'd worn over my tank top and let the warm breeze improve my mood. I could get used to a town like this. The sky is so blue I feel like I could pour it into a swimming pool.

Our cab driver plays reggae music and drives approximately nine thousand miles an hour. Sometimes I catch glimpses of the bay, a stretch of cobalt water dotted with the white triangles of sailboats. Then I'm back to holding on for dear life, watching Maggie grow greener by the second.

"Twenty-eight dollars," the cabbie says when he finally stops. I peel off a couple of twenties and hand it over. I don't bother asking for change. I'm too interested in being on solid ground again.

The house is nothing like I expected. It is a sleek, ultramodern tower, full of floor-to-ceiling windows and metal beams. It's a smaller version of the kind of house you'd imagine a rock star living in.

I blink up at the windows. I can't see anyone looking, but I still feel the chill of invisible eyes. Maybe I'm imagining it, but I turn away all the same, looking at Maggie instead.

"You okay?" I ask her. She's ghostly pale and breathing deep, thanks to the cab ride I'm sure.

"It's a miracle you're not wearing m-my lunch." She's not

exaggerating. Maggie's dealt with carsickness since I've known her. Trips to camp were always a special kind of hell.

We head slowly for the door, and even Maggie checks the address again. It doesn't seem possible, the Millers in this cold, steel-coated contraption. If the Millers I knew moved, they'd move to a cottage in the woods, where birds sing and pies are perpetually being cooled on windowsills.

The door swings open and a person who must be Mrs. Miller appears.

"May I help you?" she asks, looking at Maggie instead of me. She sounds like Mrs. Miller. She's wearing her standard summer uniform—a white polo and a khaki skirt—but Mrs. Miller does not sport nine-piece luggage sets under her eyes.

She also doesn't frown. Not ever. I saw Mrs. Miller at her father's funeral, and she smiled so much, I felt like crying for her.

Mags and I stand there, both of us trying to speak and not finding a single word we practiced the night before.

Mrs. Miller looks at me then, and the recognition is immediate.

"Oh!" she says, and her hand goes up to her mouth. Her eyes go wide, and every single bit of color drains out of her. For a minute, I'm sure she's going to scream. Or maybe even pass out. But instead, she just shakes her head, looking completely shocked.

"My Lord, Chloe Spinnaker. How did you find—" She stops herself, cementing that toothpaste commercial smile I know so well into place. "What on earth are you doing all the way out here?"

I finally find my voice. "Hello, Mrs. Miller. I'm so sorry we didn't call, but I didn't have a number."

"We brought you this," Maggie says, pulling out a gift bag of maple nut clusters, a handmade candy from a shop downtown that somehow finds its way into every Ridgeview home on Thanksgiving.

It's a weird tradition. Small town or whatever. But Mrs. Miller takes the gift like we're offering her a newborn baby to hold. Like she's never seen anything so perfect or precious in all her life.

"That's the sweetest thing," she says, still cradling her sacred plastic bag of candy. Then her smile falters, as if she's not sure what to do. She looks around once, and then her grin is back. "Won't you both come in?"

We follow her inside with little shuffling steps. I can feel Maggie's tension right along with my own. It's not like we hung out with these people. Or at least we didn't until I got sucked into the Secret Study Sisterhood or whatever.

"I'm so sorry," Mrs. Miller says. "What's your name again?"

"Maggie. Maggie Campbell."

"Oh, of course! Noreen's daughter."

"One and the s-same."

She leads us into the kitchen, and I go cold all over. It's like being in *The Twilight Zone*. The room isn't just similar to the one in their old house in Ridgeview. It's as close to a carbon copy as it can be.

The same rooster clock sits above the kitchen sink. The same country dish towels hang on the knobs of the cabinets. All of the baskets and antique crocks I remember from her old house are lined up on the concrete countertops, doing their best to battle the sterile feel of this place.

Mrs. Miller serves us hot chocolate, though it's got to be eighty-five degrees outside. Still, we sip it politely while she prattles on about the proper way to stuff a turkey. Maggie, a devout vegetarian, pales noticeably as Mrs. Miller instructs us on how to remove the bag of giblets after yanking out the turkey's severed neck.

And then, when she's finished rewiping the counter and discussing poultry technique, her smile shuts off. It's so abrupt, it's like someone flipped a switch. I half expect her head to spin around or something, but she just picks up her own mug and then sets it down again without taking a drink.

"I suppose you're here for Julien," she says.

Maggie and I exchange a quick look. I smile tightly.

"We are."

"I'll call her down if you like. She's just up in her room," she says, her smile so brief it's like a twitch. "But I should warn you…"

"Warn us?" I ask.

Mrs. Miller folds her hands, one on top of the other. "Girls, I don't know how to say this. We'd tried very hard to keep this all quiet…"

Her voice has trailed off, but I know she's not done. So we wait. And after a bit, she blinks a few times and seems to come back to life. "Julien has been…ill. We didn't want people's pity, so we decided it would be best not to reveal her diagnosis."

"Diagnosis?" Maggie asks.

"She has…schizophrenia." It's like the word is being choked out of her. She pauses to take a drink of her cocoa, and I can't help thinking she's trying to wash that word right out of her mouth. "Apparently, it's a disease that runs in my husband's family. Julien was beginning to show symptoms in the last month we were in Ridgeview."

"Is that why you left?" I ask, and immediately decide I shouldn't have. It's like laying all my cards on the table.

To my shock, Mrs. Miller nods. "We wanted a fresh start for Julien. Her disease has taken a very aggressive course. We wanted her to get the best treatment, and there are doctors here that were recommended to my husband. To both of us."

No, this isn't that simple.

"I was s-so surprised Mr. Miller could leave his b-business," Maggie says.

Mrs. Miller cringes like she's been dunked in ice. Her shoulders tense, and her eyes cut away.

"Can we see her?" I ask again, trying to bring back the open lady who seemed so ready to talk before. "I've really missed Julien."

"She misses you too," she says, smiling sadly. "She should be out of the shower, so I'll go get her. Now, again, she has been medicated, but even then her handle on lucidity isn't consistent."

"So it c-comes and goes?" Maggie asks, frowning.

Mrs. Miller's face is crunching with sadness, so I try to explain, drawing from the little I've read. "Schizophrenia can force people to sort of detach from reality. She might be fine one minute—"

"And then she might start talking about *The Wizard of Oz* as if it's happened just next door," Mrs. Miller says. Her expression is pleasant again, but her eyes hold so much pain, my own chest aches.

"Are you sure you're prepared for this?" she asks.

No. No, I'm definitely not. But I nod anyway.

CHAPTER TWENTY-TWO

· ·

Mrs. Miller leaves us to wait in a small living room with crushed velvet couches and antique tables. It's all very Jane Austen. All that's missing is a guy in a starched shirt. And maybe tea service.

We sit on the edge of the couch with our hands in our laps, too freaked out to say a thing. I hear voices at the top of the stairs and then footsteps descending. I don't even know how it's possible, but I tense up more.

Julien enters, dressed in khaki shorts and a couple of blue tank tops layered over one another. Her hair is still long and pale, curling at the edges just like a shampoo commercial. And her smile is the carbon copy of her mother's. White and wide. And one hundred percent normal.

"Omigosh, Chloe!" Julien squeals as she crosses the room, tugging me into a hug. "I can't believe you're here."

I catch Maggie's gob-smacked expression over Julien's shoulder, knowing mine has to match.

Julien pulls back from me, eager and happy. "Can you believe this house? What do you think of San Diego? Was your flight good?"

"Great!" I say, not sure which question I'm answering, but figuring it's the best word to suit them all.

Behind Julien, Maggie is still staring. I can't blame her. I mean, where's the freaking crazy girl? I was expecting some hollow-eyed horror-movie extra, the kind of girl who rocks in the corner and avoids daylight. But this is just Julien.

"Oh," Julien says, frowning and turning to Mags. "I'm so sorry, Maggie, I didn't even say hello. It's great to see you too."

"Uh, thanks."

Julien slides a slim arm around my shoulders, and I tense like she's about to snap me in half. "I'm so glad you two made up," she says. "You'd been friends for so long, and I hated seeing you fight."

Maggie and I both offer parrotlike head bobs in response. The weird factor in this room is at an all-time high. I'm beginning to wonder if I imagined the whole schizophrenia conversation in the kitchen, and then, right in front of my nose, Julien kind of fades out.

I think of a television losing signal or maybe ink dissolving in water. Her face goes dull and flat, as if everything's kind of floating around her. And then she nods, as if someone asked her a question.

"You'll have to fill me in," she says, and it's normal enough, but she's not. Something's just…off. Her voice is higher. Almost childlike.

"Of course," I say anyway, moving to sit down on the couch.

Julien plays with the hem of her tank top, twisting it over and over, her fingers flicking in tiny, rapid movements that seem at complete odds with her vacant expression.

"Where should I start?" I ask, noticing Mrs. Miller for the first time. She's still hovering by the door. Watching.

Julien looks up with that brilliant grin. "Start with the Wicked Witch because I haven't heard a thing since I've been here. I need to hear every single thing. I keep track, of course. In my diary."

I look to Maggie for help, but her expression makes it pretty clear she's checking the hell out of this adventure.

"Uh, well, I don't know much about that," I say, "but everyone's applying for colleges back home. And the winter dance is coming up after Christmas, so—"

Julien sits down beside me, slipping her arm through mine. "Oh, don't be like that. I don't want boring stuff about boys. Tell me what you've learned about the Wicked Witch."

"Julien," her mother says. It's soft, but it's a warning.

Julien doesn't even look at her. But her eyes go round and big, and she squeezes my arm until I want to pull it loose. Now her voice is pip-squeak high, like she's morphed into an overgrown toddler. "Oh no. Did she have a flying monkey go after you?"

"A what?"

"I knew she'd use them. I knew it. She did, and oh, that's terrible. I don't know what to do now. I just don't know."

Mrs. Miller moves closer, her hands clasped loosely in front of her. "Julien, sweetheart, let's not talk about that right now. Would you like to talk about the beach? You know how much you like the beach."

Julien flips her hair and sucks her teeth in a way that brings me back to middle school in the worst possible way. "I can't talk about the beach right now. Anyone could be listening, *Mother*. Anyone!"

I pull my arm free then because I have to. I just have to.

228

She really is crazy. Certifiable. I flew across the entire freaking country because I was positive this girl was kidnapped or hypnotized or some dire thing, but she's not. She's deeply mentally disturbed, and I'm here, obviously upsetting her, so I can dig into my own issues.

"Please tell me what you know about the witch," Julien says, looking at both Maggie and me, and resisting her mother's touch on her shoulder.

"I'm sorry, Julien," Maggie says, and her expression and voice are both tender. "I d-don't think we know much about her."

"I know you don't," Julien says to her, and in that moment, she looks perfectly clear. Sharp and focused. The Julien I remember. She takes my hand and looks at me steadily. "But you remember, don't you, Chloe? You know."

I open my mouth, and she squeezes my hand and then I see it, clear as day.

Dr. Kirkpatrick at the front of a classroom, that ultracalm smile on her face as she drones on about…I can't quite make it out. Relaxing.

She wants me to relax. Close my eyes and breathe deep. Let my mind open like a box.

I don't close my eyes. I narrow them and watch her through the slits. She's playing with her charm bracelet. It's pretty. I see a picnic basket and a little dog…and ruby red slippers.

I feel a hand touch my arm, and I open my eyes. I don't even remember closing them.

Maggie's standing by the couch now, watching me with worry in her face. "You all right?"

"Yeah," I say. "I'm fine." I turn to Julien, who's humming quietly beside me. She's still holding my hand, but she's not looking at me. She's not looking at anything. "Hey, Julien?"

It takes her a long while to turn to me, like the words took a winding road to get into her brain. When she does, her neatly shaped brows are knitted together above her pert nose. "Oh, Chloe! I've been waiting for you."

"Perhaps she needs to rest," her mother says. "Come on, Julien. Let's go back to your room."

"No, not yet," she says, looking at me though her words are for her mom. "Will you get me something to drink Mom?"

"Sure, sweetie," Mrs. Miller says, but I don't miss her hesitation to leave us alone. Maggie and I both try to give her a reassuring smile.

Once she's gone, I look at Julien. "You were talking about the Wicked Witch. You mean the one at our school, don't you?"

Her mouth thins into an angry line. "She tells me how to sit and how to breathe. In and out and one, two, three."

"Right," I say. I pause to give Maggie a meaningful look, but she doesn't seem convinced of anything other than Julien's heaping pile of absolutely crazy.

"I don't like her," Julien says. She's petulant, bottom lip jutting out. "Sometimes I think she's real, but maybe she's just in the movie."

"*The Wizard of Oz*?" Maggie asks.

"No. This movie. The same one I'm in," Julien says. Now she doesn't look crazy at all. She looks like a girl trapped in a glass jar.

She sees exactly where she is and what's happening, and there's not a damn thing she can do to change it.

Then Julien presses her hands to her face and shakes her head. "It doesn't matter because I can't remember. I can't remember at all."

My whole body goes tense. I lean away from Julien, heart pounding. Is this what's coming for me next? Is this what I'm going to turn into?

Julien uncovers her face, and it's like nothing happened. She's smiling and perky and groomed within an inch of her life. She's the Julien without any dark secrets or mind-altering medications. "So how about you and Blake? You still a thing?"

"Uh…sure," I say, because I can't *even* get into a breakup. Not here. Not with her.

"I dated him once, you know. Back in freshman year. But I've got to say, he was never as attentive with me. You must have the magic touch."

"Must have."

"I think I'm going to wear red to prom." Julien looks at us, biting her lip. "Do you think only sluts wear red?"

Mrs. Miller appears with a mug of tea, and I don't know about Maggie, but I'm about to fling myself into her arms I'm so grateful to see her. "How are we doing, girls? Julien, here's your tea. Just like you like it."

She offers it to her in front of me, and I catch a whiff. Lemon and herbs and something familiar in the worst kind of way. I lurch back and hold my breath, not wanting to smell it again and having no idea why I'm being so weird.

"I hate t-to cut this short, b-but we really have to get going," Maggie says, and her eyes are on me. She's worried.

I press my hands to my cheeks and try to calm down. "Right. I totally forgot. Your mom is meeting us at the station."

Julien is back to that blank stare. Her mom notices and comes closer, stroking her hair gently. "Julien? Your friends are leaving, honey."

Her face contorts, and for one second, I see the terrified confusion she's living in. Her eyes are wild, searching the room. "Wait, I didn't—there's something—"

She trails off and all but jumps off the couch. She starts pacing then, pulling away from her mother's efforts to soothe her. "Don't! I have to say this—I have to remember—"

"She's just a little upset. I'm sure she's glad you came by," Mrs. Miller says, that plastic smile melting around her obvious discomfort.

"No! I have to tell them!"

Mrs. Miller glances at us a little desperately. "Please know it's nothing you said. It's just the sickness."

"I'm not sick!" For one second, Mrs. Miller goes pale and tight. "I'm not sick, and you *know* it! I...I..." Julien trails off, pressing her temples with both fingers and looking dazed. Then she meets my eyes. "Help me, Chloe. Please."

My heart skips three beats. Maybe four. Whatever icy thing is moving through me now, it's bigger than fear. Way bigger.

"Girls, thank you so much for coming. Do you think you can find your way to the door?"

I try to nod or speak, but I can't do anything. I can't tear my eyes away from Julien. She's watching me with a look that will haunt me forever if I don't do something. But I have no idea what. Or how.

"Thank you for having us," Maggie says softly.

I can't say anything at all. I can't even wave. Instead, I let Maggie pull me through this strange mismatched house. I hold on tight to her arm, grateful that she knows the way.

CHAPTER TWENTY-THREE

. . . .

Outside, the sky is still blue. Maggie and I do not belong in this sunny day. We are white as sheets as we make our way down the stairs that lead away from the front door. We pause at the street, looking a little lost.

"What now?" I ask. Our cab is long gone.

"Now, we g-get the hell out of here. We'll walk back t-to the main road and call a cab."

Overhead, a seagull cries happily. I feel my eyes welling up, my throat getting tight. "Is that going to happen to me?"

"No." She turns back to me, finger up, looking angry. "D-don't you go there. Not even for a second. D-do you hear me? Julien is sick, Chloe. Like really sick."

"I know. I know that. But when she grabbed my hands, I remembered what she was talking about. Dr. Kirkpatrick was in that study group telling us how to breathe."

"So what if she was? I mean, I know it's creepy, and yes, you all t-turned into freaking robots—"

"So what if somehow that creepy stuff turned Julien into this? If I remember what they did, maybe I can help her. I *have* to remember, Mags."

She settles a cool hand on my shoulder. "No, you don't.

Chloe, it's schizophrenia, okay? That's not your fault. It's not *anyone's* fault."

I can't believe this. I throw up my hands in disgust. "So that's it. Julien is sick and somehow that means Dr. Kirkpatrick is innocent?"

"I d-didn't say that. I'm just saying she didn't have anything to d-do with this. And we shouldn't either."

I know she's right. There isn't a single logical explanation for anyone causing schizophrenia. But still, I can't stop thinking about her flashes of sanity. Sometimes, the lunatic shutters cracked open, and I could see the completely normal girl trapped behind them.

"Let's just get back," Maggie says, interrupting my thoughts.

I nod, scrubbing at my eyes with the back of my hands. We're just walking down the sidewalk when I hear a faint tapping from the house behind us. Maggie's glancing around, so I know she's heard it too. We search the scrubby yard and the palm tree, and then finally the house itself.

Julien.

She's standing at one of the windows upstairs, making a motion with her arms.

"Is she drawing something?" I ask. "Why doesn't she just open the window?"

"Maybe they won't open," Maggie says. "Maybe they think it'd be t-too risky."

I ignore Maggie and shake my head. I try to look as confused as I can, hoping Julien will somehow manage to read my body language.

"Let's j-just go."

"No! She asked me to help, Mags."

In the window, Julien tosses her hair. She's frustrated, I think. And then she's just gone. Maybe she sat down or walked away, but it doesn't matter. The window is empty, and there is no saving happening here. Not today.

I turn back to the road, where Maggie's already walking, but the tapping comes again. Julien, of course. She's just watching us, palms pressed to the glass and a desperate look in her eyes. Like she's waiting for me to do something.

"What d-does she want?" Maggie asks.

I sigh and push my hair behind my ears. "I don't know. You were right. We should go."

• • •

"I just don't know what she meant with all that Wicked Witch stuff," I say, doodling a cartoon of a stick figure on a broomstick on the paper place mat beneath my burger and fries.

Maggie picks at her own plate and frowns. "Maybe none of it really means anything. I don't understand why you're trying t-to make sense of it, Chlo."

"Because she doesn't make sense. Schizophrenia doesn't come on like that. It comes on slowly, like over months or even years. It doesn't just crop up at the end of one summer." I push away my plate, my appetite lost. "I don't know. Maybe there's another reason they left."

"Or maybe this is a d-dead end, like I said. Julien has problems, Chlo. And I don't know that we need to be d-digging around in her messed-up family d-dynamics anymore."

The rest of our train ride passes in silence. Maggie listens to her music, and I watch the skyline, one interesting building after the next slipping past my window. I try not to think of Adam. And fail miserably.

I want to call him. I mean, I *really* want to. But all I can think about is our last phone call. And his extracurricular visit to the local pharmacy.

What a mess.

I want to hear his side of the story. Because I know he's not a bad guy. His room, those college applications, that freaking wall of architecture? That has to mean something.

But there's another part of me that knows an explanation isn't going to fix this. My parents *already* think I'm crazy. And now I'm going to date the criminal my mom sewed up in the emergency room? They'll ship me off to a boarding school for troubled children.

God, I just wish it didn't feel so right—so *easy* with him. If it could just be hard, I'd walk away. But it's not hard. It's as simple as my own damn instinct, and that means more than whatever stupid thing he did two years ago.

I'll have to worry about the fallout with my parents later. I have to call him.

As if on cue, my cell phone rings. I spring out of my seat and into the narrow aisle, waving at Maggie to let her know

I'm stepping away. I answer it without even looking, positive it's him.

"Hello?"

"Hey, Chloe. It's Blake."

"Oh." I sound every bit as disappointed as I am. I try again, clearing my throat. "Oh, hey."

It's not much better, but I don't care. I'm not ready for this call today. Or ever, really. I reach for the wall beside me, bracing myself as the train rocks over the tracks. I'm pretty sure he'll hear the background noise, so I can't just hang up.

"So how've you been?" he asks.

His tone seems casual enough, but I feel like tiny invisible bugs are crawling up and down my arms.

"Fine," I say, keeping my tone neutral. "Is something wrong?"

He laughs a little. "No, nothing's wrong. I was just thinking about you and thought I'd give you a call. Day before Thanksgiving and all."

"Right," I say, shaking my head a little. "Happy Thanksgiving."

"Same to you. Though yours will probably be more interesting than mine since you're spending it in San Diego of all places."

My heart stops beating. I'm sure of it. My mouth drops open, but I can't form a single word right now because I'm completely paralyzed.

"I'm sorry?" I finally manage, because I had to have misheard him. I'm paranoid or tired or something.

He laughs as if it's all very funny. "Your mom told me when I called this morning. I asked if I could bring by a pie, and she told me you were in San Diego."

No, she didn't say that. She couldn't have said that because she has no idea I'm in San Diego. According to my mother, I'm in the Ritz-Carlton in Los Angeles and we told Maggie's mother that we were heading out to some botanical garden for the day. Not once, did the words *San* or *Diego* exit either of our mouths.

"So how's the weather?" he asks.

"Warm," I say, croaking it out despite my now-roiling stomach.

I will not throw up. I will not throw up or pass out, and I will not start screaming. My hand feels slick with sweat on my phone. Someone's coming toward me in the narrow little corridor, so I have to get out of the way.

"Sounds great. I've never been lucky enough to spend Thanksgiving in California."

I force a laugh, but it's worse than the canned stuff they play on sitcoms. His is as flat and as stale as mine and all I can think is *how*? How does he know where I am?

"So what are you doing all the way down there?"

My self-preservation kicks in, and the lies come pouring out of me. "Oh, this and that. Checking out the bay. I'll probably come back with a killer tan."

He murmurs something agreeable, and it's horrible and awkward and I can't believe either of us are acting like this isn't completely transparent.

"Well, I really should go," I say. "We're about to grab lunch."

"Sure," he says, and I know full well he doesn't believe me. "Oh, and happy Thanksgiving, Chloe. You've got a lot to be grateful for this year, don't you?"

"This year?"

"Well, everything is different for you now, isn't it?"

There's something to his tone I don't like. Hell, there isn't a thing about this phone call I do like, but this little preachy undertone grates me like a brick of cheese.

I guess he thinks last year was just too tragic. What with my second-rate social and academic rankings, I probably should have just stabbed myself with the wishbone and done the world a favor.

"Oh, I'm grateful all right," I say. My voice is so sickly sweet, I could pass for a flight attendant. I keep it up, like poisoned honey, as we exchange our good-byes.

I stare at the screen on my phone for a long time after he disconnects. One of the attendants asks me to take my seat. I point at the restroom like a mute and stumble toward it on legs that feel like cooked noodles.

The bathroom is cramped and loud, and I know I can't hide here the rest of the way back. But I can't tell Maggie. Our lunch made it pretty clear what she thinks of my conspiracy theories.

I palm my phone, knowing who I want to call. I can't push the idea out of my head.

It takes me two minutes to gather the courage. I half expect myself to dial the number and immediately hang up, but that's never been my style. Once I dial, I press the phone to my ear and square my shoulders.

Adam's phone rings to voice mail after four rings. I wait a minute and call back again. This time, it goes straight to voice mail. And I'm not too stupid to know what that means. Call rejected. Chloe rejected.

I think this must be what it feels like to be slapped.

I return to my seat feeling like there's a gaping hole where my important parts should be. Mags looks up briefly, returning to her notes without noticing my expression or even asking where I've been.

It wouldn't matter if she asks. She'd only think I was crazy if I tried to explain it.

And maybe I am. Maybe I'm every bit as lost as Julien now.

CHAPTER TWENTY-FOUR

. . . .

After eating for what feels like twelve straight hours on Thanksgiving Day, we take the red-eye home. We land at oh-dark-thirty Friday morning. Instead of getting sleep like a sane person, I change my clothes and brush my teeth and spend an hour reciting fun-filled antics of our trip to my parents.

And then I head out the door on the pretense of celebrating my early ungrounding with some Black Friday shopping.

Of course, I'm not going shopping. Unless I plan to buy a pack of gum from the convenience store across the street from Adam's apartment.

Mrs. Corwin's cat has probably barfed up things that look better than I do right now, but vanity will have to wait. And so will my wishy-washy pros and cons list about what I'm doing with Adam. This isn't about that. It's about Julien.

She needs help and she asked me. Which means I need to remember. And other than that brief moment holding hands with Julien in California, the only person who's made me remember anything is sitting inside this apartment.

I knock and wait at least a minute before knocking again. Adam answers maybe a half second before I lose my nerve and bolt. If I was worried about my looks, I needn't have bothered.

He's sporting four or five days of stubble at least and eyes so red I wonder if he's slept since I've been gone.

"Are you sick?" I ask.

"No," he says. He's flat. Cold. Still edgy as all hell too, looking around his apartment like he's waiting for a hit man to show up.

"I went to California," I say, but I'm not really thinking about my trip. "I saw Julien Miller."

He flinches, and for a moment, I can see the old Adam. The one who worries about me.

Then it's gone, the indifferent mask in place. "California. Sounds great. I'm really busy."

Lie. He's not busy. He just wants me to leave. It stings like hell, but it reeks like a lie too.

I should be thinking about Julien and talking about all of the things she said or hinted at, but I can't force my brain to go there. I can't think about anything other than how horrible it feels to stand here and *not* be okay with him.

"She's sick, Adam. God, she's so incredibly sick." I take a breath because I don't want to be emotional. I want to be calm and make sense, but I'm not. "She's sick, and I'm scared and I missed you. I still miss you."

His eyes meet mine then. He cuts me right to the quick with that look. And he won't say it back, I know that, but he doesn't need to. His eyes are speaking for him.

I flex my fingers and then ball them into fists because I'm aching to touch him. "I saw all these buildings. Our hotel room looked

243

over Balboa Park. The houses and storefronts or whatever—they all sort of look the same, like the same style."

"Spanish Revival," he says, and I can practically feel his eyes caressing my face. He steps closer and then backs away. It's killing me.

"Adam…"

He swallows hard and shakes his head as if he can't imagine why I'm here saying this. Acting like this. "Chlo, this needs to end. You're right to stay away from me."

"You don't believe that. I know you don't believe that."

"I do believe it. Because it's true," he says, and it's like someone's ripping the words out of him.

I feel the sting of tears in my eyes, blurring my vision. "Maybe I don't care about what's true."

Adam lets out a breath that sounds shaky. "You have no idea how hard you're making this."

"This isn't hard. You know it isn't," I say, half whining. He touches me then, hand on my face and fingers moving into my hair. Everything in me melts into his hand, drawing into the soft, warm press of his fingers.

"I wish it was different, but it isn't. Your mom was right, Chlo. I did break into that pharmacy."

"No. There's more to it than that. I know you, Adam."

He flinches, and I can tell I'm right. Still, he shakes his head. "It happened. I did break into that pharmacy, and she's right to want you to stay away from me."

I feel like I'm sinking in quicksand. Or maybe that I've become quicksand and that all of this darkness and fear is swallowing me from the inside out. "Tell me why."

He looks away and shifts his feet with a shrug. "Money."

"Liar."

That gets him to look back. He throws up his hands in surrender, and I feel cold where he's let me go. "Fine, then go with drugs. What's it going to take for you to *get* this?"

"Get what? There's nothing to get because you're not saying anything! And I know you're not a user, Adam. Give me some credit."

"What does it matter? I did *exactly* what you're so afraid I did."

"Yeah, I got that part. What's still missing is the why."

"You didn't like my why."

"That's because it's a freaking lie! Just tell me!"

Adam growls in frustration, ripping a hand through his hair. He still smells the same and sounds the same, and I wish to God I cared about what that scar on his arm means, but I don't. Not anymore.

"Tell me why you did it."

He turns, muttering something about being busy, and I can't wait anymore, so I touch him. His arms first, and that's enough for him to take a breath and hold it. He closes his eyes when I touch his face, and I take a breath as another memory runs through me.

Me a nervous wreck as Adam helps me jiggle the lock on the school cafeteria. I feel it give way underneath my fingers. Despite the thrill, I roll my eyes.

"I still don't get why I'd need to break in here."

"To study," Adam says with a shrug. Off my look, he smirks. "Well, it's a hell of a lot quieter than my house."

I pull my hands free to bring myself back to the present. Adam's here too, but there isn't anything close to a smile on his lips. Still, his eyes make me want to use big, flowery words. *Azure. Cerulean.*

Beautiful.

"I'm not giving up until you tell me," I say.

He looks away, and I can tell he's thinking it over. Maybe measuring my resolve. Finally, he nods and takes a half step back, needing the space, I guess. "She has Alzheimer's. My grandmother."

"How long?"

Adam shrugs, plunging his hands into his pockets. "Maybe three years. Do you know anything about the disease?"

"Enough to know I'm sorry she has it," I say.

He doesn't respond to that, just goes on like he's talking about the weather or something. "She gets confused a lot. She had a period where she flushed her medicine down the toilet all the time."

"Why?"

He shrugs one shoulder. "Sometimes she thought it was poison. Sometimes she thought they were mine—stolen or whatever." He waves like none of this is very important or interesting. "The doctors helped at first, but it happened too often. That month they refused. Said if she was having so much difficulty, we should consider an evaluation for assisted living."

"What is that? Like a nursing home?"

He nods. "Sort of. I told the caseworker I found the meds,

246

and she'd been doing better. We didn't have money for more. I stupidly figured the pharmacy wouldn't notice a missing bottle of blood-pressure pills."

"But you got hurt. Your arm."

"I was going to slide in through the drive-through window. The pharmacy was closed, but the owner was there. He closed my arm in the window. Glass broke…" Adam trails off, gesturing vaguely at the white scar on the inside of his forearm.

"I'm sorry," I say again.

That gets a laugh. A cold one. "Don't be. It was stupid, and I'm damn lucky he didn't shoot me."

"Adam, everybody makes mistakes."

"Yeah, but most of them don't rank up there with breaking and entering."

I want to argue, but I know it won't work. For whatever reason, he needs to own what he's done. Pooh-poohing it isn't the answer. But hell, neither is wallowing in it.

"So it was stupid," I say, throwing up my hands. "Fine. You were stupid. Now get over it. And maybe get some help for her. Have you looked into that at all?"

He scoffs, relaxing against his closed door. "Look around you, Chlo. We're not exactly wading in cash and options."

"But there are like twelve zillion social programs for senior citizens. So why not? Is she an illegal immigrant or something?"

"You don't get it, do you?" He cocks his head and narrows his eyes. "I don't have any other family."

"I know you care about her—"

"Care about her?" Adam practically sneers at that. "Yeah, Chloe, I do. But I'm not Mother Teresa, and this isn't just about family loyalty. If they find out how bad she's gotten, we'll both end up in the system."

I shake my head, still not getting it.

He leans closer. "Nursing home for her. Foster home for me. Good-bye, Ridgeview High and its reasonably decent academic program. Hello, foster care and schools with metal detectors."

I swallow hard against the lump in my throat, the one that's worked its way up from my chest. "You stole the medicine because you didn't want to go into foster care."

"Yeah. And because I didn't want my grandmother to die. She isn't perfect. But I'm all she's got."

He must take my silence for something bad because he crosses his arms over his chest and hardens his expression. "It's not pretty, Chlo. But it is what it is. And it's not right to drag you into it."

"I don't give a damn about what's right," I say.

I tug him hard by the lapels of his coat because he's so tall that going up on tiptoes isn't going to be enough.

I kiss him, and at first his lips are hard and unrelenting. I know this is some token effort at resistance, and I totally ignore it. It's a good choice because after a few seconds, Adam's hands drop to my shoulders and then he's kissing me like he's absolutely starved for it. Before long, I feel like I'm the one who needs to steal some medication.

When we finally part, his eyes are closed. His breath is coming in little shuddery bursts, and I can't quite believe I'm the one able to reduce him to this. It's dizzying.

"I'm trying to tell you I'm not good for you," he breathes, voice low and husky.

"Well, I've never been a good listener."

His mouth curls up in a smirk. "Cute. But, Chlo, there's more. There are things—"

"I don't care," I say, shaking my head. "Nothing you say is going to make me care. Not now."

"I think you'd care about this," he says.

"I wouldn't," I say, pressing my fingers to his lips. I do it because it wouldn't matter. Or maybe because I'm not ready to hear him tell me anything else.

I can see the pain in his eyes, but eventually he relents. He kisses the tips of my fingers before taking my hand in his own. "You really like to get your way, don't you?"

"Oh yeah," I say, moving in to lean against him.

Adam's arms go around my middle, and I feel perfect. The stress and fear pours out of me, like sand through a strainer. I push my face against his chest, and his chin lands softly on my head.

"Anything else you want to get out of me?" he asks, his teasing voice rumbling against my cheek.

I sigh in his embrace, wishing that this were enough. If I stayed right here in his arms, it just might be. But there's a whole world I have to deal with. School and parents and…

"Actually, there is one more thing I need."

"Name it."

"I need you to help me save Julien Miller."

CHAPTER TWENTY-FIVE

· ·

explain it all over an enormous cheese pizza. It's the place I remembered, the one with the red pop. In between greasy bites, I fill him in on everything. Maggie and me. Blake and his stalker phone call. I include everything about Julien, and even the stuff about our resident Wicked Witch, Dr. Kirkpatrick.

Finally, I stop for breath, grabbing another piece of pizza and waiting for Adam's response. I wait a while, but figure he's thinking it over. I still haven't processed it, and I've had two days.

But then, I wait long enough to wonder what expression he's wearing. Shock? Disbelief? Fear? That third one feels right, but it makes no sense at all. What the hell would he be afraid of?

"So are you going to say anything?" I ask, stabbing random ice cubes with my straw.

"I'm not sure where to start," he says, and I hear an incoming text buzz his phone.

"I guess, 'Gee, Chloe, I don't believe you,' might work," I say, but I don't sound nearly as funny as I want to.

Adam pushes away his plate and leans back in the booth. His phone buzzes again, and he presses something to silence it, looking aggravated. "Well, I don't think you can help Julien.

Schizophrenia doesn't go away, Chlo. And it's not anthrax. You can't use it like a weapon."

"Maybe that's true, but how do we know it's schizophrenia? How do we know it's not one of the weird hypno-things Dr. Kirkpatrick did in our groups?"

"Because I was in the group. It's not like she was stretching us out on couches and making us count backward."

I nod slowly, rubbing my hands clean with the napkin. "You don't believe me. Message received."

"This isn't a matter of me not believing you, Chloe. I know the lady. She's a little fixated on breathing deep, sure, but she's not the second coming of Charles Manson."

"Well, gosh, I hope she knows she can call on you for a character witness."

His expression changes. He looks tense again. Nervous, maybe. God, that can't even be right. If he is nervous, it's because I'm being a complete nut job. I sigh and lace my fingers with his over the table. "I'm sorry. I know that's not fair. I just want answers."

"I know. But I don't want to see you invent what you can't discover."

"What does that mean?"

"It means to be careful not to go accusing innocent people because you're desperate to find a reason for all of this."

"There is a reason for all of this, Adam. And Julien thinks I know what that reason is."

"Julien is a schizophrenic who probably believes a lot of things, Chlo."

"You're starting to sound like Maggie."

He looks down at his hands. "Is there any chance that's because we're both right?"

No. Ridiculous or not, I'm absolutely certain that Julien is not just schizophrenic. But knowing it isn't enough. I need proof.

• • •

"Thank you for meeting with me on such short notice," I say, settling myself onto Dr. Kirkpatrick's couch.

Dr. Kirkpatrick smiles and opens her notepad. "I'm happy I had an opening. You seemed very upset on the phone."

Good. That's exactly what I was aiming for. And if I have any luck, my mom will be home in time to see the frantic, handwritten note I left on the kitchen table. I'm pretty desperate for all of my stars to align today because this is the biggest thing I've ever tried to pull off. Ever.

"I went to California with Maggie," I say, though I have a horrible feeling she already knows that much. Something tells me she knows all kinds of things I wish she didn't.

"That's a big change from our last meeting. The two of you weren't speaking then."

"Well, I was trying to mend the bridge, but now I don't think it worked, and I just don't know what to do."

How the hell she's buying this is beyond me. It must be the nerves I've got from being here to begin with. Still, she scoots forward in her chair and asks me at least a dozen probing questions to help me gather a better understanding of the situation.

I'm barely responding. It probably looks thoughtful, but really I just can't stop watching the clock. I have fourteen minutes left. Why the hell hasn't my mom found the note? She was on her way home. Which means she would have had plenty of time to fly over here.

Surely she would have at least called, right? When your daughter leaves a full page of drama, closed with *"If you want to know what's going on with me, you can call my psychiatrist. She knows how bad it really is."*

"Chloe, I must say, you seem very distant."

"I'm sorry," I say, but I can't manage anything else. I've gone totally blank.

God, I don't know who I'm kidding. This is a ridiculous plan, and it's never going to work.

I hear the doorbell chime, and it takes every ounce of strength I have not to grin. Instead, I sniff and look down at my hands. I should probably say something. What the hell was she saying to me?

"I just want things to be normal," I say, hoping it will pass.

Outside, I hear my mother's voice. Even muffled through the walls, I can hear the commanding tone she's using. I've been on the other side of that tone, so my heart bleeds for the poor little receptionist dealing with this.

Dr. Kirkpatrick's eyes flick to the door, a frown creasing her mouth briefly before she looks back to me. "Perhaps it's time for you to redefine normal, to come to the understanding of how things are now."

"I just don't know why they can't be the same."

"There are times when change is inevitable."

"I don't want to change!"

I sound like a whiny two-year-old, but I don't care. Her eyes are on the door again, where my mom's voice is escalating into something truly scene-worthy. The receptionist is firing back, but my mother is a force to be reckoned with.

I screw up my face in a worried frown. "Is everything okay out there?"

"I'm sure it's fine."

My mother shouts something that sounds an awful lot like "sue you," and I tense my shoulders. "Are you sure you shouldn't check?"

"Would it make you feel more comfortable?"

I swallow hard, hunching my shoulders. "Definitely."

She slips outside, taking her little notepad with her. I am off the couch the instant I hear the door click shut. Her desk is small and sparse, highlighters and paper clips in the top drawer. Both file drawers are locked. Damn it.

I sigh, leaning back against the desk. A leather strap meets my eye. Her briefcase.

Through the door, I can hear Dr. Kirkpatrick working to soothe my mother. She probably won't say anything about me being here. It breaches doctor-patient confidentiality, a fact that she's probably discussing with my mother right this moment. With very little success I'd guess.

I open the heavy leather flap of her bag and flip through an assortment of invoices and educational articles. There are a few patient files with unfamiliar names, but nothing else. This can't be another dead end. It just can't be.

I go through it again, my fingers catching on a slim manila folder I hadn't noticed before. No title.

I pull it out and glance through the papers. There are documents on meditation. Documents on study strategies. I scan one set of papers that's been clipped together, and it's—oh God. Oh God, that can't be right.

But it is.

My knees threaten to give. I force them to hold by sheer force of will, my fingers pinching the clipped papers tightly.

The first page is a roster of the study group. The second is a list of chemical side effects. I see little red ticks and dots next to each of the names on the first sheet. Some sort of code. Or checklist.

I hear the door chime as I drop the folder back into her bag, holding on to those two papers. My blood is roaring behind my ears as I close the flap and shove the bag back beneath her desk. I fold the papers with shaking hands and shove them deep into my purse. I'm still fiddling my zipper closed when Dr. Kirkpatrick returns, shaking her head.

"I apologize for the interruption—Chloe, are you all right?"

Doubtful. My heart is probably beating three thousand times a minute and I'm breathing faster than a hummingbird. I say the only thing I can think of. "That was my mom, wasn't it?"

It's—oh God, it's brilliant. I didn't even think of it when I hatched this whole thing, but my mom showing up at an impromptu session? Yeah, that's definitely a valid reason to panic.

Dr. Kirkpatrick sits back down, looking like she's got it all figured out now. "Yes, it was. Something tells me you won't be surprised that she's here thanks to an alarming note left on her kitchen table."

I look down and bite my bottom lip, hoping my total incapacitating panic will pass for shame.

"Chloe, is it possible that some small part of you wanted her to come here, to prove that you matter?"

The only thing my mother proved by showing up here is that she needs control like most of us need oxygen. But I don't say that. I force a wounded look onto my face and glance up at her.

"Maybe," I say, voice soft.

Dr. Kirkpatrick tilts her head and waits a beat. It stretches too long, long enough for me to think about how close I'm sitting to the woman who stole my memories. I think of the little red marks next to our names, and it's all I can do not to bolt off the couch and run for the door.

"Chloe, it's understandable to crave attention from your mother, to need that evidence of her love. But perhaps we should talk about more constructive ways to meet your needs?"

I nod along, and it's easier than it should be considering who this high-handed crap is coming from today. But that's fine. She can preach all she wants. If I've got what I think I do in my purse right now, I'm pretty sure the next time I hear her say anything, she'll have her hand on a Bible and a judge to her right.

CHAPTER TWENTY-SIX

· ·

Adam pulls into the school parking lot five minutes before he said he'd arrive. I hop out of my car and slide into his passenger seat. He's clean and showered, but he still looks horribly unnerved. And even though he threads his hands through my hair and murmurs hello against my lips, I can't kiss that pinched look away from him this time.

"So what's up?" he asks.

I don't answer, and I don't ask about what's got him upset. There will be time for all that later. I unzip my purse and offer him the paper with the chemical name and possible reactions. I scoot back to my side of the car because I don't need to read it. I know every side effect listed.

Vivid dreams. Increased cognitive ability. Dry mouth. Excessive thirst. Sleepwalking. Headaches. Paranoid delusions. And my personal favorite—memory disturbances.

Adam scans the page, brow furrowing. "What is this?"

"Well, they don't have a kitschy name for it yet, but I'm pretty sure it's a variation of a benzodiazepine. You know, like…Rohypnol."

He looks up at me, eyes wide with shock. "Chloe, why do you have dosage and side effect information on Rohypnol?"

"Well, it's not *exactly* Rohypnol. In addition to that dratted blackout effect, Rohypnol creates drunken, sluggish behavior. Not really conducive to exceptional test results."

"What are you even talking about?"

I hand over the second paper, the one with our names and all the little red pen marks. "See, this fancy new stuff lowers inhibitions, but boy, it sure makes you a real sponge for information. As long as you don't lose huge chunks of your memories, you're golden."

He meets my eyes, and it's clear he's gotten it now. His voice is low. Different than I've ever heard it maybe. The paper shakes in his hands, and I watch it shudder. It brings me back to that first day I remember looking at him. I think of Maggie at the front of the class and me pulling the fire alarm.

"Chloe, where did you get this?" he asks, voice whisper quiet and face blanched.

"In Dr. Kirkpatrick's files. Don't worry. You and Blake don't have any marks next to your name, so it didn't affect you. But all of the rest of us have some. I have only two, so I guess I should feel pretty lucky, huh?"

"You think our study group was drugged." He sounds like a robot, like he can't believe it, can't even get his head around the possibility.

"There's no thinking to it, Adam. You are holding the proof."

He shakes his head over and over. "And you found this in Dr. Kirkpatrick's files? Are you sure?"

I roll my eyes. "Well, unless she just so happened to swap briefcases with the person who's behind my memory loss, then yes, I'm pretty freaking sure."

He looks so pale I wonder if he'll get sick. His phone buzzes in his pocket, and he silences it with a grimace. He rubs a shaking hand over his bloodshot eyes. "What are you going to do?"

"Go to the police. What else would I do?"

He shakes his head. "You can't do that."

"Excuse me?"

"What if you're wrong? What if this is a misunderstanding? I know this looks bad, Chloe, but this is the sort of thing that can end her career even if she's proven innocent."

I bristle at his words, glaring across the seat. "Are you insane? It was paper clipped together! She's in on it, Adam!"

"Or maybe she's the one who uncovered it! Have you considered that? Have you thought for one second about what you might do to her without even knowing her intentions?"

I haven't thought of that. I haven't thought of much of anything, so I stay silent, watching him like a lit stick of explosives.

He draws back from me, his face closing off as he hands the papers back. "I just think you should talk to her."

"Talk to her? Talk to the woman who might have drugged eighteen teenagers?"

"Yes, talk to her! Because if she found this, going against each other could unravel the whole damn thing. There is strength in numbers, Chlo."

Adam can see he's gotten a foothold with me because he leans in, touching my face. "I'll go with you, but you have to talk to her. Give her a chance to explain all of this."

I pull the papers from his hands and rattle them for emphasis. "I'm not giving these back to her."

He just runs a trembling hand through his hair and sighs. "Fine. Let's just talk to her. When does she leave her office?"

"Like two hours ago."

"So we'll meet tomorrow? When she closes?"

"Tomorrow's Saturday. She takes her last patient at four, I think," I say.

"Hey," he says, reaching for me. "We'll get through this. We'll get to the bottom of it."

"Okay," I say again, but for once I'm not comforted by the feel of his hand against my face. Because all I can think about is the way his fingers shake against my skin.

• • •

I drop my keys on the table inside the door. The house is warm and mostly quiet. I follow the smell of bacon and the sound of sizzling into the kitchen. Dad's hunched over a skillet, plaid shirt stretched across his wide shoulders.

"How goes it?" he asks.

"I've been better," I admit, checking the clock on the microwave. Twenty-one hours until I can do something about this. Or I could go right now. If I'm right, I could blow this whole thing open tonight.

And if I'm wrong, Dr. Kirkpatrick's career will be destroyed.

I watch my dad pull the strips of bacon out of the skillet. He lays them side by side on a nest of paper towels with at least a dozen others. "You know, your mother's worked herself into a real lather over the whole Dr. Kirkpatrick episode today."

Oh shit. I completely, totally forgot about that.

Great. I've got twenty-one hours until I confront the woman who drugged me. And I'm probably going to spend twenty and a half of those hours on the receiving end of a riot act.

"Mom would work herself into a lather if I had a tardy at school," I say, snagging a strip of bacon from the paper plate.

He turns off the burner and shoves the skillet back on the stove. He looks angry. It's a rare sight, but one I try not to mess with. "Why the note, Chlo?"

"What?"

Dad throws up his hands, clearly exasperated. "It's like throwing gasoline at a forest fire. You know how she is."

I crunch my bacon in silence and stare hard at the floor. What am I going to say to him? I can't exactly tell him that yes, I did know, and the whole point was to freak her out of her mind so I could concoct a scene and steal files from my psychiatrist.

Frankly, thinking about it now makes me feel like a complete tool.

"You going to say anything about this?" he says.

"I don't know what to say, Dad. I know it wasn't right, but I'm tired of it. We haven't seen eye to eye in forever."

"Yeah, since you started walking," he says, scoffing a little. "But this is different. You scared her, kid. And you're acting like that doesn't matter to you."

I feel a stab of guilt, and I put the bacon down, my appetite gone. "It does matter. I can't explain it all."

"Well, it's a new trend for you. And I'm trying hard not to assume it's about that Adam kid—"

"Dad—"

"Don't you 'Dad' me, Chloe. I'm in her corner on that one. I don't particularly like the idea of you dating anyone, but someone with a record?"

"There's more to that story than she knows, and more than you know too."

"I don't need to know anything else about Adam, and the truth is, Chloe, neither do you! Do you have any idea how bright your future is now? Do you have any idea what kinds of things are open to you?"

I roll my eyes, pressing my back to the wall. "Yes, Dad, I do. I know because I have a parent who's drilled me on the importance of my future every minute of every day for the past seventeen years." Then I feign a shocked gasp. "Oh, look! Now I have *two* of those."

He looks down, clearly hurt. God, what is wrong with me? What the hell am I doing? I feel knotted end over end, wrung out like an old sponge. "I'm sorry. I don't know what's wrong with me anymore."

"Why are you so sure there's something wrong? You have an open invitation to just about any college you want and parents willing to pay for it. How is that so damn bleak?"

"It isn't bleak. But sometimes it doesn't feel real. I don't even know who I am or what I want, Dad. I can't just do backflips because suddenly I'm a terrific student. There's more to me than that."

The words leave my mouth, and I feel stronger for having said them.

Before he can say anything else, the front door opens. "Hello! Guys?"

"In the kitchen!" Dad wipes his hands on a dish towel and puts the skillet in the sink.

Mom comes in wearing a gray suit and a megawatt grin. Something's up. She should be frosting me out right now, but she even includes me in that smile, though it's tighter around the edges.

"Hey," I say. "I'm really sorry about that letter. I know it was…"

Mom arches a brow, happy to fill in the blanks for me. "Dramatic? Cruel? A breach of my trust on every level?"

"Maybe all of those things," I admit, deflating. "I'm sorry. I am."

She looks at me, and I can see the temptation for her to dig into me. For once, I'm pretty sure I deserve it. Which is why you could knock me over with a feather when she shakes her head.

"We're going to put that on hold. You got mail." She holds the envelopes just out of my reach, and the big smile is back. "But before you open these, I want you to know we have a lot of things to discuss, and I'm still very angry."

"You do look furious." I can't resist it. It's hard to take her seriously when she looks like she's about to burst into song and dance.

"Fine. Open them."

I scan the return addresses on the envelopes as she hands them over. Notre Dame and Columbia. College letters. *Big* college letters. From two of the most coveted, respected universities for psychology students everywhere. I turn them over, a little struck by what I'm about to do.

"Stop dillydallying and open them!" Dad says. He's never been one for patience. I shoot him a brief glare and then tear them both open, pulling them loose at the same time. I don't even breathe as I unfold them. I feel like it's someone else's hands. Someone else's eyes. Someone else's life altogether.

And that person has just been invited to apply to Notre Dame and Columbia.

Both of them.

Which pretty much means I'm in.

I feel too light for my skin, as if my body's been filled with helium. I snag the back of a kitchen chair, desperate for something to tether me back to the here and now.

"This is it," Mom says, beaming. "This is the beginning of your future, Chloe. You did it."

They squeeze me into a hug, and we all dissolve into laughter. They keep saying it over and over. *You did it. You did it.*

Somebody did it all right. I'm just not so sure it was me.

I stare at my purse, where a different future lingers. A future of police investigations and courtrooms. All of this laughter and dancing in the kitchen will come to a screeching halt as our scores and grades are examined. Maybe even retested.

In this other future, my parents will be reminded of exactly who I really am.

CHAPTER TWENTY-SEVEN

. . . .

I meet Adam one block away from Dr. Kirkpatrick's office at five. He doesn't say anything when I slide into his car, and pulls away from the curb before I can kiss him. I hold on to the edge of my seat, shocked at his speed.

It isn't like him to drive this fast. Or to be this quiet.

He looks pale and gaunt, dark circles ringed beneath his eyes. I'm sure he hasn't slept at all. No way.

"Hey, are you all right?" I ask.

He doesn't take his eyes from the road. Just nods and checks his phone. A minute later, he checks it again. And then again.

"Is the president calling?" I ask, trying to lighten the mood.

He looks at me then. "Keeping an eye on the time."

"Okay."

But it's not okay. Something's seriously screwed up with him. And I have no freaking idea what it is or why he's acting like this. I mean, shouldn't I be the one who's wigged out right now?

This isn't the time for this. There are bigger fish to fry—hell, there's a freaking *white shark* in my skillet.

Adam pulls into the parking lot, and I spot Dr. Kirkpatrick's car. "There. That one. I'm pretty sure that's hers."

"Does anyone else work here?"

"A receptionist, but she leaves after she checks the last patient in for the day."

"What about the last patient?"

"Sessions end at ten before the hour, so we should be good. She's probably doing paperwork."

Adam doesn't park in the lot. He parks one street over, where his car won't be as noticeable. I look down at the manila folder in my trembling hands and wish I hadn't agreed to this.

I should have gone to the police. Crap, what if she calls the police?

I push the thoughts away and follow Adam into the office. The electric door chime sends a burst of adrenaline dancing through me.

"Dr. Kirkpatrick?" Adam calls out.

No answer. I clear my throat and gesture at the cracked door to her office. We step closer, still hearing nothing. I don't like it. The quiet sends cold, needling fingers up my arms and neck. I begin to shiver, though I'm not cold.

"Dr. Kirkpatrick?" Adam knocks on the door, and it groans open farther under his taps. He pushes through the gaping crack and sucks in a gasp.

"What is it?" I move around him so I can see.

I wish I hadn't.

Dr. Kirkpatrick is slumped over the desk. There's a giant red-black puddle beneath her, all over the pretty desk planner. Some small, detached part of me understands this is blood.

The rest of me demands it to be something else. That much blood would mean she's—no. She can't be.

But she's not moving at all. I take a breath and smell an

unmistakable coppery tang in the air. And the truth whooshes through me like a hurricane.

Dr. Kirkpatrick is dead.

"Oh my God." My voice splits. Cracks into pieces. "Oh my God, Adam, we have to call nine one one."

He's standing there, not merely shocked and sickened like I am, but almost catatonic. As if he can't even believe what he's seeing. And who could blame him? Because no one should believe this. No one should even see this.

There's a purse on the floor beside her desk. Her purse, I assume. The contents are spilled out across the carpet, her wallet conspicuously missing.

Is this why she was killed? For a wallet? A wave of nausea rolls through me, so I turn away from the scene. From the body. Shit, there's a *body*.

What do I do? What do I do?

I stumble backward, pulling out my phone. Suddenly, Adam comes to life, snagging it from my fingers. "No. Someone else has to call it in."

"What? What are you talking about?"

He takes me by the arm and moves fast, rushing us back out of the office and into the fading sunlight. He takes a moment to rub the door handle with his sleeve. I want to argue and pull away, but the truth is, I hardly feel present at all. A little bubble of shock is holding me away, numbing my senses.

"We have to call the police," I say again, but my voice sounds like it belongs to someone else.

He keeps walking, dropping my arm and assuming I'll follow. And I do. Because I don't know what else to do. This is way, *way* outside the realm of things I know what to do with.

I feel sick and heavy. I'm not just shaking—I'm practically convulsing.

Adam pulls out his own phone and starts texting. Furiously.

"You're texting the police?" Is that even possible?

He looks around, eyes frantic and face pale. "Get in the car, Chloe."

"Somebody robbed her! Somebody—" I trail off, bracing myself to say the word. "Somebody killed her."

"Nobody robbed her."

"I saw her purse on the floor—"

"*Nobody robbed her*," Adam says, and the certainty in his tone chills me.

What chills me more is that I know damn well he's right. This wasn't some heat-of-the-moment crime. There's nothing *random* about this.

My face is hot and my jaw aches, and I have to stop thinking. The pieces are locking together too fast, and the picture that's forming scares me to death.

I get in the car because if I don't, I will fall down. I will fall down right here. And I can't be here anymore, not knowing there's a body and so much blood inside—oh God, I might be sick.

Adam starts the engine, and I jump at the sound. Then there's another sound, one that makes my ribs ache and my throat close up. Sirens. Two police cars race past, flashing blue and red as they fly into the parking lot.

Adam swears under his breath, easing the Camaro away from the curb.

"Did you call them?" Somehow I know he didn't. I don't know why I'm even asking.

He pulls out without a word then fumbles his phone up to the steering wheel, texting again. He doesn't just look scared. He looks enraged, terrified, confused: a jumble of so many things that it makes me dizzy.

"What's wrong with you?" I ask, and my chest hurts now. Really hurts. This is bad.

He doesn't answer, and I press a hand to my sternum, willing myself to breathe deeper. But I can't. My breathing is too shallow, too fast. This isn't good. It's not good at all.

My phone buzzes, and I yank it out. "Hello?"

"Chloe, it's m-me." It's Maggie. She's crying. "You w-were right."

"Right about what?" I ask. I'm breathless and queasy, gripping my seat hard when Adam flies around a corner.

"Get off the phone, Chloe," Adam says. It isn't a request.

I flash him a glare and push closer to the passenger window. Maggie takes a shuddering breath. "I looked into the Miller family t-tree. There's n-no history of schizophrenia in Julien's family. You were right, Chloe. She's in t-trouble."

"So am I," I say.

"Get off your phone," Adam says again, almost shouting it. And then I don't have a choice because he's tearing it out of my fingers.

I'm too shocked to move. To speak.

I think of him texting at the pizza place. Checking his phone earlier tonight. And then, I remember that first night together, when we went to the tower in Corbin. When he asked me to turn mine off.

This isn't happening. It can't be.

I glance sideways at Adam as we screech to a stop at a red light. He curses again, rolling down his window. He flicks his wrist, and I jump in my seat as I hear first one phone and then the other shatter against the ground.

"What did you do?" I ask, knowing he won't answer.

I feel smothered and frozen, like the sun has been snuffed out. Darkness moves over me. Inside me and through me like cold water sucking me down fast. I know what this means.

"Adam," I say, and I know my voice reflects every ounce of my fear. I force myself not to scream. I know if I start, I will never stop. Not ever.

He turns right down a narrow side street near my house. He puts the car in park and covers his face with his hands. The scar on his arm glares at me, white and jagged like a cruel smile.

"I can't do this," he says. He sounds small and weak and shattered.

I want him to shut up. Right now. My fingers curl over the door handle because I want to run.

"I don't even know what to say or where to start, but I can't do this to you," he says. "No matter what they do to me, I can't. Not anymore."

I feel my ears ringing and my fingers going numb. It's like a blood pressure cuff has been strapped around my middle. Every breath is harder than the last.

Adam faces me, his eyes bright with the promise of tears. "You were right. Part right, anyway. Your memory loss was an accident, Chlo, but it wasn't natural. Daniel Tanner was testing that chemical in our study group. I don't know how or why, but he wants to sell it. And apparently we were the guinea pigs."

I feel like I've left my body. Like I'm floating somewhere outside, a million miles away from these words. I find my voice, but it is thin and small. "How? How do you know?"

The pain in his eyes is unmistakable. "Because I work for them. Daniel hired me to monitor the group. He said he wanted peer information on the relaxation techniques."

"Relaxation techniques," I deadpan, my lungs shriveling with each breath.

"He fed me a bunch of crap about subliminal messaging and meditation, but he never—I didn't—hell, it doesn't even matter. He sold this whole thing. He sold it to the school board as a big community service project, and he sold it to me as my only way out of this shit-hole town and I bought it, Chloe. I bought it hook, line, and fucking sinker."

The pieces are sliding together. Clicking into place. Sitting across from him for that first math test. Blake's comments in the bathroom. *I'm the boyfriend, remember?*

Blake. Blake who kissed me—I can't. I can't go there.

I shake my head, my tears hot and slick trailing down my face. How could I miss this? How?

All of the texting makes sense...tonight before he tossed our phones. Before that, even. "You were texting Daniel tonight?"

"Yes. I had no idea he could be capable of something like this, but I know it has to be him, that son of a bitch."

I shake my head, not wanting to hear any of this. Not one more word.

"I needed money for college," Adam says miserably. "I didn't—no one told me about the drugs. No one told me about *any* of this."

I shove open the door, and his hand curls gently over my arm.

"Chloe, please."

"Let me go!" I jerk my arm free and fling the door wide.

"Chloe, I'm telling you this because I'm in love with you! I've *been* in love with you since the second you pulled that fire alarm, maybe since all the way back in the fourth grade."

"Stop! Just stop!" I bite back a sob and step into the cold quiet of the evening. It's too much. And too little. And it's all way, way too late.

"Wait—"

"Stay away from me, Adam. I mean it."

I slam the door and drag in a frigid breath of November air. I sprint for the nearest yard and somehow vault myself over the chain-link fence, ignoring the sound of Adam calling after me.

Through the yard, past the next fence. I don't stop. I don't think. I just run.

CHAPTER TWENTY-EIGHT

· ·

I will go home. I will go home and talk to my parents, and we will go to the police and everything will be okay. Except when I round the corner to my street, my house is completely dark. No porch lights. No lamps inside. Not even the pale blue flicker of a television.

Saturday night. Date night. They're probably at dinner or at a movie or somewhere else. And that's just too damn bad. This is an emergency.

I immediately remember my cell phone shattering on the street. My psychologist in a pool of blood.

What if he comes after my parents? What if I get them involved and they end up like Dr. Kirkpatrick? The idea sends bile rising in my throat. God, what the hell am I going to do?

The cold has sharp teeth tonight, biting through my puffy coat and turning my jeans into sheets of ice against my legs. I can't stay out here forever. But where do I go?

Inside, my house is strangely quiet, which makes me jumpy and nervous. I scan my mother's note on the table and the plate she left for me in the fridge. Dinner and a movie. They'll be home by midnight.

I stare long and hard at the phone on the kitchen wall, but in the end, I walk away. I can't lose them. If knowing this puts them in danger, then they can't know. But I can't stay here. I can't sit in this kitchen surrounded by takeout menus and used coffee cups and pretend that my entire world isn't falling apart. And that my almost-boyfriend isn't one of the people responsible.

I need help.

Maggie.

I try her phone, and it goes straight to voice mail. Did they shut down her phone? Oh God, are they tracking her too?

I try her home number, and it rings busy. My stomach plummets to my knees. I envision Maggie slumped over like Dr. Kirkpatrick. No! No, she has to be all right. She has to.

The clock in the living room chimes six o'clock, and I cringe. One hour ago I had answers. Answers and a boyfriend and a best friend who was safe. Sixty minutes should not have enough power to change all of that.

I stumble back into the night, desperate to find Mags. To make sure she's all right.

Snow is falling, thick white flakes that cling to my hair and coat. Christmas lights shine from the windows in my neighbors' houses, mocking me with their message of peace.

I cut through the Campbells' backyard, my eyes scanning the brightly lit windows for signs of life. I jog to the back steps, steps that have seen me through skinned knees and late night truth or dare sessions. This place is full of goodness. Every step I take crosses the shadow of a game once played, a ball once thrown. It is the closest thing I have to sacred ground.

I climb the familiar stairs with my heart thundering behind my ribs. I should go around front, but I can't. My feet feel like lead weights. I have nothing else in me.

I knock hard on the door, banging and ringing the little bell next to the handle. I even call Maggie's name, but the windows stay empty and the knob won't twist beneath my fingers.

I'm alone. I don't know where anyone is or if they're okay, and it's cold. It's so terribly cold.

A sob tears out of me, and I cross my arms over my chest. I'm no better off than Julien now. If I go to the police, they will see a lunatic. The poor, crazy girl with big stories and a ruined future.

The panic that's been buzzing along my skin for the last hour seizes me like an iron fist, squeezing hard around my chest. It hurts to breathe. Hurts like blades are slipping between my ribs. I try to remember Dr. Kirkpatrick's words, but all I can think of is the blood on her desk. So much blood.

My arms and legs go numb, and my vision blurs. I feel myself falling, hands flailing at empty air before I hit the steps hard.

The mix of pain and fear takes me like the tide, rolling me under and pulling me out to sea. My eyes drift closed, and I can't even fight that. I can't fight anything anymore.

• • •

"Chloe!"

My name, in stereo, drags me back. Two voices: one high, one low. They are shouting back and forth to each other, words bouncing between them so quickly I can't pull them apart. They make no sense to me—only noise.

I feel my body lift, the ruthlessly cold concrete giving way to something warm. And then I'm moving. Being carried, I think. The air changes. I feel it happen, the cruel wind giving way to stillness. I feel the heat at once, seeping into my clothes, melting the snow on my face and hair.

"T-tell me she's b-breathing."

Maggie. I turn my face toward her but can't seem to manage to open my eyes. She's not the one carrying me though. She's not strong enough.

"She's breathing," Adam says.

Adam. Adam's carrying me. I take a breath of cinnamon and soap and leather. And then I open my eyes.

"Oh, thank G-god," Mags says. I hear her sniffle.

Adam doesn't say anything. He just tips his head skyward and breathes hard. The fragile flesh beneath his eyes is so dark it looks bruised. I know that I should be mad at him, but it hurts me to see him like this.

I touch his face without even realizing I moved. He looks down at me, anguish etched in every feature.

"I did this to you," he says.

His words lance through my middle, bringing tears to my eyes. I bite my lip and turn away from his face, but somehow I move tighter against his chest too. I don't know why.

I think I might hate him.

And I know I love him.

I don't even know which is worse anymore.

Maggie looms into view, eyes puffy and red. "You s-scared me half to d-death."

"I'm sorry," I say. My voice is stronger than I thought it would be. My mind, though, is still reeling. "How are you here?"

"I live here," Maggie deadpans.

"And I was convincingly desperate," Adam adds.

Maggie nods in agreement, but it seems impossible. She all but commanded me not to trust him. Now they're all buddy-buddy?

She seems to read my mind, waving a hand dismissively. "We'll cover all that later. Let's g-get you on your feet."

Adam scoots back from me, giving himself the space to stand up. I shiver on the floor. It's colder here without him against me. When I look up, I see them both, hands outstretched to help me up.

I reach for Maggie with my right hand and Adam with my left. Our fingers connect, and the floodgates open.

I shouldn't be driving. I don't even know why I'm in the car or where I'm headed, but my head is pounding and swimming at the same time and it's hard to see the road with the snow pouring down like this.

I lick my lips, recoiling at the acrid, lemony tang in my mouth. An image of Blake flashes through my head. We're in his house. In his father's office. We're shouting and then we're not. I shove something into my purse when he's not looking. I try to remember what, but it's all in jagged pieces now.

I'm terrified. Struggling against someone. No, it's fine. I'm fine. Blake kisses me at the car. Smiles and tells me to take care of my head.

No, it doesn't make sense. I was at Blake's but…There is nothing but blankness. I feel stuck, like a badly copied music track. There are blips of silence in my evening.

Not right. It can't be right. My head hurts so bad. And I'm so cold. Where the hell is my coat? Why am I driving?

My car slides a little coming up to a red light. I try to pump the brakes, but the back end fishtails to the left. I hear my purse slide off the seat, dumping on the floor. The car comes to a rest, and I grope blindly through the mess on my passenger mat: lipstick and wallet and my iPod and then—what the hell?

My fingers close around a black box. Something rattles inside, tinkling like glass. The sound turns my stomach to lead.

I have to hide it.

The snow falls and my head reels. Everything blurs. There are snowy streets. And then I am walking. I watch my feet crunching through a thin layer of snow. I hear myself grunt and feel the agonizing burn of the snow I'm shoveling away barehanded.

My head spins and spins. It aches and I feel sick. Just sick. I open my eyes and I am back in my car. Driving again. I see dirt under my fingernails. The box is gone. I don't know how. Oh God, I don't know.

I feel a sob shake my shoulders. I'm so cold. So sick. I pull out my phone and blink hard, trying to clear my vision. I tap out the only number I can think of and wait for it to ring.

"Don't tell me you're stuck on number twenty-nine," Adam says by way of greeting.

I try to keep my voice normal. "Can you meet me?"

"Yeah. What's wrong? You don't sound right."

"I'm okay," I say, swerving over double yellow lines. I'm not okay. I'm a million miles from okay. I glance around, getting my bearings. The school bus lot blurs by on my right. "Maybe we'd better meet at the school."

"I'll be there in fifteen minutes."

I shove my phone deep into my jeans. Then I park in the front lot. I'm shivering in my sweater, so I can't stay out here. The latch on the cafeteria door is ice-cold, but I move it up and left, leaning on it hard like Adam taught me.

I slip inside and feel the quiet surround me completely.

It's darker than dark. I feel my way through the tables, my eyes fixed on the red exit sign glowing at the back doors. I need to sit down. Like now.

I don't understand why I'm here or why it's so dark or what I'm so freaked out about. I just need to rest for a minute. I just want to close my eyes. I stop in the first classroom I find, study hall from last year. Thank God. I can just sleep. Just for a minute.

Everything feels slow and dull. My eyelids droop as I slide into my seat from last year. I sink down low in the desk, watching the snow fall like tiny white butterflies. It is the last thing I see.

CHAPTER TWENTY-NINE

. . . .

Chloe!" Adam's voice brings me back to the present. His hands are on my face now. Maggie is clasping my hands. I'm sort of sandwiched between them, only half upright.

I gasp, filling my lungs with the sweet, yeasty air of the Campbells' kitchen. "I remember. I remember the night I woke up."

"What n-night? What are you t-talking about?"

"The night in the classroom?" Adam guesses. "The night I met you there?"

I nod, feeling stronger and warmer with them so close. "I was at Blake's. I found something. They did something to me, but they didn't take what I found. I had it."

My heart is still racing. I feel Maggie's hand, a soothing pressure against my shoulder. But it is Adam's eyes that anchor me. "I remember calling you, Adam. I remember the box, but I don't know what was in it. I hid it though. It had to be important."

"They would have never let you leave with any evidence. Hell, after tonight—" He stops, taking a harsh breath. "God, after tonight, who knows what they would have done to you."

I remember myself, remember exactly who it was I called that night and all the lies he's told me since. I pull away from his touch. "*They?*"

He has the decency to flush, dropping his hands to his side. "I was never one of them. I was a guy who worked for them."

"And how do I know you're not working for them right now?"

"Maybe you don't, but I d-do," Maggie says. "He let me tape a confession from him detailing everything he knows. It's on my phone."

"That doesn't fix this," I tell him. "Dr. Kirkpatrick is dead. You can't fix that, can you?"

Adam doesn't say anything at all. He nods once and then slips outside to the back steps where they must have found me. I half expect him to keep walking, but he doesn't. He just stands there waiting, his profile frozen in the moonlight.

"It's real, you know," Maggie says quietly. "The way he feels about you."

"Funny, I thought you were Team Stay-the-Hell-Away-from-Adam like two days ago."

"I was."

"And what? You find out he really is just as bad as you thought—hell, worse than that—and suddenly you think he's hero of the day?"

"I d-didn't say that. I'm still not sure what I think of him."

I glance outside the back door again. He's still there. "I know what I think. I think he betrayed me."

Maggie sinks into a chair, sighing. "Yeah, well, d-don't start flinging stones in your little g-glass house."

"What does that mean?"

Mags looks at me with a flinty expression. "It means you b-betrayed me too."

I wince at her words, torn between curiosity and dread. "What happened, Mags? Tell me what happened to us."

"*They* happened to you, Chloe." Her face goes dark and sad. "I t-told you that group was wrong. It was almost like a cult. You hung out at the same places, wore the same kind of clothes. You started d-dating each other, for God's sake."

I shake my head. "It still doesn't make sense, Maggie. We didn't stop being friends when you went through your Danny obsession or when I was on the volleyball team and at practice ten thousand times a week."

"That's because you didn't insult me!" She takes a shuddery breath, and I can see that her eyes are too bright. Her chin trembles when she speaks again. "When I t-told you something felt wrong, you said I was paranoid. Time after time you blew me off, and then when ignoring me wasn't enough, you staged an intervention. You sat me d-down with a couple of your study bitches and t-told me you wanted to help. You told me that maybe if I spent a little more t-time centering myself that maybe I w-wouldn't, that m-m-maybe I wouldn't…"

I fill in the blank with a hollow voice. "Stutter."

It can't be true. I can't be capable of that. But somehow, her words prickle at my mind, whispering of a memory that's waiting to be recovered.

"You always p-protected me," she says, swiping tears off her cheeks angrily. "Even way b-back in the second grade, you never t-treated me different. Not until that d-day."

I slump back against the wall, my heart in pieces.

We're both crying now, quiet sniffs punctuating the silence of her kitchen. I finally brave my voice, which is every bit as weak and shaky as I feel. "I don't even know what to say. I know sorry isn't enough. I don't know what would be. I don't know how I could ever believe…"

She picks up where I trail off, stepping closer. "*They* made you believe. You b-believed these people and all the b-bullshit they fed you, Chloe. Maybe not as much as the others, but they had you."

I repress a shudder, still revolted by the idea of those words on my lips. Maggie isn't looking for me to talk yet though. She looks right past me to the back door where Adam is still waiting. I see his hard profile in the moonlight, his sharp jaw and thin nose.

"They had him too."

• • •

I step outside and he turns to me. He is prettier than a boy has any right to be and far too beautiful for the ugly things he's done.

"I don't trust you," I say.

He doesn't look at me, but he flinches like it stings. But also in a way that tells me he gets it.

"It doesn't change the fact that I want to help," he says.

"Maybe I don't want your help."

Adam turns toward me then, his expression stony. "Then I'll go to the police and tell them everything I know."

"What?"

"You heard me."

I feel fury under my skin, heating me up despite the snow. "If you do that, we have nothing. We might never find the evidence I had."

Adam shrugs and I feel my jaw clench.

"It'd be my word against Daniel Tanner's, Adam! Do you understand that the only proof I have was stolen from a recent murder victim? He'd come through this smelling like a rose, and I'd probably look like the killer!"

"I don't care."

"You don't care? You don't care about the possibility of me being a murder suspect?"

"That's right, I don't! Because you'd be alive! If I go to the police, they'll launch an investigation and you will be watched. Protected. He'd be too smart to come after you then because it would lead a trail of bread crumbs back to the study group and eventually to him."

"So you'd let him get away with what they did to Julien? You'd just walk away?"

He closes in on me, his head bending down until his face is lost in shadow. His hand reaches for my cheek, and I hold my breath. When he speaks again, his voice is so low I can feel it as much as I can hear it. "You have no idea what I'd do to keep you safe, do you?"

The back door opens, and Maggie lets herself out. I'm half irritated when I turn to her, but the look on her face shuts my mouth. Her skin is pale and her eyes are wet. Too wet.

"What's wrong?" I ask her.

"Look," she says, pointing blindly back to the house. Her laptop is open on the kitchen counter. "I was j-just checking my stuff, and—"

"And what?" Adam asks. He moves his head, like he wants to see the screen. "Are they looking for us?"

Maggie shakes her head, and I see that her cheeks are wet. She's crying. I reach for her hands. She's cold. Shaking. "What is it, Mags?"

"It's Julien. She's d-dead."

• • •

The bright future of a former local honor roll student was cut tragically short when she took her own life—

I stop reading. I've already read the post a half dozen times. We all have. I don't know why. Maybe we think reading it over and over again might make it untrue.

But it is true. Julien is dead. Mrs. Campbell found her hanging in her bedroom two days ago.

I try to think of Julien dead, but the truth is, I don't really know what death looks like unless you count my glimpse of Dr. Kirkpatrick. I mean, I saw my grandpa Frank at his visitation, but I was eight and all I remember thinking is that he looked kind of orange and that he probably wouldn't really like the lacy satin pillow under his head.

But he was old and Julien isn't.

Wasn't.

God, this just shouldn't be possible. I'm pretty sure I should feel something other than this. Because I don't feel anything. I'm just…numb.

Adam lets out a low sigh and pushes his fingers into his hair. Maggie sniffs into a tissue, and I wince. Her crumpled face makes me ache, but is that for Julien or for Maggie?

And what about Mrs. Miller? I remember her so vividly, her soft hands closing around the bag of maple nut clusters. Her tired eyes and perfect smile. She found Julien.

She found her daughter hanging in her room.

"We need to do something," I say. Not that I really have any ideas. I had to say something though. Because I can't think about Mrs. Miller. Not for one more second.

"L-like what?" Maggie asks.

"We can't bring her back," Adam says. He too looks shaken. Stunned.

And I'm still sitting here, cold and hard like a stone while, somewhere in California, Julien is dead. She killed herself, and it wasn't because of a bully or a bad breakup. It wasn't anything stupid or childish. It was because of Daniel Tanner.

"We can't let him get away with this," I say.

"No," Maggie says, and her eyes go flinty.

"How?" Adam sits back in his chair, shoulders slumped. "I'll do whatever you want. You know that. I'll do anything. But we don't have proof."

"I do have proof!" I say, and then I wince. "I did. I had it before."

"Do you remember anything?" he asks.

Swirling snow. My tires slipping on the pavement. Dirt crusted on my half-frozen fingers. I remember so much. And nowhere near enough.

I shake my head, and Maggie touches my hand. "It's okay."

"No, it's not okay. I need to figure it out."

"It's locked somewhere in your head," Adam says. "It's not like you can just force something like that out."

I don't say anything, but I know he's wrong. They've already forced my mind to forget things. And if they can do that…

"Let's go," I say, standing up.

"W-what? Where are we going?"

"We're going back to the school."

"Why? What for?" Adam asks, though he stands up with me.

I know what I have to do. It scares me to death, the idea of someone poking around in my head for the second time. But I can't let this rest. I have to try.

I push down my fear and square my shoulders. "What do you guys know about hypnosis?"

• • •

We decide to meet at the school. Mags needs to check in with her mom, who's still at the bakery, and I need to pick up a couple of reference books from home, including the one I checked out of the library. I don't know why I have Adam drive me, because I don't exactly trust him. But the world still feels steadier when he's close.

I'm grateful that I don't need to explain this to Maggie, who watches us from her front window as we drive away.

Adam tunes the radio to a station playing Christmas carols, and I stare out the window. Houses draped in pine swags and twinkle lights drift past. For a moment, I can almost pretend this is a date. That we're two normal people, stretching out the last bit of a perfect evening.

"It's different now," I say, maybe to remind myself more than anything.

"Maybe," he says. "But it doesn't change anything. Not for me."

He pulls to a stop at the curb beside my driveway, and then he comes around to my side of the car, and everything's just like it was before. Except we don't touch. We don't hold hands or sling arms around each other's shoulders. We just walk side by side, crunching up the snowy sidewalk until we're at the foot of my porch steps.

"Chloe," Adam says, moving in front of me.

I suddenly feel like I've run a marathon. Breathless and light-headed, I can't seem to do a thing but watch him as he slides his hands to my face. "I'm a liar and a thief and thousand other shitty things, but I would *never* hurt you. I need you to know that."

I nod because I know he wouldn't. Truth told, I don't think he'd hurt anyone. Except maybe himself.

"I don't deserve you." He moves in, and I could sooner resist breathing than I can resist curling my hands in the edges of his coat, pulling him until I can feel the heat from his chest and breathe in the smell that I now know as well as my own.

My hands are shaking and cold when I press them to his cheeks. He doesn't flinch or pull away; instead he breathes harder, like every whisper of my fingers is magic.

"No more lies," I say.

He nods but doesn't say anything. Like he knows I'm not done.

"I don't know what this means," I say. "I don't trust you now. I don't know if I ever will."

"I'll wait," he says, and I think he will. I think he'll wait forever if that's what it takes. And it might.

Still, I pull him down and kiss him until the cold disappears. His hands are tangled in my hair, and the world is a tiny, insignificant thing sliding sideways beneath my feet. It feels better than good. It feels right.

When we pull apart, the snow has stopped. The moon is bright and full in the star-pricked sky. I gaze at the pale ring around it, remembering that it's an omen of something the future will bring. I wish I could remember if it's good or bad.

CHAPTER THIRTY

• •

We sit in the parking lot behind the school, waiting for Mags to show up. My parents, for once, will be out too late to notice my absence.

We keep the radio low and read through the sections in my books that cover hypnosis. I highlight a section and hand it over to Adam.

"Okay, here's the bit on imagery. *It's often helpful to use imagery in a sequence to bring people into a hypnotic state.*"

He frowns. "What imagery?"

"I can't tell you. There are case studies in the back, but it's not something I can rehearse. If I think about it from your point of view, it won't work on me. Keep a steady, soothing tone."

"I don't like this, Chlo. This is like *The Idiot's Guide to Psychology*. Enough people have messed with your head already."

"It's fine," I say, but of course it's not fine. It's an insane idea born out of pure desperation. As tense as I am right now, it'd be a miracle if a trained hypnotist could put me under, let alone a couple of amateurs with a textbook. But we have to try.

Adam's face makes it clear he doesn't agree. "It's dangerous, Chlo. We don't know what we're doing."

"Yeah, well, clearly neither did Dr. Kirkpatrick. They obviously killed her for a reason, and I'm thinking a botched attempt at cover-up is probably said reason."

He trails a hand down my cheek. "I just want you to think about this. There's a lot that could go wrong."

"I've done nothing but think about this." I sigh. "I'm done thinking. We're doing this, Adam. We have to. It's simple. You're going to lead me through some relaxing imagery and count backward and gently lead me through the night at Blake's house."

His jaw goes tight. "And what if you do remember? Are you ready to remember everything that might have happened that night?"

"Yes, everything! Why would you—oh. Oh."

Everything that might have happened starts to sound a lot like *sex things that might have happened.*

My stomach does an ugly barrel roll. I take a breath and press my lips together. Could I forget something like that? I think about Blake's familiarity in my room, the way he'd tossed our books aside like there were better things to do.

No, I wouldn't have done that with him. But a devil's voice reminds me that not so long ago, I would have done *anything* for Blake Tanner. And I'm just kidding myself if I try to pretend that anything wouldn't have potentially included sex.

I turn to Adam, biting my lip. "Were we...serious? Blake and me?"

Adam shakes his head slowly, looking pained. "Don't make me go there."

"Are you saying this because you don't know or because you don't want to talk about it?" I ask.

"Both, if you want the truth," he says.

I scoot away from him. "Because it would change the way you feel about me, right? Because you were fine and dandy with the whole fake dating gig right up until you had to think of me as leftovers."

"First off, you're nobody's leftovers. Second, until that day at the tutoring center, I had no idea Blake being with you was actually his dad's sick new way to keep a thumb on you."

"What, you thought he was *sincere*? Why on earth would someone like Blake date *me*?"

Adam's eyes are narrowed, his voice too loud. "I don't know, Chloe, maybe because he's met you?"

The compliment doesn't faze me. Maybe because as far as I remember, I haven't had sex with anyone. So yeah, I'm a little preoccupied with the fear of it happening with somebody who was getting paid by the hour.

Maggie taps on his window, and we both look up. I climb out of the car, trying to look nonchalant. "Where's your truck?"

"I walked. I was t-too paranoid someone would see it," she says. Her brow is furrowed in a way that tells me she doesn't buy my glib attitude. She can tell I'm upset.

Adam heads in first, and Maggie snags my sleeve at the door. "What's wrong?"

I take a long breath. "How about what isn't? It's a shorter list."

• • •

An hour later, Maggie bites her lip and looks around the silent study hall room. "Okay, this isn't working, and I'm nerved out. When d-does the cleaning crew get here?"

"They don't come on weekends. We're fine," Adam says.

She's been edgy since we got here. Maybe the school wasn't the best idea, but we need privacy and I figured being in the place where it all started might jog my memory.

I open my eyes and shift in the chair, my gaze going to the window beside me. It's creepy thinking about the last time I looked at that rectangle of glass. If I fall asleep now, will I wake up to flowers?

Adam adjusts his coat behind me, and I frown up at him. "I'm sorry. I thought it would work faster."

"Don't be," he says. "I'm probably not doing it right."

"Me either," Mags adds.

I shake out my shoulders and clear my throat. "Let's go again. I just need to be a little more receptive."

Maggie gives me an appraising look, one that tells me she's pretty sure I'm not going to be receptive to anything even remotely like what they're doing. She exchanges a look with Adam that makes it pretty clear it's a shared opinion.

"We could try the lake imagery again. That was nice." My voice sounds unconvincing. Even to me.

"Maybe Adam is right. We could g-go to the police," Maggie says.

"We've been over this," I say. "I need that box. I wouldn't have hidden it if it wasn't seriously important." Their silence seems to agree with me, so I push my hair behind my ears. "We have to do this."

Adam nods and scoots closer, reaching for my hand. I feel the roughness of his fingertips against my palm. A flash of him walking down the stairs at school rushes back at me. *Halfway down the stairs, he turns over his shoulder, giving me a smile that makes my insides curl warmly.*

I gasp and squeeze his hand harder. "Wait. I know what I need. I need you to touch me."

He smiles a little wickedly, and I smack his arm, flushing to the roots of my hair. "Not like that. I mean—"

"You've remembered things when I touch you," he says, filling in my awkward silence.

"Yes. That." I turn to Maggie, willing my cheeks to cool down. "That's how I remembered that night at Blake's. When you held my hands to help me up, it all came back to me."

"How?" Maggie asks.

"I don't know," I admit, lacing my fingers with Adam's. "Maybe it's because of my connections with you."

"Would that b-be stronger than the drugs?"

"It can be," Adam says softly, and I squeeze his hand, too overwhelmed to voice my own opinion. The truth is, my connection with both of them might be the strongest thing I know. Maybe the strongest thing I'll ever know.

"Okay, we'll d-do it again. Holding your hands," Mags says.

She scoots her chair closer to me. Her hand is small and cool, and Adam's is wide and warm. They are absolute opposites, and they both fit me just right.

"Close your eyes," Maggie says.

Something in me struggles, still afraid of what will be waiting when I open my eyes. Most of all, I fear the truth of the six months I can't remember. Knowing there will be pieces I wish I could forget.

No. This is not me. I jump off bridges. I pull fire alarms. I don't have a place in me for this kind of fear. I push it back, tamp it down, and focus on Maggie's words.

"Should we start with the lake?" she asks, voice gentle.

I feel the rising panic as the unknown draws closer. I think of the person I've been. Of the things I might have done and said. And then I feel the welcome softness of Adam's lips against my temple. It's featherlight, nothing like the heat and pressure he usually delivers.

I feel his lips near my ear, then a soft whisper. "We find what we find. And we move on."

"We leave it in the past," Maggie whispers.

I let out a sigh, one that comes from the deepest parts of my soul. Maggie starts to count, and they both hold me tight. Finally, I begin to let go.

• • •

I look around the blurred edges of this memory, down at my black sweater and jeans. At the wet snow clinging to my boots. Something dark peeks out from my curled fingers.

"I'm holding the box," I say, but my voice comes out somewhere else. I'm here but not here. Watching it like a bad movie, where the color is distorted by static.

I move through the yard, my steps pushing through the snow to the wet grass underneath. A familiar house stands across the yard, the back steps covered in snow.

"I'm at Maggie's house."

I walk away from the house, my feet slipping through the slushy backyard. Am I going home? No. Not home.

I know where I'm going. Around the compost pile and down to the base of the tree. I drop to my knees and wipe the snow away with my bare hands. My fingers burn and ache from the cold. There's a shovel in the tree, but I don't use it. I just rip the loose chunks of dirt away until I see the metal rectangle.

The Not Treasure Box.

"I found it."

I wrangle it out and wrench it open. Bracelets and bookmarks and coded letters in Maggie's writing and mine. Tears sting my eyes, but I don't let them fall. I put the new plastic box inside, pulling the latch open to look at the contents.

Four syringes rest side by side in the bottom. I snap the lid shut and tuck the container beneath an old Tinker Bell T-shirt. Then it all goes back into the ground. I scoop mounds of half-frozen dirt back over the hole, stomping it down with my feet. The snow turns the dirt to mud, but it's good enough. It will have to be.

Are you still at Maggie's house?" The voice is nowhere and everywhere at once.

"Yes." My own voice is still crisp and clear in that other place. "I'm leaving now."

I find my car parked crookedly two streets over. I turn the key in the ignition with shaking hands and slip-slide my way back to the main road.

Lights flash overhead, green and red. I don't know if I stopped. I don't even know if I was supposed to. I'm on autopilot with no destination, turning blindly from one street to the next. This is crazy. I have to stop this.

I pick up my phone, dialing the only number I can think of.

"Don't tell me you're stuck on number twenty-nine," Adam says by way of greeting.

I try to keep my voice normal. "Can you meet me?"

"Yeah. What's wrong? You don't sound right."

"Chloe, are you ready to come back now?"

"Yes."

The faraway voice begins to count. It pulls me away from the cold and the snow, tugging me closer to the sound. Then it is right there with me. Only inches from my ears.

I am back.

I hear the soft drone of the radiator and the shuffle of Adam's boots against the floor. It's okay. Everything is okay this time.

"I know where I hid the drugs," I say.

I open my eyes.

I'm facing the window I saw the first time I woke up. This time there's a man standing in the snow beyond the glass. He's tall, graying, and either he can read lips or he has mutant hearing. Because the smile on his face tells me he knows what I said.

CHAPTER THIRTY-ONE

· ·

A dam?"

The terror must be as clear on my face as it is in my voice. Adam swears softly under his breath. His back is to the window, but he knows who's out there. I'm sure of it.

Daniel Tanner.

Out of nowhere, Adam lunges out of his chair, hands reaching for us. His chair knocks backward, and I hear him whisper even as he hooks his fingers in my shirt. "Run!"

I jerk back, shocked, and he kicks at the chair, like he's tangled up in the legs. I can't do anything but stare, my mind reeling to catch up. He fumbles for my sleeve, but Maggie yanks me free, dragging me toward the door.

Daniel is watching us. Adam nods and waves him toward the cafeteria before reaching for me again.

"You're not going to get out of here until you tell me where they are!" Adam yells, but the sharp edge in his voice doesn't match the worry in his face.

My face feels hot, my jaw too tight. This can't be happening. He can't have fooled me for this long. But he told me to run. I heard that. I'm sure I did.

Something flings past me. Maggie's thrown a chair. It hits

Adam in the shoulder, and I don't know if she's acting or if he's acting. I don't know what's happening, but I run. We rush into the hallway and around a corner with Adam right on our heels.

He grabs both of us by the shoulder, hauling us back easily. I take a breath, feeling a scream build, but then Adam's hand is over my mouth and his cheek is pressed to the side of my face.

His voice is low. "I'll keep him off your trail, but you have to get out fast."

Relief floods my senses. I nod and curl my fingers around his wrist as he pulls his hand away.

"H-how? Where w-will we go?" Maggie asks.

"Get the drugs and go to the police." Adam holds my gaze. "You can do this."

Distantly, I hear a scraping squeak. The cafeteria door squealing open. Daniel's inside.

"Okay, I need you to hit me and run," Adam says.

My head feels loose and fuzzy, like static is buzzing through my brain. "No! We can't just leave you."

"Yes, you can. Use the back door in the library then cut away from the school. Now, hit me."

I shake my head. "Adam—"

I see something flying by my face and then I hear the sickening smack of flesh against flesh. Adam's jaw whips back, and I cry out as I see blood bloom on his lip. Maggie pulls her fist into her open hand, rubbing her knuckles as red blotches rise on her cheeks.

"Maggie!" I cry.

"Good hit," Adam says.

I hear footsteps in a nearby hall. The sound sends ice up my spine. I turn to Adam, feeling my heart spiraling into my throat. I don't want to go. I don't want to leave him.

He reaches for me, his fingers warm against my cheek. "Be safe," he says softly. And then he slaps his open hand against a locker. The crashing makes me jump. "Stop, you little bitch!"

We race back down the hallway, hearing the distant mutter of footsteps and then male voices in the front of the cafeteria. We cut across the back instead, passing the stairs where we eat lunch, and then the school office. We file into the library, wide-eyed and panting.

It's darker than dark in here. The smell of aging books and new highlighters tickles my nose.

Mags volunteers in the library, so she knows it like the back of her hand, thank God. She slides along the south wall, and I follow her, spotting the muted red glow of the emergency exit at the end of a narrow row of shelves.

The door is old and wooden, a relic of a school with a limited remodeling budget. I twist the knob and push hard. Nothing. I twist again, grunting with the effort.

Maggie's hand clamps like a vise into my shoulder. I'm about to yelp when I hear footsteps thundering toward the library.

I freeze in place, afraid to release the handle. Afraid to breathe. "They're probably at the front by now." It's Adam. I'm sure of it. "You'd better be right, Reed."

The footsteps move past, and the grip on my shoulder loosens. I take a single shuddering breath, and Maggie presses her hands to the door as well. Our eyes meet and we share a slow nod.

I lift up my fingers one at a time. One, two, three. We slam into it together, and the door flings loose.

We're out.

We fly into the parking lot in a full sprint. My feet slide on the asphalt, but it's Maggie's gasp that stops me in my tracks.

"What is—" I cut myself off because I see what it is. A black Mustang, engine purring and headlights on. Blake.

I keep my eyes locked on the car, on the dark square of glass that hides Blake's face from me. My hand searches blindly for Maggie until I find her coat sleeve and pull.

"Run," I say.

"Where?" Maggie asks, her voice shrill. She's got a point. High fences and thick brush surrounds the high school lawn. From this side, the only way out is the driveway, which means moving straight into the parking lot. We either take our chances of dodging Daniel again in the school—or we run for it.

"We have to book it," I say.

Maggie follows me as I half run, half slide into the slick, white lot. Running isn't going to be possible. Ice-skating would be closer to the truth.

I don't look up, but I hear Blake's door open and his feet hitting the ground. "Chloe, stop! Nobody's going to hurt you."

I just move faster, ignoring the way my feet slip and the way the cold air burns my lungs. We can do this. We *have* to do this.

Blake is closing in behind us. The sound of his footsteps sends me rushing faster, but every step is a chance to fall. And we can't afford to fall. I hear a scuffling and turn to see Blake in an awkward stance, his arms stretched wide for balance. I square my shoulders. We've got the edge for now.

And that's when Maggie goes down, hitting the ground knees-first with a cry. I pull her up and look at the road beyond the school. We're close now. The street and sidewalks are clearer, probably thanks to the last dusting from the salt trucks.

"C'mon," I say. We head for the road and hear a desperate scrabble of boots on ice. I glance back to see Blake on the ground now, swearing.

I don't look back again. Not when I hear him limp his way back to the car. Not even when I hear the crunch of his tires on the fresh snow. He's coming for us.

"Chloe?" Maggie's voice is small.

All I can do is nod. The sidewalks are better, so we pick up speed. But Blake is right beside us, that big engine growling as he keeps pace with our jogging. I don't know why he doesn't stop. I guess he doesn't need to bother. It's not like we can outrun him.

Not on the street anyway.

Nudging Maggie, I veer into a yard, cutting toward the narrow space between two of the houses near us.

I hear the whirring of a window rolling down and then Blake's voice.

"Don't be stupid, Chloe. My dad called. Just show me where it is and nothing bad happens."

I ignore him and my burning lungs. We climb a chain-link fence and move diagonally across a snowy backyard. Blake speeds up, no doubt trying to cut us off. We switch directions halfway through the yard and cut through to Beech instead of Maple.

Not that it matters. This isn't Manhattan. He can loop all the streets in town until he finds us. We're like rats running in a maze.

Maggie stays close as we head back to the road, trying to stick to the shadows. It's six blocks to her house, and my boots are soaked through. I can hear Maggie's teeth chattering. How the hell are we going to get there without him seeing us?

"W-w-why is he staying in the car?" she asks.

"Because he knows he has a better chance of keeping an eye on us."

"So he's just waiting t-to tire us out?"

"He doesn't need to catch us, Mags. He just wants to know where I'm going. Let's cross here."

We move quickly and quietly across the street, eyes darting in both directions, but there is nothing. No headlights, no rumbling engines. The quiet is almost enough to convince me that I've lost him. We're in and out of a half dozen lawns, zigging and zagging through the growing blanket of snow.

Sometimes, I hear a car that sounds like his. But it's not. We're getting lucky. At Main Street, we finally stop. Maggie braces her hands on her knees while I wipe sweat from my brow.

"We have to keep moving," I say, too nervous to be standing on this corner.

"The p-police," she gasps out, nodding left.

"Your house is closer. That's where the drugs are."

"You d-didn't bring me anything, Chlo. I d-don't have them."

"The Not Treasure Box," I say, and it is all she needs.

We start to cross the deserted street and then I hear it. A rumble that settles in my bones in all the wrong ways. For a moment, I think of turning back, of slipping into the shadow of the pine trees.

"Run!" I say.

But it's too late. The engine speeds up, and I know he's seen us.

Maggie and I are bolting across, but he's going to be right on us. It's a straight shot to her house from here. He'll know there's nowhere else we could be going.

I change my mind and reach for Maggie's hand. "Let's double around. We'll go by the doughnut shop."`

Blake's already approaching the intersection when we change directions. The car starts to turn, but he's going too fast. The tires slip, and I hear the rapid *thud-thud-thud* of antilock brakes kicking in. He tries to swing back to the right, but the Mustang shudders on the slick pavement. The rear fender squirrels to the left. Too far left.

He's going to hit something.

I jerk Maggie the rest of the way across the street, my fingers curling hard in her jacket. I can see Blake through the windshield, his face pale and tight with fear. And, just like that, he hits. The right front fender slams into a telephone poll. The smash of metal into wood is like a scream.

And then it's over.

• • •

All is quiet and still. The only thing moving is the airbag sagging behind the windshield. I hold my breath and watch it, looking for Blake.

"Is everyone all right?"

Maggie and I spring apart in shock, looking up. There's an older guy looking down at us. He's still zipping his coat up over his pajamas, so he must have heard the wreck.

"Are you all right?" he repeats. "Did you get hurt?"

"Yes," I say, pointing at the wreck automatically. "No, we're fine. It's—"

The sound of Blake's door grinding open chokes my words off. I see one of his feet hit the ground outside the car. Then a second one. Maggie's grip on me tightens.

"Blake? Is that you?"

Someone else has pulled up. She's got a coat pulled around her and a scarf knotted at her neck. I don't know her, but she looks like someone's mom. Behind her, I see the gray minivan she obviously just stepped out of.

"Honey, are you all right?" she asks, gingerly crossing the road.

"I already called the police," the guy says. We are instantly forgotten as he walks into the street, checking out the front of Blake's car with a low whistle. "I'll call for a tow too."

Blake steps out of the car then, and his gaze doesn't stay on his rescuers. He looks past the wrecked car and the melting snow and the people who are gathered in close. Instead he looks at me. His eyes go as hard as Maggie's grip on my arm.

The mom-type touches his sleeve. "Sweetheart, let me call your mom."

I see the resignation in his eyes. Because he can't just leave his wrecked car and chase me through town. He's stuck here with the concerned neighbors and the police who are already en route. And I can't help but to smirk at him before I turn away.

"Come on," I say, as I tug Maggie along with me.

"Wait," she says quietly. "The police."

I keep walking, and she trails after me, asking again. "Where are you g-going? The police are coming."

I don't answer until I'm sure we're far enough away that no one will hear. "So what, we just run up to them in the middle of an accident scene? They'll think I'm crazy, Mags. Honestly, until I see these drugs myself, I'm not sure they'll be wrong."

I hear the soft wail of a siren from the opposite end of the street. Maggie looks over her shoulder longingly before speeding up to keep pace with me.

Maggie's yard is empty when we arrive. Neither one of us says a word. Talking about the Not Treasure Box is a little like talking about where we're going to eat lunch. We just don't. She grabs a shovel from the shed, and we run to the tree where we've spent countless summer afternoons burying sentimental junk or digging it back up.

It was supposed to be a time capsule. We'd created it in the second grade, some notes and a current newspaper, stuff like that. I'd put in my favorite pencil, and Maggie had included a pink plastic ring that she'd worn all year long.

She'd cried all night over that stupid ring. The next morning, I woke up early and trudged through the dew in her yard. I came back with muddy feet and a piece of pink plastic jewelry. It wasn't technically a time capsule after that. But it was something else. Something good.

The ground is hard like clay beneath my shovel, but it isn't buried deep. I chip away at the dirt until I feel my shovel strike something hard. This is it.

I wrestle it out, fingering the rusting latches with a sense of déjà vu. I pop it open and touch the black box inside. And then, just like that, the pieces of my lost summer snap back into place.

I remember being here. I remember burying this box and calling Adam. I remember everything before it too. The months slide back into place like a key tumbling in a lock. The afternoons in study group. The evenings with Blake. It's all there. The hole in my mind is gone. Dr. Kirkpatrick's hypnosis sessions. New friends. Cup after steaming cup of that damn lemon—

My head snaps up, tears clouding my vision. "The tea. Oh my God, they put the drugs in the tea."

Maggie just watches me, one hand at her chest.

I leave the box where it is and lean back on my heels, letting out a long breath. It steams around my face and mingles with my tears as I remember my words to Maggie, my voice so awful and superior. I can see her like it was yesterday, back against the lockers and an expression of dark betrayal on her face.

I take a breath—so cold it stings my lungs. "Maggie…"

Snow is still falling thickly, but I can see the realization dawn on her face. "You remember, d-don't you?"

I nod, swallowing thickly, wishing I could claw the awful images back out of my head. And maybe the memories of Blake too, his mouth on mine and hands under my shirt. I feel my throat close up, a gag rising through me.

Maggie grips my shoulders and shakes me. She isn't gentle. "D-don't!"

I scrabble away from her desperately, away from the little black box and all the months I wish to God had never happened.

"Maggie, I said things—I did things—you and Blake and—" I cut myself off because I can't even talk about the images running through me, the ugliness in these memories. Ugliness in me.

"You *did* things, Chlo. Past tense."

I shake my head, ball my cold fingers into fists. "No."

"Look, it wasn't pretty, b-but there was drugged tea and creepy hypnosis, right?" She stops until she's sure she's got my attention. "Look, it's time for you to let it go. Do you hear me? You need to move on. We b-both do."

She puts the black box in my hands, and I feel the edges, clean and smooth. Smooth like Maggie's speech used to be around me. Come to think of it, it's pretty smooth right now. Is it really so easy? Am I forgiven, just like that?

I pull the latch open, finding four syringes like I remember them. The label on the syringe reads "High Concentration—Test Lot 1." My fingers tingle as I read that. God, wasn't it concentrated enough already?

It doesn't matter. What matters is that they used this on us. They drugged us. They put this poison into our tea, maybe straight into us through needles like this. And now I can prove it. "Let's get this done," Maggie says, pulling her phone out of her pocket. "My phone is dying. We'll c-call from inside."

I close the box with a nod and tuck it in my pocket, not trusting my voice as I stand up. We slip back through her yard and up the steps. The idea of her warm kitchen is like heaven. The only thing that would be better than being warm would be knowing that Adam is safe.

But he is safe. He has to be. I can't have come this close to lose now.

Maggie heads through the back door, and I'm right on her heels. Everything is warm and perfect. I take a breath…and Maggie screams.

Something's coming at me. It hits fast and hard, and then there is nothing but darkness.

CHAPTER THIRTY-TWO

· ·

The pain wakes me. For a moment, I think I'll just go back to sleep. Or maybe I'll get something from the medicine cabinet because my head feels like it's turning itself inside out and my stomach is rolling in all the wrong ways.

I smell yeast and cinnamon, which tells me I'm not at home. I'm at Maggie's house. On Maggie's floor to be precise.

The memory of Maggie's scream comes back to me, and I try to bolt upright. My body doesn't comply. I groan and try to open my eyes instead, but my vision swims through the slits I manage. Oh God. I'm going to vomit. I'm sure of it. I breathe deep and will the nausea to pass. Around me, the muddy blurs try to slide into focus.

I see fragments. Maggie's shoes. A pair of gray pants. Adam slumped on the couch.

Adam?

I sit up again. Too fast. The room spins, and I fall right back down.

"Oh, I think you should stay still for a bit longer, Ms. Spinnaker."

The voice makes everything in me recoil. My body tenses, and I gingerly push up on my elbows.

What I see makes me wish I were still knocked out. Maggie,

gagged and tied to a kitchen chair. Adam on the couch, eyes half-closed and arm extended. Daniel sits between them, pulling a needle out of Adam's arm. The syringe attached to that needle is empty.

"Do you know why I love this drug?" Daniel says, capping the needle and putting it back in the case he's holding. "I call it liquid cooperation. A little of this in your system, and you're happy to think or do or remember anything I want you to."

"How? He would never let you…" I trail off, dumbstruck that Adam just sat there, rolled up his sleeve and let Daniel pump a mind-altering poison into his veins.

"Well, I didn't ask permission when I injected him the first time," he says, smirking. "But your little boyfriend was feisty. An extra dose has made all the difference, hasn't it?"

Adam blinks blearily, looking lost.

I lumber to my feet, wobbling around like a marionette. Daniel watches me from the couch. He knows he can take me if he needs to. I'd like to think otherwise, but he's not small. Plus, he didn't just get knocked upside the head.

I ball my hands into fists and try to look taller than I am. "What do you want from us?"

"I want you to show me where you put the drugs."

"No way."

He sighs like it's really not a big deal to him. Then he opens the leather case again and pulls a new needle out. My eyes fix on that syringe, on the clear liquid inside it. "You know, this drug could change the world. Imagine criminals reformed. Students with perfect marks. Soldiers without fear. Do you know what governments would pay for something like that?"

"That's what this was about for you?" I feel the horror twisting my face into something ugly. "This is why you killed Dr. Kirkpatrick? For money?"

Daniel looks up at me. "Killed her? Now, who would believe I'm the killing sort? That kind of crime takes someone with a dark side. A record, perhaps. Someone like your boyfriend here."

"Liar," I say, shaking my head.

"Am I? But he's already a criminal, isn't he? A criminal and a liar. What else is he hiding? Who's to say he wouldn't confess to *unthinkable* crimes?"

The smile he gives me is the purest form of evil I've ever seen.

"Were you there with Dr. Kirkpatrick's body?" Daniel asks Adam.

"Yes."

"You saw her on that desk, didn't you? All that blood, Adam," Daniel says, shaking his head. "How could you?"

"Did I hurt her?" he asks, his brow furrowing confusion. "I don't—"

"You didn't hurt anyone, Adam," I say. And then I turn to Daniel with a scowl. "You're a twisted bastard."

"And you're stalling." Daniel's face contorts, and he rears back, backhanding Maggie in the mouth.

I'm not sure whose cry is louder, hers or mine.

Adam struggles weakly to get up, and Daniel pushes him back. "You aren't going anywhere. You're going to sit right there and think of all the ways you're not good enough."

Adam shrinks back from his words, and I try to lunge, hearing the syringes rattle in my pocket. Daniel has Maggie's arm in his hand and the needle at her flesh before I can take a step.

"Think very carefully about how you want this to go," Daniel says. Then he presses the needle in, just a little. Maggie whimpers softly, and my stomach curdles like day-old milk. "You show me what I want or we'll see just how much of this I'll need to knock her out for a month."

Adrenaline surges through me, hot and hungry. My whole world is reduced to the sight of that needle at Maggie's arm.

"The drugs, Ms. Spinnaker!"

"Okay, I'll show you," I say, shoving my hands into my pocket. I feel the cap on one of the syringes and think of the life Dr. Kirkpatrick doesn't get to have. The life Julien doesn't get to have either.

"You have it with you?" he asks, looking skeptical.

I do.

I do, but I cannot let this happen. I will not let him win.

I try to form the words with my lips, but Maggie's eyes are pleading with me. Not for herself. She's begging me for courage. For the strength to do the right thing.

"Show me what you have!" he shouts, jabbing the needle in farther.

I hold up one hand. "It's a map, okay? I'm getting it out."

But I'm not getting it. I'm getting a syringe. And I don't know how I'll do this because he's staring right at me, but I can't not try. I have to try.

While I wrestle to find some way, some sliver of a window of possibility, Maggie suddenly moves. She lurches wildly , leaning away from him until her chair topples over onto its side.

"You conniving little bitch!" he says, leaning to grab her.

This is it.

My one chance.

I pull the cap off and lunge. I stab the closest thing I can find and push the plunger hard and fast.

For Dr. Kirkpatrick. For Julien. For all of us.

He roars and slams his hand against my arm, batting me away. The needle still dangles from his neck when he punches at me again. This time I'm faster. I dodge left.

Daniel pulls the syringe from his skin, reading the label with obvious horror. I grab the nearest heavy thing I can find—a vase from the coffee table.

I wield it like a bat, ready to strike. But I won't need to hit him. He reaches for me and stumbles, one knee hitting the ground in front of the couch. He's panting and pale.

"You have no idea what you're dealing with," he says, slurring his words. "Those needles are concentrated…" He trails off, swaying on his feet. "It hasn't been tested like that."

I force air into my lungs and courage into my voice. "Well, then consider this my experiment. That's what we were to you, right? Experiments?"

He stares at me then at his feet. He shakes his head and looks around. I think of a deer in headlights. And I decide to use his own bag of tricks against him.

"You look so tired, Mr. Tanner," I say, tilting my head in mock concern. "I heard you say you want to sit down."

"I didn't say—" He cuts himself off, looking at Adam on the couch and Maggie beside him. He tries to take a step, but his knees buckle. I watch him land on the couch gracelessly, his long legs bent at awkward angles.

"You want to rest," I say. "You're so tired. So weak. You want to sleep."

His eyes are glazed, pupils too wide. I see him shake himself, trying to clear his head. "I don't…I'm tired."

"You are tired," I say, feeling a cold rush of power. "And now you're going to close your eyes until I tell you to open them again."

Maggie wriggles out of the rope around her legs after I free her hands. She sets to work tying Daniel up while I call the police.

When it's done, I go to Adam.

I approach him on soft feet, and he watches me through half-mast eyes. He looks like he's in agony. It makes my chest ache, seeing him broken like this.

"The police are coming," I say.

"The police," he repeats. And then he stiffens, looking alarmed. "You've got to get out of here. You didn't have anything to do with this, Chloe."

I try to touch his arm, to be soothing. "Adam—"

"Go, Chloe! You are too good to get mixed up in this. This is my fault. I'm the problem. Please. Just go." He's pushing at my hands, and he's so strong, even like this. It's all I can do to keep myself close to him.

I look to where Daniel is passed out on the other end of the couch. The feeling that goes through me is too hot, too red to just be anger. I remind myself that the police will come, that this man will leave here in handcuffs and he will go to jail.

It isn't enough for me.

I could hurt him the way he hurt us. With whatever creepy drug that is running through his veins, I could wake him up and say things that would torture him for the rest of his life. I could feel the weight of his justice in *my* hands.

"You are too good for me," Adam says, breaking my focus.

I'm not too good for him. But I am too good to turn into Daniel Tanner.

I slide into the space between Adam and the couch arm. I touch his face and he frowns, still looking groggy and confused.

"You deserve better, Chloe. I keep trying to tell you."

"Then it's a good thing I never listen."

When he tries to pull free, I kiss him. He makes a halfhearted effort to stop me, but I fight harder. When we separate, I can see his eyes are clearer. His touch brought my memories back. Maybe mine is doing the same to him. It's a crazy idea, but it still makes me smile.

"You know, I remember everything now," I say. "All my missing time came back."

I see the worry in his face before he manages to hide it. "Yeah? Any big surprises?"

"Nothing worth mentioning. I mean, I already knew I love you."

He's halfway through a nod when it catches up with him. I

see the way he hesitates, feel the way the intensity in his eyes changes, his whole face going soft. "Chloe, you can't—"

"Yeah, well, I do. And I'm *way* stubborn, so you're just going to have to deal with it."

I see the barest hint of a grin before he pulls me in. His kiss is sweet and lingering, his hands trailing up my back and into my hair. It pushes out all of the cold and the fear of this night, leaving me warm and strong.

When we break apart, Adam smiles with his eyes closed. "Stubborn works for me."

I laugh for the first time in forever. And that feels even better than the kiss.

CHAPTER THIRTY-THREE

· ·

The reporter's face on the screen is full of concern. "How do you feel about the school board's voluntary retesting invitation?"

I bite my lip. I wish I hadn't. It's not pretty in person, but with my head filling up the entire television screen—remind me to thank the cameraman for that one—I look like a nervous wreck. But, then again, I was a nervous wreck.

"I haven't thought much about it."

"So you haven't made a decision on how you'll proceed?"

"Oh, no. I've decided. I'm retaking the test."

The reporter tips her head in that way reporters do when the answer they receive isn't quite what they expect. "Like many of the other students involved in this scandal, your SAT scores were exceptional, correct? Some have suggested it might be the one benefit to your suffering."

On screen, I shake my head. I look revolted. "I guess I don't think there were any benefits. There's really no silver lining here. Not for me."

"Do you find some satisfaction in being the one to bring him to justice? Your courage to come forward with this story has given other victims the strength to speak out as well."

She lays eight pictures on the table between us. It's all a concoction for the segment—a news trick to visualize the magnitude of Daniel's impact. As if somehow the number of pictures on that table is directly proportionate to how big a hero I am.

But I'm not a hero at all.

"You gave these students a voice. That's something."

They were my friends then. And we are something different than friends now, tied together in a way we can never unravel.

On the screen, I close my eyes and take a breath. In the here and now, I feel Adam's hand reach across the couch for mine, his fingers lending me strength.

"It isn't nearly enough. But it's all I could do."

The reporter closes with a reminder of the upcoming trial for Daniel and the investigation that's still underway on two unnamed, involved minors. The minors have names: Blake Tanner and Adam Reed.

I still don't know what will happen to them.

"Don't start worrying about that," Adam says, reading my mind.

Maggie, who's curled up on the other side of me, turns off the television. "She's n-not the only one who's worried about it."

"Coming from my fan club, I'll take that as a compliment," Adam says, but he's mostly teasing. The two of them probably aren't going to start trading secrets or braiding each other's hair. But they love me. And that seems to be enough for both of them.

"Well, I, for one, am proud of you," my mom says from the love seat. Her smile wavers a little, which tells me that's not all she wants to say. "I still wish you'd reconsider the test. There's no harm in you keeping that score—"

I roll my eyes. "Mom. We've been over this."

She relents with a sigh. It's almost like she's letting it go, but we both know better than that. Beside her, my dad makes a cuckoo sign with his hand. "Don't listen to her. You'll probably get even better scores."

"I doubt that," I say.

"I don't," my dad says. "And, as you know, I'm always right."

I laugh. "Well, brace yourself for reality."

"One of these days you're going to figure out how smart you actually are," Adam says quietly. "Then you'll be the one bracing."

My dad notices. He's been doing that with Adam. Noticing things.

It's kind of weird, still, me dating this guy with a record. Not exactly everything they'd dreamed, and I get that. Hell, Adam's worse than them. He wouldn't even come in the house at first. But one day, Maggie and I dragged him inside, and we forced the elephant out from under the carpet.

Awkward does not begin to cover it. But here we are. And it's okay. Good even.

"When's your next meeting with the detective?" my dad asks.

Maggie looks right at me, her brows arched. I force myself to close my mouth and watch as Adam looks down. He takes a breath before he answers.

"Friday."

"Will your grandmother be there?"

"She's not…well," he says, and I squeeze his hand. He's barely comfortable having a soda from the fridge. Dragging his senile, alcoholic grandmother into the mix is probably somewhere he doesn't want to go.

"If it's all right with you, I might give him a call," Dad says.

Maggie and I both whip our heads to stare at him. Mom's gaping too.

"What?" he says, looking at us like we're crazy. "Is it so strange that I want to put in a good word for the guy?"

Um, yes, it's strange. My dad defending a boy I'm making out with on a regular basis is pretty much a portent of impending apocalypse.

"You don't have—" I cut Adam off with a hard squeeze to his fingers and a very pointed look. His eyes soften and he tries again. "If you'd like, that would be great. Thank you."

Mom claps her hands together and offers pizza, and my dad joins her as she heads into the kitchen talking toppings and pickup versus delivery.

Maggie pulls out at least four stacks of flash cards, thumping them on the table in a line. "Now that that's out of the way, we need t-to get down to business. Where are your highlighters?"

I stare at the mountain of work on the coffee table with a frown. "They're in my backpack. Tucked in beside the last shred of hope for a fun weekend."

Adam laughs.

His laugh was the first thing I remembered all those months ago. It's still one of my favorite sounds on earth.

• • •

Six minutes. In six minutes I will walk through those double doors and sit down at a desk, and it will change my future.

I wait in a row of orange plastic chairs with Adam and three dozen juniors I don't really know. Everybody else kept their scores.

The other kids here look like they've had three cups of coffee with a Red Bull shooter. They're twitchy and sweaty, shifting in their seats and watching the clock with dread etched in their faces.

"I thought I was the calm, cool, collected one," Adam comments.

I shake my head. "No, you're the smoking-hot, irresistible one."

"Am I?" The smile he gives me is probably illegal in four states. Sadly, even the promise of an impromptu make-out session wouldn't outrank what we're waiting on. Not for him, at any rate.

Not for me either, really. Maybe once. But things are different now. I look at the closed double doors on the south wall. White SAT testing signs are taped to both doors. Maybe I'm crazy, but the sight of them makes me grin.

"You're scaring the natives," Adam says.

I kiss him, and he makes a humming noise in the back of his throat when I pull back. "Hey, don't stop on my account."

"Oh, that's not for you. I need a clear head."

"Right. Clear heads." He shakes his head and straightens up in his chair, looking grave. Like he needs to bother. He'll walk out with a score that should land him in any school he wants.

Should but probably won't.

And as for me—

"So what's your goal?"

I think about it. About the 2155 that was framed on my fridge. The score I probably don't have a snail's chance of getting again.

"Don't think negative," Adam says. "You've studied your ass off."

"I know, and I'm good with it. No matter what it is, it'll be mine."

"It'll be good enough for Brown," he says with absolute conviction.

I take a breath and hold it in because it might not be. The truth sits low in my chest. It's solid and ugly, but I can swallow it. I can keep breathing.

"Maybe. Maybe not." I shrug. "It doesn't matter. I know what I want. And I'll find a way to get it."

He gives me a pointed look. "Well, God knows that's the truth."

My too-loud laugh earns a stern frown from the proctor. I'm never going to be the teacher's pet. Or the top of the class. It's fine. I kind of like the view from where I'm standing.

"When the doors open, please find an open desk and be seated," the proctor says.

The doors swing wide open. Just like my future.

ACKNOWLEDGMENTS

· ·

This is harder than I thought it would be. I want to thank everyone I've ever met and maybe a few random strangers—and it probably looks like I have. But truthfully, I know I will think of others later and wish I'd mentioned them too. I hope they'll have the grace to forgive me.

My first thanks is to God, for planting this dream and giving me parents that would let me chase it. To my mother, who I hope is looking down with pride, and to my father, who teaches me every day what the word *perseverance* actually means.

Six Months Later was championed by an unbeatable publishing team at Sourcebooks Fire. Kim Manley, Cat Clyne, Jillian Bergsma, Derry Wilkens, and, most of all, Leah Hultenschmidt, thank you so much for believing in me and in this book. You have made every part of this process lovely.

I wouldn't be where I am today without the hard work of my agent, whose wisdom and kindness are unmatched. Cori Deyoe, as always, thank you so much for being in my corner.

I am blessed with an amazing group of supporters, some friends, some relatives—all family to me. Angela, Debbie, Tori, Tiffany, Leigh Anne, Sharon, Christy, Esther, Jon, Melissa, Kathy, Paul, my cousin Jennifer (who just "knew" this book would sell), and my stepmom Karen (who read this long before it was actually good)—I'm more grateful than you know for your encouragement.

A special thanks to some of my writer friends, my awesome fellow Doomsdaisies and my chapter mates at COFW. In particular, I'd like to thank Karin, Susan, and Margs, who've taught me so much and been such good friends. Also, to Robin, for sound advice, homemade meatballs, and thirty-five visits to the Disney store in forty-eight hours. Last but certainly not least, I'd like to thank Sheri, who's probably spent a year of her life on the phone with me dissecting one story issue or another. I have no idea why you still pick up the phone, Sheri, but I'm so grateful.

Of course, writing with three young children would be impossible without the unfailing support of my wonderful husband. David, you never, ever doubted. I love you for that and for so much more.

In closing, I'd like to thank my three children who make my world brighter and more beautiful. Ian, Adrienne, and Lydia, I love you to the moon and back times infinity. *You* are the magic in every one of my stories.

ABOUT THE AUTHOR

. . . .

At seven, Natalie D. Richards wrote about Barbara Frances Bizzlefishes (who wouldn't dare do the dishes). Now she writes about awesome girls, broody boys, and all things dark and creepy. Natalie lives in Ohio (Go Bucks!) with her husband, three kids, and a seventy-pound dust mop who swears he's the family dog. You can visit her at www.nataliedrichards.com or follow her on Twitter @NatDRichards.

Check out more YA thrillers from Sourcebooks...

TRULY, MADLY, DEADLY

Hannah Jayne

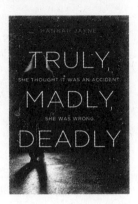

They said it was an accident...

Sawyer Dodd is a star athlete, straight-A student, and the envy of every other girl who wants to date Kevin Anderson. When Kevin dies in a tragic car crash, Sawyer is stunned. Then she opens her locker to find a note:

You're welcome.

Someone saw what he did to her. Someone knows that Sawyer and Kevin weren't the perfect couple they seemed to be. And that someone—a killer—is now shadowing Sawyer's every move...

Praise for *Truly, Madly, Deadly*:

"A fast-paced thriller." —*Kirkus Reviews*

"What a ride! Full of twists and turns—including an ending you won't see coming!" —April Henry, *New York Times* bestselling author of *The Girl Who Was Supposed to Die*

BROKEN

CJ Lyons

All Scarlet Killian wants is a normal life.

Diagnosed with a rare and untreatable heart condition, Scarlet has come to terms with the fact that she's going to die. Literally of a broken heart. It could be tomorrow, or it could be next year. But the clock is ticking...

All Scarlet asks is for a chance to attend high school—even if just for a week—a chance to be just like everyone else. But Scarlet can feel her heart beating out of control with each slammed locker and vicious taunt. Is this normal? Really? Yet there's more going on than she knows. And finding out the truth might just kill Scarlet before her heart does...

Praise for CJ Lyons:

"Everything a great thriller should be—action packed, authentic, and intense." —#1 *New York Times* bestselling author Lee Child

"Laurie Halse Anderson's *Speak* meets Kathy Reichs' *Virals*." —Jill Moore, Square Books, Jr., Oxford, MS

And coming in January 2014…

SEE JANE RUN

Hannah Jayne

I know who you are.

When Riley first gets the postcard tucked into her bag, she thinks it's a joke. Then she finds a birth certificate for a girl named Jane Elizabeth O'Leary tucked inside her baby book.

Riley's parents have always been pretty overprotective. What if it wasn't for her safety…but fear of her finding out their secret? What have they been hiding? The more Riley digs for answers, the more questions she has.

The only way to know the truth? Find out what happened to Jane O'Leary.

For more YA thrillers, visit teenfire.sourcebooks.com.